Crime Wave

TOO FEW TO COUNT

TOO FEW TO COUNT

Canadian Women
in Conflict with the Law

edited by

ELLEN ADELBERG
& CLAUDIA CURRIE

press gang publishers

Canadian Cataloguing in Publication Data

Too Few to Count

Includes index.
Bibliography: p.
ISBN 0-88974-009-7

1. Female offenders—Canada.   2. Sex discrimination against women —Canada.   3. Sex discrimination in criminal justice administration— Canada.   I. Adelberg, Ellen. II. Currie, Claudia.
HV6046.T66 1987   364.3'74'0971   C87-091440-5

Edited by Penny Goldsmith and Barbara Kuhne
Type produced by Baseline Type & Graphics Cooperative
Cover design by Debbie Bryant
Book design and layout by Jean Macgregor

Photographs copyright ©Tom Skudra. Some photographs included here were first published in *Equinox*, Number 14, March/April 1984. Reprinted with permission.

First printing October 1987

Printed in Canada by the collective labour of Press Gang Printers.

Bound in Canada

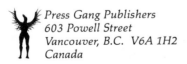
Press Gang Publishers
603 Powell Street
Vancouver, B.C. V6A 1H2
Canada

Acknowledgements

We would like to thank the many people who gave generously of their time to help us complete the book: Christie Jefferson, Ken Hatt and Carol LaPrairie who supported our application to the Canada Council; Joan Holmes and Cynthia Telfer who provided editorial comments and publishing advice; Wendy McPeake who provided a wealth of good advice and encouragement; Marion De Vries who typed and re-typed drafts under tight deadlines with the help of Janet Currie and Gay Firth; Margaret Barker for proofreading assistance; the ten women we interviewed for our chapter; Darlene Lawson of the Toronto Elizabeth Fry Society, Barb Coflin of the Elizabeth Fry Society of Ottawa and George Caron of the Prison for Women, who helped us contact women in conflict with the law; Holly Johnson for providing additional statistics; and Jim Davidson for his ongoing support.

This book was made possible by the receipt of a Canada Council Explorations grant.

*For all the women we have met
who have come into conflict
with the law.*

Contents

Introduction

by ELLEN ADELBERG
& CLAUDIA CURRIE

Women, crime, Canada... three topics of heated discussion, although rarely in the context of women in conflict with the law. Yet approximately 98,000 charges were laid against women in Canada in 1984, and at least 8,000 served time in prison.[1] Long a forgotten minority, women who commit crimes have received scant attention in Canada from scholars, feminists and the correctional system itself.

Both of us have worked in the criminal justice system; as a result of our experiences, we feel compelled to break the historic silence surrounding women offenders. As social workers, we witnessed events while working with convicted women in the community and in Canada's only federal prison for women which left deep imprints on our hearts and minds. The wasted lives and intense pain and anger of those behind prison walls have engendered in us a commitment to explore how and why this destructive system is sustained.

We were both employed as halfway house directors for the Elizabeth Fry Society of Ottawa. During that time, we met dozens of female residents who had committed petty offences such as shoplifting, fraudulent cashing of welfare cheques or selling small amounts of street drugs (usually as fronts for male marijuana or hashish dealers). Their crimes made us question the economic conditions and life circumstances which surrounded them. The significantly smaller numbers of women we met who were charged or convicted of assault, or other forms of personal violence (which usually took place in the context of an abusive domestic situation), made us question the social conditions of women's lives that led to such events.

We entered the correctional system as professional "helpers," but quickly realized that far from needing help, our "clients" needed liberation—both economic and social—from a patriarchal system based on male dominance and male property rights. We also realized that as social workers with community-based social service agencies, we were cogs in the larger wheel of social control which the state exercises to protect such rights. Because non-profit organizations are funded by provincial and federal departments of corrections, in essence we were paid by those departments to monitor and enforce sentences handed down to women in the justice system. No matter how good our intentions to help women surmount the system, we were restricted to acting as arms length law enforcers by relying on the state for funding.

Most of the women we met were young and poor. Very few had finished high school, and still fewer had any training for the job market. However, as a result of coming into conflict with the law, their lives were laid open for inspection and judgement by various people in the justice system, and they were expected by judges, correctional officials and ourselves to attain respectability by finding employment, paying off fines and debts, and, frequently, learning to be better mothers.

It became obvious that, despite our best intentions and those of women offenders, their chances of finding employment, furthering their education, or regaining custody of their children, were virtually nil. Few jobs existed for unskilled, uneducated women, particularly those with criminal records. Those jobs that did exist, such as waitressing or office cleaning, paid poorly and demanded hours incompatible with other duties expected of mothers. Training and academic upgrading programs were scarce and provided such miserly living stipends that it was virtually impossible for anyone to survive financially while enrolled in a program. No amount of good will on our part made up for the appalling lack of resources for poor, uneducated women in this country.

Despite the existence of voluntary social service agencies and state-run probation and parole programs, women offenders' lives did not seem to improve after coming in contact with the criminal justice system. In fact, quite often just the opposite occurred. As a result of trauma experienced in the courtroom and in prison, which often included loss of their children, many women we knew developed physical and mental ailments which compounded difficulties they already faced in the struggle to survive on low incomes. These problems continue to be encountered by women who come into conflict with the law.

It became clear to us that the vast majority of Canadians know little about the actual workings of the justice and correctional systems, and still less about women who enter that system as offenders. Media images of courtrooms, prisons and criminal acts serve as the source of public knowledge about offenders. Particularly in the case of women, these images are hugely distorted from reality. As documented in Karlene Faith's article, women offenders tend to be uniformly portrayed in television shows and movies either as violent individuals and/or predator lesbians. This book is intended to provide a more accurate portrayal of women's conflict with the law and their experiences in and outside of prison.

During our years as students of criminology and social work, and later while working in the criminal justice field, we scoured libraries and bookstores for literature on the subject of women and crime that would inform and assist us. Little was to be found, at least about Canadian women.[2] Although some women and women's organizations had made significant inroads researching women in conflict with the law, little of their work had been published or disseminated.

Canadian publications have been restricted for the most part to a few government studies and documents, and a small number of minor publications from organizations such as the Canadian Association of Elizabeth Fry Societies (CAEFS).[3] In recent years, both the federal and provincial ministries responsible for justice and corrections have funded some initial research projects pertaining specifically to women and crime. Some are available to the public in the form of published documents.[4]

Status of Women Canada, the federal government department responsible for women's issues, released a ground-breaking report in 1986 entitled *A Feminist Review of Criminal Law*. This report was the first to approach Canadian criminal law from the perspective of women's interests. It challenged the existing assumptions about legal concepts such as property, morality and protection, and stressed that criminal law seeks to preserve an order established strictly through male consensus.

The writing in this book brings Canadian content further by exploring many unpublished dimensions of women offenders' experiences. What have been the consequences for women caught up in a system created for, designed, and controlled by men? Are there aspects of women's subordinate status which relate to the crimes they commit? What have women done to attempt to change the criminal justice and correctional system? These are some of the questions addressed by contributors to this volume. We and our contributors look at women and crime not only through women's eyes, but with a critical view of the male-dominated criminal justice system. This view is distinctly feminist in that it studies a social phenomenon from the perspective of women's history and experience, recognizing the unequal social, political and economic positions of the sexes.

Intended to provoke debate and discussion about the treatment of women by the courts and prisons, the book provides a starting point for the development of feminist analysis on these issues, and not any final words on the subject. The lack of good statistical data on women in conflict with the law leaves all of the authors making tentative, as opposed to written-in-stone conclusions about why women have committed certain types of offences (such as fraud and shoplifting) more frequently than others, and what is needed to help women offenders live better, crime-free lives. While discussion of some issues related to oppression in women's lives (such as rape, pornography and economic discrimination) has been well-developed in the past twenty years, women who break the law in Canada have been largely ignored by the mainstream male society, and by the feminist movement. This book is a pioneering effort to define the problems related to women's conflict with Canadian law, and to point out avenues for change.

In every section there are gaps in the discussion where better numbers are needed to document the past and present patterns of women's offences and women offenders' lives. Hopefully, in ten years' time, we will be able to look back at this anthology and say, "Did we really not know the average level of education of women who go to prison? Did we really not know how many were mothers, or how old their children were, or how much money they earned, or if they came from abusive relationships?"

At present, the sad truth is that we have very few statistics to document these kinds of problems. And while the available data is used, all of the authors rely, to varying extents, on their own and others' first hand impressions of the lives women offenders lead before, during and after imprisonment.

Holly Johnson, a researcher for the Solicitor General of Canada, documents that women are charged largely with petty property offences, and comprise less than fifteen per cent of all offenders. Her article presents demographic data that suggests a link between Canadian women's crimes and their generally inferior economic and social position compared to men. Johnson provides as complete a statistical picture of women offenders as possible, given the large gaps in data collection in this area.

Her discussion of the data raises a multitude of questions about women in conflict with the law, some of which are addressed by other contributors. The statistics showing a disproportionately high rate of certain offences by Native women are addressed by Carol LaPrairie. The nature of women's imprisonment is discussed by Liz Elliott and Ruth Morris. Gloria Geller analyzes the entry and subsequent treatment of young women in the criminal justice system.

The way that theorists have analyzed women's involvement in crime is explored by lawyer Shelley Gavigan. As she points out, until fairly recently, criminological theory has portrayed women offenders as deviators from their socially-defined feminine and sexual roles (Gloria Geller also found this to apply in the case of young women, as she describes in her article). Gavigan first discredits these traditional theories, then examines the work of a number of theorists who maintain that "women's liberation" is responsible for growing female crime rates. She demonstrates that these rates may be due instead to a more punitive attitude towards women on the part of those who are threatened by the women's movement.

Gavigan argues that feminist theory in criminology, which tries to redress the mistakes of earlier approaches, must begin to incorporate historical, economic and social factors relevant to the subordinate position of women in society in order to fully understand the relationship of women to the criminal justice system. The implications of theory are not restricted to the academic world. Many of the sexist views found in the theoretical treatment are replicated in correctional practices. The articles by Sheelagh Cooper, and Ruth Morris and Liz Elliot, which explore in detail the discriminatory treatment of women in prison, testify to the accuracy of Gavigan's point.

Without hearing first hand the voices of women offenders, the theory, data and history of women in conflict with the law seems less than real. In our article we interviewed seven women convicted of serious offences and they told us their stories. As well as the women's perceptions concerning significant events in their lives, the larger factors related to the tragedies they experienced and the crimes they committed are discussed. The women's experiences bring to life the statistics in Johnson's article and their stories reveal some of the most brutal examples of the condition of women under patriarchy. Their experiences of physical and sexual assault, child abuse, and powerlessness within the family and the economy are common to many women in Canada. Our view is that there is a strong relationship between those traumas and the crimes these women committed. For the most part, it is difficult to imagine their offences occurring in a society characterized by economic and sexual equality.

Carol LaPrairie, like Johnson, is a researcher for the Solicitor General of Canada. In her article, she explores the historical and material conditions which lead to the over-representation of Native women in the criminal justice system. LaPrairie examines the link between the oppression of Native people by white colonizers and the consequent breakdown of Native family structure. She argues that Native men who have lost traditional roles in this process may act out their frustration by turning on themselves, and on women and children in their families. Native women who attempt to escape this abuse by moving to large urban centres become particularly vulnerable to crime and arrest, due to their lack of job skills and consequent poverty and visibility. Those who commit crimes of violence, she suggests, are often retaliating against men who have violated them.

LaPrairie's work builds on the statistical profile of Native women offenders provided by Johnson, although LaPrairie is careful to note that detailed data on Native women is almost non-existent. Her argument is corroborated by anecdotal information from sources such as the director of a Native women's transition house in Thunder Bay. LaPrairie helps us to understand the high incidence of Native women's offences. She suggests that fundamental changes to the position to which Native people have been relegated are necessary to reduce Native women's conflict with the law.

Historically, the treatment of young women and girls in conflict with the law has been based on sexist assumptions of appropriate female behaviour. In her article, Gloria Geller provides testimony to this assertion by tracing the fate of young women offenders in our courts and training schools. Geller, whose doctorate was on female juvenile delinquency, discusses the types of offences for which young women are usually prosecuted as compared to young men. One of her most frightening findings is that young women have been locked up in institutions more readily than young men for committing non-criminal offences such as running away from home, truancy and sexual immorality. She suggests that judges and correctional officials have felt they were doing their paternalistic duty by "protecting" young wayward women in this way. She also argues such treatment is destructive and misguided; that young women need instead supportive structures and positive role models in the community.

Sheelagh Cooper traces the imprisonment of women serving federal sentences, since the time incarceration was first used to punish women in Canada. Like Gavigan and Geller, she finds the perceptions of correctional administrators have reflected narrowly-restricted female role definitions.

Cooper demonstrates that treatment of federal female prisoners has consisted of "a fascinating mixture of neglect, outright barbarism and well-meaning paternalism," not unlike the history of women's treatment in society at large. According to Cooper, as a group, women prisoners have received only the crumbs from the predominantly male correctional establishment. This is particularly true with respect to the facilities used for their incarceration. In the 1980s, the majority of federal women inmates still cannot serve their sentences in their home provinces. Cooper reveals this policy was ill-advised from its inception sixty years ago, but is maintained for bureaucratic reasons, at an exorbitant cost to both the prisoners and the federal government. In providing this historical base, Cooper lays the foundation for further discussion of women's imprisonment by Berzins and Hayes, and Elliot and Morris.

A vivid description of life behind the walls of the Prison for Women (P4W) in Kingston, Ontario, is provided by Liz Elliott and Ruth Morris. Based on their experiences as feminist social workers and prisoners' rights advocates, the authors discuss women's experiences in the federal prison system. Interviews with women who have served time in P4W reinforce the authors' description and analysis of the prison as a patriarchal and destructive environment which does little to promote women's success upon their release.

Lorraine Berzins is a social worker with many years experience in the prison system. In their article, she and Brigid Hayes, a feminist social reformer, discuss their efforts as change agents in the criminal justice system. Their experiences provide lessons for all women working to improve the status of women offenders. They document the obstacles placed in their way by a sexist system resistant to transformation. Such obstacles even included, in Berzins' case, the loss of employment. Berzins and Hayes point out that women in the community must lobby for change, because governments have neither the motivation, the interest nor the tools to find solutions on their own.

In the final article, Karlene Faith analyzes the messages behind popular media portrayals of women in prison. She explains how these depictions have generated public misconceptions about female offenders, and how they serve to maintain stereotypic images of criminal women as lesbian, and somehow, by association, masculine and violent. Faith draws on her past work in the U.S. (where she completed her doctorate) and on her current work in Canada with imprisoned women.

Throughout this book, several common threads emerge. Women who have broken criminal laws and been caught are often victims of economic deprivation, social subjugation to men, and restricted options in life. Youth or adult, Native or white, first offender or seasoned inmate, women caught up in the system are treated in ways that only reduce their status further.

Cooper calls it "afterthought" planning in her discussion of the policy treatment of women offenders by the federal government. From collecting data, to researching the causes of women's crimes, to locking women up, historically all have been done in a sexist and intransigent way.

To change this tradition, all of these areas need to be reassessed, and new tools to tackle the problems need to be developed. The necessary basis for good policy-making and the evolution of useful programs is a sound data base. We need to know more about the backgrounds of women who enter the court system in order to work with them effectively. For instance, what is their class background, what kinds of experiences have they had before being arrested, and what is their aptitude for future skills and educational development? If we could answer questions like these, we might be able to demonstrate that new approaches to working with women offenders, including incest and sexual assault counselling, educational and skills training in non-traditional areas, and assertiveness training, would help women in prison to change their lives more than learning to work in the prison kitchen, or the laundry, or the hairdressing salon do now.

We also need better documentation of the effect on women of the court process and imprisonment. As Liz Elliot and Ruth Morris point out in their article, prison programs are poorly equipped to assist women re-entering the world after incarceration, but little time is actually spent analyzing the usefulness of the programs. We believe that the entire structure of the prison system needs to be changed, if it is to produce any positive effect. One significant step would be to reduce the use of imprisonment, so that any woman who is not a physical danger to others would not be placed behind bars. Supervised settings in the community (like the halfway houses we supervised in Ottawa) are cheaper, more humane ways of censuring women offenders' illegal activities, while at the same time providing constructive alternatives that build self-esteem, skills and relationships. Each author in this book suggests new ways of meeting the needs of women and girls in conflict with the law, so that we can begin to challenge the status quo.

While the relatively small numbers of women, compared to men in conflict with the law, has been used in the past to rationalize paying them little attention in research studies or policy development, these small numbers would make it easier to collect data, analyze the women's needs, and plan programs to assist them, *if the political will were there* to order such data collection, and plan such programs. As Berzins and Hayes and Cooper all demonstrate in their articles, political will to do anything new and creative about women offenders has been sadly lacking until now. Its only fleeting appearances have occurred when media attention has turned to issues such as the successful Human Rights Commission complaint by Women for Justice in 1983.[5] Clearly, in this era of political rule by public interest poll, members of the public must emphasize repeatedly their desire to see progressive policies developed for improving the status of women offenders.

Many important issues concerning women and crime are not addressed in this book. The effects of imprisonment on mothers and their children is a topic that needs to be addressed, if we are to stop damaging young people's lives by incarcerating their parents with no thought of the effects on family relationships. Prostitution has received some attention in recent years,[6] but most of the attention has focussed on the nuisance factor of soliciting for "law abiding citizens" in urban neighbourhoods. That women in this society are a sexual commodity to be bought, and that prostitutes must operate without protection from violence and intimidation, are issues which relate very directly to the status of women in conflict with the law.

As mentioned earlier, Native women are highly over-represented in Canadian prison populations. While LaPrairie's article explores the reasons why, it is only a tentative beginning in our understanding of the situation of Native women in conflict with the law. Native women themselves will hopefully share their perspective and lead the way in the process of change.

In this book, the sections on women's imprisonment deal primarily with the situation for federal offenders. Yet the majority of women prisoners in Canada are incarcerated in provincial prisons, serving sentences of under two years, usually for minor offences. Those prisons range from the Vanier Centre for Women in Brampton, Ontario to the Sleepy Hollow Correctional Centre in Charlottetown, Prince Edward Island. The former offers varying types of accommodation, and an array of education and vocational programs; the latter provides almost nothing for female inmates to do to fill their time. In western Canada, co-ed institutions have been operating for several years, and the extent to which mixed-sex institutions serve the needs and interests of women is an issue worthy of debate.

The province of Quebec has had its own traditions in imprisoning women. Francophone women in Quebec as well as in other parts of the country have a distinct history and experience to share.

It is left to future writers to document these provincial conditions, and to point the way towards progressive change.

Part of reclaiming women's history is documenting our oppression in all facets of life. Women who come into conflict with the law, although they constitute a small minority of all women and historically have been considered too few to count, suffer the ramifications of sexual discrimination most acutely of all. But the feminist movement, as mentioned earlier, has paid scant heed to the plight of women offenders. When issues such as rape, or wife battering, or incest, or job discrimination are taken on by feminists, a special effort should be made to consider how they affect women in conflict with the law, and to ensure that remedies such as support services, and job training programs, are also made available to women convicted of crimes.

It is heartening that a feminist group such as the Legal Education and Action Fund (LEAF) has taken on a Charter of Rights challenge on behalf of women in the federal prison. LEAF also funded an action against discrimination in Ontario's welfare laws which, until the laws were abolished recently, landed dozens of women in prison each year for collecting welfare while co-habiting with a male.[7]

Any progressive feminist movement must take into account the role the criminal justice system plays in perpetuating our inferior status. A first step was taken by Status of Women Canada in distributing *A Feminist Review of Criminal Law*, the report which first identified how Canadian criminal law and policy contribute to the oppression of women. In this book, the next step, but by no means the last, is taken towards understanding this reality.

Ellen Adelberg and Claudia Currie
August, 1987

21

NOTES

1 Holly Johnson, *Women and Crime in Canada* (Ottawa: Solicitor General Canada, User Report No. 1986-28), p. 5 and p. 38.

2 Contrary to this state of the art in Canada, significant progress has been made in this area in Britain and the United States. See, for instance, from Britain, Carol Smart's *Women, Crime and Criminology: A Feminist Critique* (London: Routledge & Kegan Paul, 1976); Pat Carlen's *Women's Imprisonment: A Study in Social Control* (London: Routledge & Kegan Paul, 1983) and *Women and Crime* (Cropwood Conference Series No. 13), eds. Allison Morris and Lorraine Gelsthorpe (Cambridge: Inst. of Criminology, 1981). Ground-breaking American literature has included: Dorie Klein and June Kress, "Any Women's Blues: A Critical Overview of Women, Crime and the Criminal Justice System," in *Crime and Social Justice* 5 (Spring-Summer 1975): 34-39; Dorie Klein, "The Etiology of Women's Crime: A Review of the Literature," in *Issues in Criminology* 8 (Fall 1973): 3-30; and Eileen Leonard, *Women, Crime and Society: A Critique of Theoretical Criminology* (New York: Longman Inc., 1982).

3 The most recent and comprehensive work to come from the private sector is *A Forgotten Minority: Women in Conflict with the Law* (Ottawa: The Canadian Association of Elizabeth Fry Societies, 1985). And just as this book was being completed, Bonny Walford, a P4W inmate, helped to fill the gap by writing *Lifers: The Stories of Eleven Women Serving Sentences for Murder* (Montreal: Eden Press, 1987).

4 Johnson; Linda MacLeod, *Sentenced to Separation: An Exploration of the Needs of Mothers Who are Offenders and their Children* (Ottawa: Solicitor General Canada, User Report No. 1986-25); Robert R. Ross and Elizabeth Fabiano, *Correctional Afterthoughts: Programs for Female Offenders* (Ottawa: Solicitor General Canada, User Report No. 1985-18).

5 See Berzins and Hayes' article in this book.

6 *Report of the Special Committee on Pornography and Prostitution* (Ottawa: Department of Supply and Services, 1985).

7 See Berzins and Hayes' article in this book.

Getting the Facts Straight: A Statistical Overview

by HOLLY JOHNSON*

W omen who come into conflict with the law have long been excluded from the serious study of crime. The justification for this typically has been that women account for a minority of all persons charged by police in Canada each year, and rarely pose the same kind of threat to public safety as the more numerous and more violent male offenders. Yet the number of women who are charged with Criminal Code offences amounts to thousands each year. There is also evidence to suggest there are thousands more who, because of poor economic and social standing, may be at risk of becoming involved in criminal activities. Until recently, very little effort has been devoted to understanding who these women are, why and how they develop criminal careers, what resources are available to them, and what can be done to reduce crime by women.

Statistical profiles of women offenders are particularly problematic because of significant gaps in data at all stages of the

* For expanded statistical information, see H. Johnson, *Women and Crime in Canada*, Technical Report No. 9 (Ottawa: Ministry of the Solicitor General, 1986).

criminal justice system, from arrest to incarceration. National police statistics have been published annually since 1963, but while the sex of persons charged is specified, age, race and other socio-demographic characteristics are not. Nor do police statistics count individuals they know have committed an offence but who are not formally charged. Data on sentencing is limited to the provinces of British Columbia and Quebec — and only up to 1980 when the Courts Program at Statistics Canada was disbanded. We know little about women sentenced to short terms of imprisonment or remanded in prison awaiting sentence or trial. Somewhat more detailed is the data concerning the small group of women serving lengthy terms in the federal prison system. In effect, official crime data yields a very incomplete picture of women offenders.

Nevertheless, important observations can be made from official statistics about crime involving women. The purpose of this chapter is to document what is known about women in Canada who come into conflict with the law, to discuss the data within a feminist framework, and to suggest directions for future developments in this area. The ultimate aim is to increase public understanding of women offenders and hence the ability to respond appropriately to their needs for services both before and during involvement with the criminal justice system.

THE STATUS OF WOMEN IN CANADA

The achievements of the contemporary women's movement have meant significant gains for many Canadian women. Over the past decade or so, women have made dramatic inroads into traditionally male-dominated areas in education, the labour force and the political arena. The benefits of these advancements have not been shared equally, however. Unemployment, underemployment, poverty and abuse are still the lot of large numbers of women in Canada today. It is estimated, for example, that one in ten women who lives with a man is abused by him,[1] and one in two females will be the victim of unwanted sexual acts at some point in their lives.[2] Statistics also show that ninety-eight out of every one hundred women will marry during their lifetime and sixty-eight will end up living alone.[3] Upon divorce, the average woman's income goes down forty per cent, while the average man's disposable income goes up seventy per cent. The number of families headed by single female parents has increased by sixty per cent over the past decade. The average income of families headed by women is half the average income of families headed by men. Fully forty-five per cent of female headed families live below the poverty line compared to ten per cent of male-headed families.

This imbalance can be explained in part by women's poorer standing in the employment market. Women remain concentrated in part-time jobs and low-paying occupations. In 1981, seventy-five per cent of all minimum wage earners were women. The "ghettoization" of much of women's labour has served to maintain their average earnings at sixty-four per cent of the average earnings of men. Even those with university degrees earn an average of only $1,600 per year more than men with high school education. For the most disadvantaged women, those who comprise the majority of women who come into conflict with the law, equal opportunity remains a distant reality.

The lower socio-economic status of Canadian women can be traced to paternalism and gender-based roles through which women's participation in a wide range of economic activities is limited and advancement curtailed. Restrictive generalizations and overt discrimination, justified on the basis of women's maternal functions and physical differences, place them at a distinct disadvantage in all aspects of social and economic life.[4] Women continue to be socialized to expect a limited range of functions in life which for the most part preclude economic independence and foster low expectations and low self-esteem.[5] An appreciation of these aspects of women's experience is central to understanding female criminality.

WHO IS THE WOMAN OFFENDER?

The public image of women offenders has suffered enormously in the absence of comprehensive data and a focussed perspective on female crime. In her article "Women's Crime: New Perspectives and Old Theories," Gavigan explains in some depth how criminally deviant women have been characterized by early theorists as morally deficient, devious and deceitful, or maladjusted to their "natural" roles as women.[6] Some recent theorists contend we are witnessing an historical upsurge in crime by women and point to the contemporary women's movement as the root cause.[7] We are warned, in particular, that the increased willingness of women to emulate the behaviour of men is closing the gaps in the incidence and types of crimes committed by women and men, and that a new breed of violent female criminal is on the rise.[8]

As in the past, these new theories suffer from outdated notions and a lack of scientific rigour. Canadian statistics suggest a link between the social and economic status and the criminality of women, and the status of women on the whole remains poor in comparison to men. In the experience of correctional workers, women who come into conflict with the criminal justice system tend to be young, poor, under-educated and unskilled. A disproportionate number are Native. Many are addicted to alcohol, drugs or both. Large numbers have been victims of physical and sexual abuse, and many are emotionally or financially dependent on abusive male partners. This type of information about the lives of women offenders is essential for a better understanding of their needs for services, but is generally lacking in available statistical data.

Police statistics show that over the past twenty years, recorded female crime has increased steadily (Table 1 in this section). Women offenders doubled from seven per cent to fourteen per cent of all persons charged with Criminal Code offences. Offences which account for the bulk of the increase in female crime are non-violent. In 1965, forty-five per cent of all charges against women were for property offences; by 1985 this proportion had increased to almost sixty per cent. More than one-half of all women charged with Criminal Code offences in 1985 were charged with theft or fraud.

Figure 1 in this article shows the relative distribution of charges laid against women and men in 1985. The proportion of women charged with theft and fraud was more than twice the proportion of men charged with these offences. Men were more likely than women to be charged with violent offences, impaired driving and other property crimes such as breaking and entering and possession of stolen property. Women's participation in property

Table 1

WOMEN[1] CHARGED WITH CRIMINAL CODE OFFENCES, 1965-1985

	1965		1975		1985	
	Number	Percent	Number	Percent	Number	Percent
Violent Offences						
Murder/Manslaughter	22	0.2	71	0.2	81	0.1
Attempt Murder/Wounding/Assault	1,006	7.2	2,942	6.6	6,168	8.6
Rape/Other Sexual	23	0.2	44	0.1	168	0.2
Robbery	125	0.9	398	0.9	474	0.7
Total	1,176	8.4	3,455	7.7	6,891	9.6
Propery Offences						
Break and Enter	303	2.2	1,098	2.4	1732	2.4
Theft over $200	894	6.4	1,405	3.1	3,942	5.5
Theft under $200	3,857	27.6	17,426	38.8	24,897	34.9
Possession of Stolen Goods	275	2.0	1,056	2.4	1,574	2.2
Fraud	984	7.0	3,954	8.8	9,387	13.1
Total	6,313	45.1	24,939	55.5	41,532	58.1
Other Offences						
Prostitution	1,274	9.1	2,372	5.3	566	0.8
Impaired Driving[2]	754	5.4	5,148	11.5	9,956	13.9
Other CC Traffic[3]	434	3.1	1,345	3.0	812	1.1
Other Criminal Code[4]	4,040	28.9	7,659	17.1	11,680	16.4
TOTAL CRIMINAL CODE	13,991	100.0	44,918	100.0	71,437	100.0

1 *Double counting occurs if an individual is charged in more than one incident during the year.*
2 *Includes driving while impaired, fail or refuse to provide a breath sample.*
3 *Includes criminal negligence, failure to stop at scene of accident, dangerous driving, driving while disqualified.*
4 *Includes gaming and betting, offensive weapons, arson, kidnapping, wilful damage, abduction and other Criminal Code offences.*

Source: Statistics Canada, *Canadian Crime Statistics* (Ottawa: Ministry of Supply and Services, 1966; 1977; 1986) Annual, No. 85-205.

Figure 1
CRIMINAL CODE OFFENCES, 1985

WOMEN CHARGED

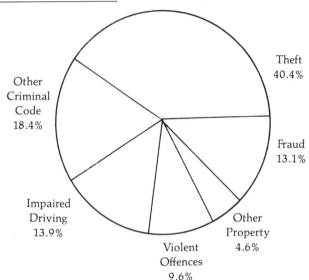

Theft
40.4%

Other
Criminal
Code
18.4%

Fraud
13.1%

Impaired
Driving
13.9%

Other
Property
4.6%

Violent
Offences
9.6%

MEN CHARGED

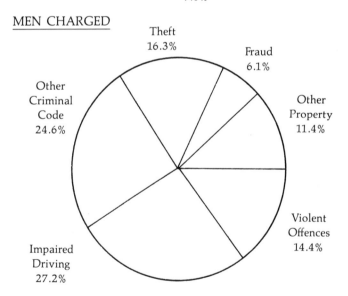

Theft
16.3%

Fraud
6.1%

Other
Criminal
Code
24.6%

Other
Property
11.4%

Violent
Offences
14.4%

Impaired
Driving
27.2%

Source: Statistics Canada, *Canadian Crime Statistics* (Ottawa: Ministry of Supply and Services) Annual, No. 85-205

offences is consistent with their traditional roles as consumers and, increasingly, as low income, semi-skilled, sole support providers for their families. In keeping with the rapid increase in female-headed households and the stresses associated with poverty, greater numbers of women are being charged with shoplifting, cheque forging and welfare fraud.

Also in keeping with women's social and economic status is the number of young women who turn to prostitution. The 1985 *Report of the Special Committee on Pornography and Prostitution* concluded that because of the difficulty of detecting some practices of prostitution, it is impossible to know whether the number of prostitutes in Canada has increased in recent years, but there undoubtedly has been an increase in the number working on the streets.[9] Police records of prostitution-related offences which show dramatic fluctuations over the past two decades must be viewed with a great deal of caution. Rather than indicating the actual participation of women in prostitution, police data (shown in Table 1) reflects the impact of prevailing social and legal definitions of this behaviour on police activity. By altering the legal definition of these offences, court decisions have had a tremendous impact on the number of women charged. For example, the offence of soliciting for the purpose of prostitution was severely limited in scope by a Supreme Court of Canada decision in 1978 which said that soliciting was illegal only when "pressing and persistent." In the same case, it was decided that a private vehicle on a public thoroughfare did not constitute a "public place" for the purposes of a conviction. The number of women charged with soliciting dropped off sharply in 1978, due largely to realistic assessments by police of the chances of successful prosecution.

Prostitution thrives in a society which values women more for their sexuality than for their unskilled labour, and which puts women in a class of commodity to be bought and sold. Research has shown one of the major causes of prostitution to be the economic plight of women, particularly young, poorly educated women who are unable to find other employment.[10] Entry into prostitution is also typically characterized by running away from home, often to escape physical and sexual abuse.[11] Rather than providing a refuge from ill-treatment, however, street life puts women at great risk of further violence and abuse, and significantly increases their vulnerability to identification and arrest by police.

One area in particular for which there exists a serious lack of information about women offenders is their role in crimes of violence. Almost 7,000 charges were laid against women in 1985 for acts of violence, up from less than 1,200 in 1965. Although police statistics hold no clues about the nature of these violent acts, the small body of research in this area suggests that violence by women for the most part consists of acts of rebellion or retaliation against abusive or exploitative domestic situations. One Canadian study of women imprisoned for violent crimes found the incidents occurred primarily within the family milieu.[12] While homicide by women is relatively rare, 1985 statistics show that sixty per cent of the victims in these offences were domestically related to the offenders, and were usually a spouse or common-law partner.[13] The increase in violence by women over the past twenty years may very well reflect an increase in the incidence of family violence in which women are ultimately both victim and offender. Further research and statistical information in this area is critical if we are to understand and respond to the violence in the lives of women who are charged with crimes of violence.

The criminality of women may also be explained as symptomatic of a sense of futility with a desperate life situation, perhaps following from poverty, homelessness or abuse. In 1985, approximately 18,000 women were charged with violations of provincial liquor laws such as drinking in a public place or under age; an additional 10,000 were charged with impaired driving, and 4,000 with drug offences.[14] These figures almost certainly understate the number of women who find escape through alcohol or drugs, and who suffer severe health and social consequences as a result.

Hysterical predictions of a female crime wave are fuelled by a misrepresentation of police statistics. The worst offenders are the mass media, also the principal source of public information on crime and the criminal justice system.[15] It is common practice in news reports to compare percentage increases in Criminal Code charges laid against women and men, which is essentially a meaningless comparison. Because of the much lower base *number* of charges against women for any given offence, *percentage* increases consistently give the appearance of greater increases in the number of women offenders relative to the number of men, no matter how small the increase in actual numbers may be.

For example, a total overall increase of 400 per cent in women charged with Criminal Code offences over a period of twenty years represents a difference in actual numbers of about 57,000, whereas a percentage change of only 150 per cent represents a real increase of 272,000 men charged over the same period (see Tables 1 and 2). The increase in the actual *number* of men charged is almost five times the increase in the actual number of women charged.

Similarly, an increase of almost 300 per cent between 1965 and 1985 in charges against women for homicide offences reflects a real increase of only 59 women. To claim that crimes by women increased 400 per cent and crimes by men only 150 per cent by comparison, or that homicides involving women grew by 300 per cent, is an irresponsible approach to crime data analysis if actual number of offenders are not also given emphasis. It becomes evident that sensationalistic reports of escalating crime by women are simply untrue. If police charges against women follow recent trends, the gradual increase in base numbers in most offence categories will yield increasingly smaller percentage changes, and not the "crime wave" predicted.

"Official" crime statistics are subject to a number of influences independent of the volume of crime that comes to the attention of the police, factors which have considerable bearing on how women are labelled criminal. Although empirical evidence is scarce, it has been argued, for instance, that crimes by women are less likely to be reported to the police than crimes by men, and that criminal justice officials, who are usually male, give preferential treatment to women who come into conflict with the law.[16] Consequently, the argument goes, women offenders are seriously undercounted in police statistics.

Certainly the reverse is true where juvenile offenders are concerned. Under the Juvenile Delinquents Act,[17] girls were routinely charged with "status" offences which normally would not result in charges against adults or boys.[18] Although male delinquents outnumber females about five to one, girls tradi-tionally have been dealt with much more severely by the social

Table 2

MEN[1] CHARGED WITH CRIMINAL CODE OFFENCES, 1965-1985

	1965 Number	Percent	1975 Number	Percent	1985 Number	Percent
Violent Offences						
Murder/Manslaughter	169	0.1	451	0.1	490	0.1
Attempt Murder/Wounding/Assault	17,522	10.0	29,998	7.3	51,520	11.5
Rape/Other Sexual	2,786	1.6	3,467	0.8	7,120	1.6
Robbery	1,901	1.1	5,549	1.4	5,461	1.2
Total	22,378	12.8	39,465	9.6	64,591	14.4
Property Offences						
Break and Enter	12,592	7.2	30,381	7.4	39,473	8.8
Theft over $200	13,686	7.8	18,519	4.5	24,472	5.5
Theft under $200	14,198	8.1	38,741	9.4	48,437	10.8
Possession of Stolen Goods	3,557	2.0	9,040	2.2	11,688	2.6
Fraud	8,324	4.8	16,788	4.1	27,484	6.1
Total	52,357	29.9	113,469	27.6	151,554	33.8
Other Offences						
Prostitution	459	0.3	696	0.2	385	0.1
Impaired Driving[2]	35,353	20.2	137,889	33.5	121,770	27.2
Other CC Traffic[3]	19,589	11.2	38,163	9.3	10,482	2.3
Other Criminal Code[4]	45,266	25.8	81,832	19.9	99,091	22.1
TOTAL CRIMINAL CODE	175,402	100.0	411,514	100.0	447,873	100.0

1 Double counting occurs if an individual is charged in more than one incident during the year.
2 Includes driving while impaired, fail or refuse to provide a breath sample.
3 Includes criminal negligence, failure to stop at scene of accident, dangerous driving, driving while disqualified.
4 Includes gaming and betting, offensive weapons, arson, kidnapping, wilful damage, abduction and other Criminal Code offences.

Source: Statistics Canada, *Canadian Crime Statistics* (Ottawa: Ministry of Supply and Services, 1966; 1977; 1986) Annual, No. 85-205.

welfare and criminal justice systems. Girls are expected to be passive and obedient and when they aren't, the police and courts have been quick to classify them as abnormal or disturbed. This practice has been defended under the guise of paternalism and a belief that the virtue of girls is more highly valued and in need of protection than the virtue of boys. It is impossible to determine from police statistics the extent to which fluctuations in the number of charges laid against adult women are the direct result of changes over time in the attitudes of police officers toward women offenders.

The steady increase in recorded crime involving both women and men is occurring in direct proportion to the ability of the police to detect and record crimes. As technology advances, so does the ability of the police to respond quickly, track offenders and record criminal incidents. The size of the increase in the rate of any one offence is affected by the enforcement practices and priorities of local police, changes in legislation and legal precedents. Fluctuations in the number of drug offences recorded by the police in Canada over the past two decades, as an example, are tied not so much to the actual occurrence of these offences as to societal tolerance and local political pressures which cause police to target certain offences and offenders for arrest. Legislative changes and legal precedents established with respect to prostitution-related offences, as discussed earlier, have had a profound effect on the level of enforcement of these and other related offence categories and on the number of women charged with criminal offences. These are only a few examples of the sensitivity of crime data to external forces which are commonly ignored in analyses of women and crime.

WOMEN IN PRISON

There are no nationally collected court statistics to describe the kinds of sentences women in Canada receive. In 1980, the last year for which court statistics are available, women convicted of criminal offences in British Columbia and Quebec were proportionally less likely than men to receive prison sentences (fifteen per cent compared to twenty-five per cent).[19] The lower incarceration rates for women may be related to the comparatively minor nature of the crimes in which women become involved, their shorter criminal histories, and the often ancillary role women play to men in serious crimes. The statistics on fines are mixed: in British Columbia women were less likely than men to receive a fine, while in Quebec the reverse was true. Nevertheless, given the social status and economic disadvantage of women, and the growing number of women who are likely to have sole responsibility for young children,[20] the impact of criminal sanctions such as fines and jail sentences are almost certainly felt more acutely by women than by men.

Women who are sentenced to terms of imprisonment may be held in provincial or federal institutions depending on the length of the sentence they receive. Those serving sentences of two years or more are the responsibility of the federal government, while those sentenced to less than two years, or who are remanded in custody awaiting sentence or trial, come under the jurisdiction of the province or territory in which they are tried. The majority of men and women incarcerated each year serve sentences of less than two years. The Canadian Centre for Justice Statistics has only recently made available very limited statistics on women admitted to provincial or territorial institutions. Between 1978 and 1985, women admitted under sentence to all provincial and territorial correctional institutions each year increased from almost 5,000 to 8,000, and women admitted under remand increased from about 3,000 to 5,000.[21] These are only very rough estimates of the actual number of women admitted to jail each year, however, since some are admitted more than once in a year on remand, under sentence or both, and are counted separately each time. We do know, for instance, that one-half of the 8,000 sentenced admissions in 1985 had been incarcerated at least once before.

Virtually nothing is known from official statistics about women who are remanded in custody. All that is known about those who are sentenced to imprisonment is the length of the sentence and the type of offence that leads to conviction. As Figure 2 illustrates, less than ten per cent of women admitted under provincial sentence in 1985 had been convicted of a violent offence.[22] Three of every ten women were admitted for property offences, and the remainder for impaired driving, violations of provincial liquor acts, drug offences, other Criminal Code

Figure 2

OFFENCE TYPE FOR WOMEN ADMITTED UNDER SENTENCE TO PROVINCIAL INSTITUTIONS, 1985

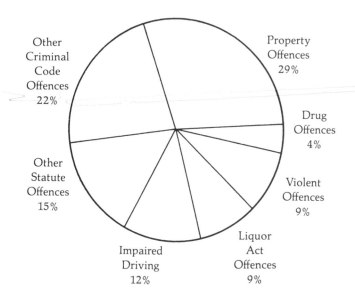

Other Criminal Code Offences 22%

Property Offences 29%

Drug Offences 4%

Other Statute Offences 15%

Violent Offences 9%

Impaired Driving 12%

Liquor Act Offences 9%

Source: Statistics Canada, Canadian Centre for Justice Statistics, Corrections Program, unpublished data.

offences, and infractions of other statutes and by-laws. Almost half received sentences of less than fourteen days and two-thirds received sentences of less than one month.

Descriptive information about the inmates themselves is unavailable but from what we know about the type of offences for which women typically are charged, convicted and sentenced to jail, it would appear that the large majority are non-violent. For many, the indirect cause of imprisonment is alcohol abuse. Most importantly, for one third of all women admitted to provincial jails in Canada each year, their greatest crime is poverty:

approximately thirty-four per cent were incarcerated in default of fine payment. For some, life is a revolving door of theft or alcoholism and jail.

The large number of non-violent offenders who are jailed for short periods of time, often when incarceration was not the intended sentence (as in the case of inability to pay a fine), should be of utmost concern for those interested in the needs of women offenders. The high rate of women being sent to jail more than once for minor offences is evidence of the failure of the penal system to deter these women from further criminal involvement. Viable programs for women are visibly lacking in most provincial jails where the majority of women serve less than thirty days. At a minimum, greater emphasis must be placed on programs and services to enable women to serve their sentences in the community, particularly those women unable to meet the requirements of a financial penalty. Programs for women in need of educational training, skills development, addiction counselling and the like are much more readily implemented and utilized in the community than during a few days or weeks of incarceration.

The smallest group of women offenders within the criminal justice system are those serving prison terms of two years or longer and who come under the jurisdiction of the federal government. The number of women admitted to federal penitentiary increased from eighty-nine in 1975 to 141 in 1985, remaining at a steady two per cent of the total penitentiary population.[23] Women are also being admitted to federal prison with increasingly longer sentences, and this has resulted in an expanding female inmate population. Between 1975, when Correctional Services Canada began collecting detailed data on federal inmates, and 1985, the total number of women on register under federal sentence increased from 173 to 235.

The trend towards longer sentences follows from an increase in the number of women admitted to federal penitentiary for crimes of violence, particularly in the categories of murder, manslaughter and serious assault (Table 3). The number of women sentenced each year to terms of ten years or more increased from nine in 1975 to fifteen in 1985 (Table 4). By 1985, there were forty-nine women in Canada serving minimum twenty year sentences and sixty serving sentences of ten years or more. The likelihood that federal women inmates will have served a federal

Table 3

OFFENCE TYPE FOR WOMEN AND MEN
ADMITTED TO FEDERAL PENITENTIARY, 1975-1985

		1975 Number	1975 Percent	1985 Number	1985 Percent
Murder/Manslaughter	F	10	11.2	20	14.2
	M	231	6.1	283	6.0
Attempt Murder/	F	5	5.6	10	7.1
Wounding/Assault	M	150	3.9	334	7.1
Rape/Other Sexual	F	0	0	2	1.4
	M	226	5.9	132	2.8
Robbery	F	11	12.4	18	12.9
	M	980	25.7	1,051	22.2
Break and Enter/	F	15	16.9	29	20.7
Theft/Fraud	M	1,498	39.3	1,833	38.8
Federal Statute	F	33	37.1	40	28.6
Drugs	M	334	8.8	374	7.9
Other Criminal Code/	F	14	16.8	21	15.0
Federal Statute	M	389	10.2	720	15.2
Total	F	88	100.0	140	100.0
	M	3.808	100.0	4,727	100.0

Identifying information such as the offence type of persons granted a pardon or released with convictions quashed are retroactively deleted from the O.I.S. data base. This practice may be the cause of discrepancies in totals appearing in Tables 2 and 4.

Source: Solicitor General, Correctional Services Canada, Offender Information System, unpublished data.

sentence previously is also on the rise, a factor which has been shown to have considerable bearing on sentencing.

Despite this increase, the number of women serving lengthy sentences at any one time remains small, and this adds to the difficulty and the urgency of providing adequate programs and services for them. Particularly where the growing prison population of "lifers" are concerned, female inmates are limited in many of the more basic options open to male offenders, and at the heart of much of the controversy over the delivery of services to women is the issue of correctional facilities (see "The Diaries of Two Change Agents" by Lorraine Berzins and Brigid Hayes). Whereas there are over forty prisons in Canada for men serving sentences of two years or more, the Prison for Women in Kingston, Ontario is the only institution operated by the federal government for women offenders. As a result, women are denied the same opportunities as men for transfer to facilities with a

Table 4

LENGTH OF SENTENCE OF WOMEN AND MEN
ADMITTED TO FEDERAL PENITENTIARY, 1975-1985

| | | 1975 | | 1985 | |
		Number	Percent	Number	Percent
Less than 2	F	5	5.6	18	12.8
years[1]	M	473	12.3	835	16.3
2-3 years	F	30	33.7	33	23.4
	M	1,313	34.3	1,602	31.2
3-5 years	F	26	29.2	42	29.8
	M	1,097	28.6	1,540	30.0
5-10	F	19	21.3	33	23.4
	M	618	16.1	783	15.3
10-20 years	F	3	3.4	6	4.3
	M	169	4.4	169	3.3
20 years to life	F	6	6.7	9	6.4
or indefinite	M	163	4.3	202	3.9
Total	F	89	100.0	141	100.0
	M	3,833	100.0	5,131	100.0

1 *Federal sentences of less than 2 years reflect sentences recalculated due to day parole revocation or being unlawfully at large, or readmissions due to parole or mandatory supervision revocation with a new indictable offence.*

Source: Solicitor General, Correctional Services Canada, Offender Information System, unpublished data.

reduced security classification, special program options, or to a preferred geographic location.

Agreements between the federal government and all provinces except Ontario and Prince Edward Island have been in effect since 1973, allowing women under federal sentence to apply to serve their sentences in provincial correctional institutions closer to their homes and families. But the lack of uniform guidelines governing transfers, and the disparity in availability of local facilities, have resulted in unequal opportunity to participate in this option. By 1985 there were 157 women on register in the Prison for Women and 108 federal women inmates in provincial institutions, primarily in Quebec and the western provinces.[24] Forty-five women in the Atlantic region received federal sentences between 1980 and 1984, and only four remained in the Atlantic region to serve their sentences in a provincial institution.[25] Two-thirds of women admitted under federal sentence between 1975 and 1985 were under thirty, the age at which women are most likely to have responsibility for young children. In a report prepared for the Ministry of the Solicitor General, Linda MacLeod estimates that four per cent of women admitted to correctional institutions are pregnant, fifty per cent have borne children and thirty per cent had been living with their children prior to incarceration.[26] Extra hardship is placed on both women and their children when mothers are incarcerated for long periods at great distances from their homes and families.

NATIVE WOMEN AND CRIME

Native people are over-represented among the number of Canadians who are arrested and incarcerated and the disproportionate presence of Native women incarcerated is even greater than for Native men. Although Native people (status and non-status Indians, Metis and Inuit) make up an estimated two per cent of the Canadian population, in 1985 they accounted for an average of eighteen per cent of all admissions to provincial and territorial institutions and more than ninety per cent of admissions in some areas.[27] This high rate of criminalization of Native people is clearly linked to their bleak socio-economic profile. That Native people live in deprived conditions relative to Canadians generally is beyond dispute. The situation is aggravated for Native women who suffer racial discrimination, gender discrimination and, until 1985, when section 12(1)(b) of the Indian Act was amended, legislated discrimination that deprived some women of Indian status, forced them off reserves and denied them rights (see Carol LaPrairie's article, "Native Women and Crime in Canada.").

The 1981 census reports that single parent families are twice as common among Native Indians as among non-Native families, and that families with five or more children are five times more common.[28] The high incidence of birth outside marriage among Indian people (four to five times the national average) may be attributed in part to the reluctance of women to relinquish their status by marrying non-Indian men.[19] In 1981, only one-quarter of Native women in rural areas and less than one-half of those in urban areas were employed, compared to forty per cent and fifty per cent of non-Native women. In 1980, almost one-third of Native women had no income, compared to one-quarter of non-Native women and seven per cent of non-Native men. This reflects low education and the substantially lower rate of full-time, full-year employment among Native people, and Native women in particular.

The rate of violent death among status Indians is more than three times the national average.[30] Young Indians aged fifteen to twenty-four have the highest suicide rate in Canada, more than six times the national rate. It is estimated that over one-half of illnesses and deaths suffered by Indian people are alcohol-related. In addition, Native people living on reserves have a higher than average incidence of respiratory and infectious diseases, reflecting poor housing and living conditions and poorer access to medical facilities.

These statistics offer only a glimpse of the consequences of a near complete breakdown of the Native culture and traditional way of life. The number of Native people who leave their homes for work in cities is growing, and when this occurs, lack of experience in an urban environment, poor support systems and visibility to police almost certainly increase their chances of coming into contact with the criminal justice system. However, official statistics which trace the involvement of Native people in the justice system are extremely limited. Police statistics do not identify the ancestry of persons charged, and details about offenders are available only for those sentenced to prison terms of two years or longer. It is instructive, therefore, to look to small local studies which have succeeded in gathering critical information about Native people and their conflict with the dominant legal system.

A study of charges by the Winnipeg City Police in 1969 found a shockingly high incidence of arrest among Native women. While Native people comprised approximately three per cent of the urban Winnipeg population, charges against Native women accounted for seventy per cent of all charges against women, and charges against Native men accounted for twenty-seven per cent of all charges against men.[31] Native women were twice as likely as Native men to be charged with violent offences. Although these statistics cannot be generalized to areas of Canada outside Winnipeg, they raise some important questions about violence

Table 5

OVER-REPRESENTATION OF NATIVE WOMEN
IN PROVINCIAL AND TERRITORIAL
CORRECTIONAL INSTITUTIONS

Province	Percent Native in general population, 1981	Number non-Native women inmates 1982[1]	Number native women inmates 1982[2]	Percent Native in female inmate population
Yukon Territory	18	0	3	100
Northwest Territories	58	3	9	75
British Columbia	3	52	13	20
Alberta	3	99	41	29
Saskatchewan	6	14	46	77
Manitoba	6	11	27	71
Ontario	1	232	46	17
Quebec	1	143	2	1
New Brunswick	1	15	2	12
Nova Scotia	1	20	0	0
Prince Edward Island	1	2	0	0
Newfoundland	1	0	8	100
Canada	2	591	197	25

1. One day snapshot
2. Ibid

Source: C. Misch, et al., *National Survey Concerning Female Inmates in Provincial and Territorial Institutions* (Ottawa: Canadian Association of Elizabeth Fry Societies, 1982).

Statistics Canada, *Canada's Native People* (Ottawa: Ministry of Supply and Services, 1984) No. 99-937.

in the lives of Native women and the lack of alternate social support systems for Native women in urban communities.

According to a "snapshot" survey of provincial and territorial institutions by the Canadian Association of Elizabeth Fry Societies, one-quarter of female inmates incarcerated on one day in 1982 were Native.[32] The over-representation of Native women in the female inmate population varied considerably among provinces, with Alberta, Saskatchewan, Manitoba and Ontario showing the greatest concentration (Table 5). Native women were much more likely than non-Natives to have been incarcerated for a violent offence and for an inability to pay a court-ordered fine.

According to the annual report of the Ontario Ministry of Correctional Services, Native women accounted for fourteen per cent of all women admitted to provincial institutions in 1984 in a province where Native people make up less than two per cent of the total population.[33] A study to determine the problems faced by Native persons incarcerated in Ontario correctional institutions concluded that alcohol abuse, unemployment and poor living conditions were critical factors in the high incidence of arrest and incarceration of Native people.[34] The rate of unemployment among the women in the sample was over eight times the national average, and any employment they had was almost always temporary. Many women were dependent on some form of social assistance. Native women were twice as likely as Native men to be incarcerated for liquor-related offences and default of fine payment. This study also reports that Native inmates are seriously isolated from their culture and their families, and that distance from their communities, the expense of travelling to institutions, and a breakdown in family relationships contribute to this isolation.

In a report to the government of the Northwest Territories, Native women were found to account for over ninety per cent of women admitted to local institutions in 1983, even though Native people comprise less than sixty per cent of the total population.[35] One-half of the women admitted to correctional institutions that year were under twenty-one years of age. While only one in five was married at the time of incarceration, one-third had at least one dependent. Only two per cent completed high school.

Statistics collected by Correctional Services Canada offer some insight into the background of Native women sentenced to federal penitentiary, which differs in some important respects to that of non-Native women. Native women admitted to federal terms of incarceration are more likely than non-Native women to have served a federal sentence previously, and are twice as likely to be incarcerated for crimes of violence. Sentences, however, were shorter overall for Native women owing to the minimum mandatory sentences given for the drug offence of importing (more often a white woman's offence) and the greater likelihood of Native women to be convicted of manslaughter, which does not carry a minimum life sentence, compared to murder, which does.[36]

Isolation from family and community support is even more severe for Native than non-Native women inmates. Three-quarters of Native women who receive federal sentences are from the Pacific and Prairie regions, yet seventy per cent are incarcerated in the Prison for Women in Ontario, great distances from where they were admitted and presumably from where they will eventually return.[37] This likely has a very negative effect on release plans and on chances for early release. Research has shown that Native women are less likely to be granted full parole, and those who are released early are more likely to have parole revoked,[38] a situation which may be affected by isolation from families while incarcerated and poor support in home communities upon release.

CONCLUSIONS

This statistical overview, though necessarily incomplete, describes women offenders as a microcosm of women in society at large. For the most part, women in conflict with the law are non-violent offenders who commit petty crimes of economic gain. Their offences are concentrated in the types of property crimes that could well be considered means of survival in a time when employment options for unskilled women are becoming increasingly restricted. For some women, sexual or physical abuse as a child mark passage into a life of street prostitution; for others, years of physical or emotional abuse as an adult culminates in a single act of violence. Many women offenders are at the same time victims.

The response of the justice system in many cases has been to impose jail sentences, often for the inability to pay a fine. The options these women have for alternatives to the lifestyle they experienced before arrest are few. In fact, a criminal record usually guarantees immobility on the social status ladder and reduced opportunities for success.

The needs of women who come into conflict with the law, or are at risk of joining the ranks of offenders, extend beyond the criminal justice system. Statistics suggest that offenders, like a great many Canadian women, need greater opportunities for advancement, job re-training and economic independence.

To begin to address these needs, more data must be collected at all stages of the justice system. Little can be said with confidence at this point about the type of counselling or treatment programs that would benefit women offenders. We need to know, in greater detail, the specific life situations of women who are charged with criminal offences. On the basis of this knowledge, programs could be designed to divert offenders into non-criminal life-styles and improve the life situations of thousands of would-be offenders.

NOTES

1 Linda MacLeod, *Wife Battering in Canada: The Vicious Circle* (Ottawa: Canadian Advisory Council on the Status of Women, 1980), p. 21. See also Linda MacLeod, *Battered But Not Beaten: Preventing Wife Battering in Canada* (Ottawa: Canadian Advisory Council on the Status of Women, 1987).

2 Canada, *Report of the Committee on Sexual Offences Against Children and Youths* (Ottawa: Ministry of Supply and Services, 1984), p. 175.

3 Statistics Canada, *Women in Canada: A Statistical Report* (Ottawa: Ministry of Supply and Services, 1985), No. 89-503E.

4 Canada, *Report of the Royal Commission on the Status of Women in Canada* (Ottawa: Ministry of Supply and Services, 1970), p. 11.

5 Canada, *Report of the Commission on Equality in Employment* (Ottawa: Ministry of Supply and Services, 1985), pp. 133-164.

6 See also Cesare Lombroso, *The Female Offender* (Littleton: Rothman, 1895), p. 151 and Otto Pollak, *The Criminality of Women* (Philadelphia: University of Pennsylvania Press, 1950), p. 3.

7 Freda Adler, *Sisters in Crime: The Rise of the New Female Criminal* (New York: McGraw-Hill, 1975) and Rita Simon, *Women and Crime* (Toronto: Lexington Books, 1975).

8 Adler, p. 14.

9 Canada, *Report of the Special Committee on Pornography and Prostitution* (Ottawa: Ministry of Supply and Services, 1985), p. 369.

10 Ibid., p. 353.

11 Canada, *Report of the Committee on Sexual Offences*, pp. 980-984.

12 Ellen Rosenblatt and Cyril Greenland, "Female Crimes of Violence," *Canadian Journal of Criminology and Corrections* 16 (1974): 173-180.

13 Statistics Canada, Canadian Centre for Justice Statistics, Law Enforcement Program, unpublished data.

14 Statistics Canada, *Canadian Crime Statistics* (Ottawa: Ministry of Supply and Services, 1966; 1977; 1986) Annual, No. 85-205.

15 See for example "Crimes by Women Increasing," *Montreal Gazette* 19 June 1986 and "Women Turning to Violent Crime," *Winnipeg Free Press* 27 June 1983.

16 Pollak, p. 2.

17 The Young Offenders Act was passed in 1982 and came into effect in 1985, replacing the Juvenile Delinquents Act.

18 Barbara Landau, "The Adolescent Female Offender: Our Dilemma," *Canadian Journal of Criminology and Corrections* 17 (1975): 146-153.

19 Statistics Canada, Canadian Centre for Justice Statistics, Adult Court Program, unpublished data.

20 Statistics Canada, *Women in Canada*, p. 6.

21 Statistics Canada, *Adult Correctional Services in Canada* (Ottawa: Ministry of Supply and Services, 1979; 1986) Annual, No. 85-211.

22 Statistics Canada, Canadian Centre for Justice Statistics, Corrections Program, unpublished data.

23 Solicitor General Canada, Correctional Services Canada, Offender Information System, unpublished data.

24 Ibid.

25 Ibid.

26 Linda MacLeod, *Sentenced to Separation: An Exploration of the Needs and Problems of Mothers who are Offenders and their Children* (Ottawa: Ministry of the Solicitor General, 1986), p. 11.

27 Statistics Canada, *Adult Correctional Services in Canada* (Ottawa: Ministry of Supply and Services, 1986) Annual, No. 85-211.

28 Statistics Canada, *Canada's Native People* (Ottawa: Ministry of Supply and Services, 1984) No. 99-937.

29 *Indian Conditions: A Survey* (Ottawa: Department of Indian Affairs and Northern Development, 1980), p. 24.

30 Ibid., p. 18.

31 Rita M. Bienvenue and A.H. Latif "Arrests, Dispositions and Recidivism: A Comparison of Natives and Whites," *Canadian Journal of Criminology and Corrections* 16 (1974): 105-115.

32 Cindy Misch, Christie Jefferson, Brigid Hayes and Candis Graham, *National Survey Concerning Female Inmates in Provincial and Territorial Institutions* (Ottawa: The Canadian Association of Elizabeth Fry Societies, 1982).

33 Ontario Ministry of Correctional Services, *Annual Report 1984-85* (Toronto: Ministry of Correctional Services, 1986).

34 Andrew Birkenmayer and Stan Jolly, *The Native Inmate in Ontario* (Toronto: Ministry of Correctional Services and the Ontario Native Council, 1981), p. vi.

35 *Female Offender Study Committee Report to the Minister* (Government of the Northwest Territories, Department of Health and Social Services, 1985).

36 Solicitor General Canada, Correctional Services Canada, Offender Information System, unpublished data.

37 Ibid.

38 Robert Hann and William Harman, "Full Parole Release: An Historical Descriptive Analysis," prepared for the Ministry of the Solicitor General, 1986.

Women's Crime:
New Perspectives
and
Old Theories

by SHELLEY GAVIGAN*

U ntil very recently, it was possible to condemn criminologists both for their near silence on women and criminal law, and for their sexism when they did speak. The most recent wave of feminism has witnessed two seemingly contradictory developments in theories of women and crime. First, feminism has kindled interest in women's studies in various academic disciplines. Criminology has been no exception: the sexist treatment of women victims and offenders by police and other criminal justice officials, the sexism of traditional theories of crime and the concept of victimless crimes have all been under attack.[1]

But, there have also been arguments that women's crime has increased as a result of the women's liberation movement. This belief has been called "the most powerful and widely held... concerning the topic of female criminality,"[2] and its impact has been felt by women offenders being punished for their supposed acts of liberation.[3] Feminist criminologists now must do more than denounce mainstream criminology for its failure to acknowledge the significance of female crime. It is not simply enough to

* An earlier version of this paper appeared in *Canadian Criminology Forum* 6, (1983): 75-90.

resurrect the neglected female offender. We must transcend the traditional boundaries of criminology and examine the role of the state and the law in reinforcing the position of women in contemporary society.

Criminologists often assume that definitions of crime and categories of offences apply equally to all historical periods and to all cultural and social groups. However, it is important to be precise in studying crime to avoid the assumption that women's crime (or anyone else's for that matter) is always and everywhere the same. The formal definitions of the law and the ways particular activities are criminalized, as well as the underlying social and economic structures, must be understood. For instance, the early criminologist Cesare Lombroso[4] studied prostitutes, but if prostitution had not been a crime in late nineteenth-century Italy, there would have been none in prison for him to study. Similarly, abortion in the early months of pregnancy did not become an offence in England until a statute enacted in 1803 prohibited the practice for the first time. Thus prostitution and abortion, now often considered to be women's crimes, would in other times not even have been the subject of criminological investigation.

Two criminological issues merit attention. First, women's crime has been explained in terms of sexuality and psychology, and invariably in reference to "real" (male) crime.[5] Given this, it is necessary to consider what *image* of women is reinforced by various theoretical perspectives. In other words, does criminological literature reproduce conventional wisdom about the inherent nature of women and their proper sphere?

Criminologists' images of women tend to be inconsistent and contradictory. For example, women's crime has often been explained in physiological terms, as resulting from raging female hormones (as in cases of theories that are based on premenstrual syndrome, pregnancy, postpartum depression and menopause). Other times, the very lack of "female" qualities and the "masculinization" of women is blamed for women's involvement in crimes.

A second issue is the relationship between equality, liberation and crime. This has been a recurring theme throughout the twentieth century. It has been the focus of contentious debate[6] ever since Freda Adler[7] argued that the rise of American feminism in the late sixties and early seventies caused an increase in women's criminal activity. These are the two themes—the representation of women in criminological literature and the impact of feminism—addressed in this article.

THE BIOLOGICAL IMPERATIVE: LOMBROSO'S LEGACY

Cesare Lombroso, a nineteenth-century Italian physician, is commonly regarded as the first criminologist. His first study of female criminality was undertaken with a colleague and "the help of 26 skulls and 5 skeletons of prostitutes."[8] It served as the basis for future work by criminologists such as Otto Pollak who will be discussed later in this article. Lombroso and his colleague Ferrero reported:

> We have seen that women have many traits in common with children; that their moral sense is deficient, that they are revengeful, jealous and inclined to vengeances of refined cruelty. In ordinary cases these defects are neutralized by piety, maternity, want of passion, sexual coldness, by neatness and an undeveloped intelligence. But when piety and maternal sentiments are wanting, and in their place are strong passions and intensely erotic tendencies, much muscular strength and a superior intelligence for the conception and execution of evil, it is clear that the innocuous semi-criminal present in the normal woman must be transformed into a born criminal more terrible than any man.[9]

For Lombroso, the "normal" woman's criminality was kept in check by fulfillment of her maternal role and by repressing her sexuality: "in the ordinary run of mothers the sexual instinct is kept in abeyance."[10] He implied that women not kept in check in this way were destined for crime.

The work of two feminists is helpful in understanding Lombroso's significance. The first is that of Susan Edwards,[11] a British criminologist, who has analyzed historical shifts in the description of women in medical and legal literature. Her central concern is the social and legal definition of female sexuality. She argues that a paradoxical image of female sexuality (i.e., both sexual passivity and sexual aggressiveness) is reflected in criminal law and medical practice.

Although protective criminal legislation is supposed to safeguard women from aggressive male sexuality, in practice women are often seen as seductresses.[12] Edwards points out that the contradictory images of women as chaste yet unchaste, good yet bad and virgin yet whore[13] have had an important impact on nineteenth and twentieth century English criminal law. She argues that control, not protection, of the sexual behaviour of all women was the objective of nineteenth-century criminal law. Further, the degree and form of this control has varied according to women's social class:

> Ladies of the middle classes were as a general rule considered passive and therefore to be protected. . . It was control under another guise nevertheless. The social and sexual behaviour of middle-and-upper-class wives and daughters was also controlled via the father's and husband's right to consortium, which was determined in part by the "value" of the wife or daughter with regard to her chastity. The behaviour of working-class women was regulated and rigorously controlled via the laws relating to vagrancy and prostitution.[14]

Edwards also examines definitions of femininity based on gynaecology which have been of profound significance for women in the criminal law. She argues that English legal practice in the nineteenth century:

> . . . [was] increasingly influenced by medical and especially gynaecological precepts of sexuality which came to inform the various stages at each and every level of the criminal justice system. As law breakers women were rarely, if ever, recognized as criminals. . . Instead, the female law breaker was defined as "sick,"and the origin of her sickness was located in her gynaecology.[15]

The historical development of criminal law concerning infanticide supports this analysis.[16] Medical and legal experts regarded all aspects of reproduction as crises for women. They claimed that menstruation and menopause, in addition to pregnancy and childbirth, contributed to female instability.[17]

The assumption that physiological factors contribute to women's involvement in crime has never been abandoned, even to this date.[18] In the 1950s, criminologist Otto Pollak[19] made the argument that "because of woman's irritability at certain times, she is often a disturber of the peace."[20]

In Canada, reference to premenstrual syndrome first appeared in the courts and the press in the early 1980s. One newspaper, under the headline "Women's crime spree linked to pregnancies," reported:

> A Mississauga woman's six-year crime career seems clearly linked to
> her pregnancies, a judge conceded, but she will still face a lengthy jail
> term as soon as she has delivered her fourth baby.
>   Lawyer Kenneth Anders argued his client. . .had a "personality
> flaw" that led her to become dishonest when she became pregnant.[21]

The discussion of premenstrual syndrome and pregnancy[22] in
the media and its incorporation into criminological literature,[23]
illustrates that attempts to understand women and crime have
never lost their intimate connection to an analysis of the inherent
nature of women.

OTTO POLLAK
AND THE MASKED WOMEN
OF HIS IMAGINATION

Otto Pollak, who became a major figure in criminology, distanced
himself from absolute biological determinism.[24] In his attempt to
be more sociological than his predecessors, he noted the importance of the family in structuring women's activities. He also
noted the prevalence of a double standard of sexual conduct
which was particularly harsh for women.[25] He argued for instance,
that in western culture, deceit is a "socially prescribed form of
behaviour" for women.[26] It follows that "many crimes which are
considered highly detectable (e.g. murder) lose this quality when
they are committed by women because of the way they are
carried out."[27] Women, Pollak argued, compensate for lack of
physical strength by devising covert and deceitful methods of
crime (e.g. poisoning). Women's crime, he implied, is masked
crime.

Historical research on the criminality of women in eighteenth-
century England challenges, indeed contradicts, Pollak's assumption.[28] Feminist critics have also argued that Pollak did little
more than reinforce prevailing myths of women's peculiar pre-
disposition to be "strange, secretive, and sometimes dangerous,"
thereby giving "folklore a pseudo-scientific status."[29] And, as
Australian criminologist Jocelynne A. Scutt[30] demonstrates, if
one accepts Pollak's definition of masked crime, then much crime

51

(e.g. corporate crime and sexual assault) is equally masked, because of the way it is carried out.

Pollak displayed a healthy skepticism about the reliability of official statistics to measure criminal activity. In his view, however, the primary reason for the small number of women in criminal statistics was male chivalry: "...in many instances, police, prosecution, and the courts are biased in favour of women offenders and...criminal statistics must be analyzed with corresponding caution."[31]

Pollak did not support this suggestion with empirical data and feminist criminologists have explored and debunked the notion. American feminist criminologist Meda Chesney-Lind rejects the whole concept of chivalry. She argues that discretionary and differential treatment of women by the police is essentially harassment of women who are not "sexually monogamous and indoors at night." The police, rather than responding chivalrously to women, are "patrolling the boundaries of the female sex role."[32]

Other studies have shown that police tend to respond similarly to both men and women whose demeanour is polite and respectful, and who have not been involved in a violent crime.[33] It would appear that deference to authority is much favoured by them. Furthermore, when women are subjected to the formal processes of criminal law and justice, they are not always treated differentially and favourably by police and the courts. Chesney-Lind's characterization of the police patrol is clearly significant for women as *both* offenders and victims:

> The police force operates according to particular assumptions about gender; they are, for instance, reluctant to intervene in cases of even the most brutal marital violence because they see themselves as respecting the privacy of "the family." In rape cases the police are well known for subjecting the victim to an offensive and degrading inquisition in which her own sexual history is on trial. It is the police, too, who enjoin women not to go out alone at night when they have difficulty in tracking down a still-active rapist or murderer, thereby adding a secondary element of control to the original threat.[34]

The most disquieting aspect of Pollak's work on female criminality is his consideration of a possible correlation between formal equality and criminal behaviour:

> One of the characteristic phenomena of our time is women's progress toward reaching equality with men. This raises the interesting question

whether we may assume that, in consequence of this development, female crime will change its nature, become masculinized as it were, and lose its masked character.[35]

Given that his hypotheses tended to proceed from folklore and unexamined assumptions, it is perhaps not surprising that he also assumed women's "equality" might lead to the "masculinization" of women's crime. He was aware of the adverse impact of male-dominated culture on women's lives,[36] but as Smart suggests, he was not critical of this inequitable social order: "it serves as merely another causal factor in his study."[37] He simply pondered what might happen if women ever achieved equality, without considering whether real equality would ever be possible in a society characterized by sexual, economic and racial inequality.

Mary Eaton[38] illustrates that if one posed the question in terms of "differential treatment," one missed the subtle processes by which gender divisions are reproduced by the courts.[39] Eaton found that men and women defendants who were guilty of the same offences, and who were in the same circumstances (e.g. single, no previous criminal record) received the same sort of sentence. However, she found that men and women defendants were rarely *in the same circumstances*.[40] Both Eaton and Carol Smart[41] argue that criminologists should research the unexamined assumptions of the courts and lawmakers about women's sexuality and women's place in society.

THE WOMEN'S MOVEMENT AND WOMEN'S CRIMES

Freda Adler's work on women and crime cautions against the achievement of equality because it will lead to more women criminals. She purports to document the changing pattern of female crime in the United States, noting the women's convictions for theft and other property offences have increased, while conviction rates for murder and aggravated assault "curiously have remained the same."[42] In her view, "Women have lost more than their chains, they have lost many of the restraints which kept them within the law."[43]

Adler implies that criminal activity is historically a male prerogative, and that the "new female criminal" is breaking with her sex role. She equates the feminist movement's struggle for formal equality and legal rights for women with the achievement of real equality, suggesting not only that women have come a long way, but they have "made it." Adler's work has been criticized as neither theoretically nor methodologically sound.[44] She cannot, however, be ignored: her work "captured the imagination of the media and practitioners."[45]

According to a chief of police in one major American city, the women's movement triggered "a crime wave like the world has never seen before."[46] A police official in another city indicated that a "breakdown of motherhood" was the result of the feminist movement and the cause of this crime wave.[47] Morris and Gelsthorpe, using English newspapers, refer to this theme in media coverage, of which the following are but a few examples:

"Equal crimes for women!" (*Daily Mail*, 23 February 1977)

"Gangster Lib." (*Sunday Mirror*, 2 April 1978) of an event that occurred in 1965.

"Women's Lib 'pushes up crime'" (*Daily Mail*, February 1980)

"A TOUGH new breed of criminal is emerging—young women whose behaviour is increasingly masculine..." (*Daily Mail*, 12 April 1978)[48]

Similar themes have surfaced from time to time in the Canadian press:

"Lib takes the lid off the gun moll" (*Toronto Star*, 15 May 1975)

"Equality equals equal jail for pregnant woman" (*Globe and Mail*, 1 July 1975)

"Women's Lib linked to soaring crime" (*Toronto Star*, 7 August 1975)

"New female boldness is spawning more crime by women" (*Toronto Star*, 3 November 1975)

"Female crime rate soaring" (*Toronto Star*, 18 September 1983)

The argument that women's crime is rocketing ever upward rests entirely on official statistics. The Canadian figures show however that the headlines are misleading. A report of the Solicitor General's department observed that in 1964 there were ten times more men than women charged with Criminal Code offences, and that by 1974, the ratio was only six to one.

However, the Report noted with concern:

> With the exception of "rape/other sexual offences," . . . the increase
> in the number of women charged for each criminal code offence
> outstripped the increase for males. The most noticeable variation
> occurred in fraud offences with the increase for females (306%) being
> five times greater than was the increase for men (59%).[49]

Fraud and other property-related offences continue to indicate
higher rates of change for women than for men: the changes in
the numbers of adults charged with property offences indicate a
ninety-four per cent increase for women and a seventy-two per
cent increase for men; the change in violent crime has been
sixty-eight per cent and twenty-five per cent for women and men
respectively.[50]

But the actual numbers behind the percentages tell an interesting
story. As Holly Johnson notes in her article, there is a great
danger in comparing percentage increases when the base numbers
are small. This is particularly true when dealing with official
statistics of crime and conviction rates, because they may tell
us more about enforcement than about any real increases or
decreases in criminal activity. Morris and Gelsthorpe argue that
it is possible for actual crime to decrease while recorded crime is
increasing, because we do not know the relationship between the
actual amount of crime committed and crimes traced to offenders by the police.[51] There are many factors which intervene
between the commission of a criminal act and that act becoming
a statistic. Such factors include decisions by victims to report or
not report offences, decisions by police officers as to whether a
charge should be laid and if so, how the act should be defined in
order to lay the charge, and enforcement priorities of police
departments.

Nevertheless, although far fewer women than men are convicted of criminal offences, the statistics from the 1960s and
1970s do indicate a real increase. We still have to ask *why*
women's recorded crime is on the increase. Is this where the
women's movement has had an effect?

Smart argues the existence of the women's movement affects
not only the women to whom it is directed, but also "the consciousness and perceptions of the police, social workers, magistrates, judges and others, who may well interpret female behaviour in the light of the belief that women are becoming more

'liberated'."[52] Chesney-Lind suggests that any change in numbers of women charged, convicted or incarcerated could easily be the product of an "if it's equality they want, we'll see that they get it" attitude on the part of law enforcement personnel.[53]

Morris and Gelsthorpe suggest that unemployment, low wages and social alienation are good reasons for the jump in female crimes.[54] Along with Carol Smart[55] and Victoria Greenwood,[56] they reject simplistic explanations. However, they speculate that recorded crime has risen primarily because the women's movement has been seen as a change that threatens and challenges the social order.[57]

The notion that women offenders are influenced by feminism or "political and social beliefs and ideologies"[58] has to be addressed, although the number of "radical" women offenders is extremely small. As Weis[59] pointed out over a decade ago, the "new female criminal" was personified in the media by Bernadine Dohrn, Susan Saxe, Emily Harris and a few others associated with American groups such as the Weather Underground and the Symbionese Liberation Army. In Canada, we can count on one hand the number of women members of the FLQ or Direct Action who were convicted or imprisoned.

Women involved in political crimes are not numerous, however notorious or celebrated they may be. Neither are they a new or universal phenomenon, as even Lombroso acknowledged in reporting on his extensive examination of the skull of Charlotte Corday, the eighteenth-century French revolutionary executed for the assassination of Marat.[60]

The assumption that feminism is a significant factor in relation to women's offences has been challenged by American criminologist Cathy Spatz Widom,[61] who (while noting a dearth of empirical research in this area) has found in her own research that female offenders tend to be "more conservative and traditional in their attitudes toward women than [comparison groups of] non-offender women."[62]

Regarding increases in women's recorded criminal activity in the area of property crime (e.g. fraud and shoplifting), British criminologist Jeanne Gregory's assessment seems accurate: "far from providing proof of liberation, these increases can be understood as a response to deteriorating economic conditions, as they occur mainly in non-occupational areas such as welfare fraud and minor property offences."[63]

FEMINIST ATTEMPTS
TO RECONSTRUCT CRIMINOLOGY

Carol Smart wrote her landmark work in feminist criminology to redress the male-oriented biases integral to criminological theory.[64] Feminists were the first to challenge the marginalization and invisibility of women's crime, and to insist that it be taken seriously. They were also the first to point to the falseness of research which characterized "female crimes" such as prostitution and abortion, as "victimless."[65] As well, the oppression of women in the criminal justice apparatus by its non-treatment of sexual offences and wife battering was brought to the fore by feminists.[66]

But two problems in feminist theory as it relates to women and crime must be addressed. First, as Mary McIntosh has pointed out, in emphasizing the sexism of criminological theory, feminist critiques of criminology do not "locate its weaknesses at a deep enough level."[67] In other words, it is not enough to say criminology has been wrong in ignoring women's inequality. This leaves intact the notion that the criminality of *individuals* is the appropriate target of investigation and research.[68] Greenwood argues that focussing on the neglect of women's crime and criminality steers one away from the necessary analysis:

> . . . whilst criminologists have undoubtedly been biased and prejudiced against the study of women's crime, they have equally shown bias and prejudice in selecting certain topics for scientific scrutiny. For instance, even if the rate of women's crime was very high, it might well have been neglected just as the study of corporate crime was neglected until recently by criminologists. . . . The scientific study of criminality has focussed on blacks and not whites, on the poor and not the rich, on men and not women. This reflects the concerns of a policy-oriented, correctionalist criminology.[69]

Greenwood argues that criminology has relied on stereotypes of men as well as women:

> . . . our aim should be to develop a criminology which recognizes assumptions about gender and analytically locates crime and criminality within the sexual division of labour. The particular condition of women requires a specific form of analysis which cannot be similar to that used for men.[70]

By examining late nineteenth-century British penal statistics, she demonstrates that prison sentences have not always been imposed on only a small number of women. She argues this raises questions about the changing nature of the control of women.[71] She rejects the notion that women who have been imprisoned are inherently different from male prisoners; on the contrary, her close examination of the British statistics shows that like men, women in prison are working class, black, poor, with little or no education.[72]

Support for her analysis (and indeed the most damning challenge to the "equality, liberation and crime" thesis in the Canadian context) emerges when one considers the position of Native women. For while all women account for only a small fraction of persons incarcerated in Canada, [73] it is clear that Native women comprise a disproportionately high percentage of the female inmate populations of Canadian penal institutions.[74] In Saskatchewan and Manitoba, Native women account for over seventy per cent of women imprisoned in the provincial correctional centres; in the federal women's penitentiary, thirty-six Native women represented 21.7 per cent of the women incarcerated at the prison in 1982.[75]

Native people in Canada represent only a small fraction of the total population (although admittedly this varies by province and territory), and the poverty, destitution and racism that characterize the experience of many defy quantification. The unemployment rate for Native women is many times higher than the national average, and studies confirm what the street suggests: half the Native women in jails studied in Ontario and Manitoba had less than high school education and most had been unemployed prior to incarceration.[76] It becomes crystal clear that within criminology and criminal justice, as in social life, issues of gender cannot be considered in isolation from "the more specific factors of class, race and social position."[77]

The second problem for feminist criminology concerns the role of the state. Although some Marxists may disagree,[78] the state is not simply a coercive institution. Indeed, some feminists have insisted that the state and its law enforcement personnel provide women with social support and protection from violence at home as well as on the street.[79] But as Mary McIntosh suggests, the state is not equally concerned about the behaviour of everyone.[80]

One indication of the complex relationship between women

and the state is found in the criminal law. Historically it has been indifferent to lesbian sexuality, yet punishing in its treatment of male homosexuality.[81] This is not to say that lesbianism has not been punished by the state. Although criminal codes have not been invoked as controls, the mental health system's coercion of lesbians and the incarceration of lesbians in psychiatric institutions have been well documented.[82] Lesbians have almost always had their children taken from them in custody battles in court if they live openly as lesbians.[83] Clearly, we need to look beyond the formal sanction of the criminal law to understand the oppression of women.

CONCLUSIONS

The understanding of women and crime must be broadened to include the general position of women within a given social context. This concern is not abstract or simply of academic interest. Criminology developed as a policy-oriented discipline and criminological theories find their way very directly into correctional practices. For instance, the notion that female offenders are inherently different from male offenders has long pervaded penal policy and criminological writing.[84]

In 1938, the *Report of the Royal Commission to Investigate the Penal System of Canada (Archambault Report)*[85] suggested that female delinquency was not a particularly serious problem in Canada:

> . . . when the sick have been deducted, the number of trainable women is very small, and the women prisoners apart from young prisoners who are capable of deriving benefit from continued education would constitute a small class.[86]

In the *Report's* conclusions regarding the thirty-two prisoners of the Kingston Penitentiary for Women in 1936 it was noted:

> . . . murder, attempted murder and manslaughter account for approximately 47 per cent, or nearly half. These women are not a crime problem but are of the occasional or accidental offender class, who have been carried away by the overmastering impulse of the moment, often the outbreak of long pent up emotion. They are not a custodial problem, and could be cared for as well in a reformatory as in a penitentiary. The same is true of the other seventeen female penitentiary inmates.[87]

Three decades later, the *Report of the Canadian Committee on Corrections (Ouimet Report)* (1969)[88] tended to echo its predecessor:

> There are certain differences in the criminality of women, as compared with men, which have implications for correctional planning. The most outstanding single difference is that of numbers. . . many more men than women are dealt with by the police and the courts. . .
>
> There is some indication that the difference in numbers between men and women offenders tends to be lower in highly industrialized societies than in less developed ones.[89]

Addressing an apparent increase in women's crime, a more recent federal report (1977) noted:

> With the pressure for equality for the sexes is coming reduced paternalism on the part of the police and the judiciary. This could lead to increased charges against women and longer sentences if convicted.[90]

Because of the way female criminality has been perceived, women prisoners have not been of great concern to correctional officials of the Canadian state. At the same time, however, the assumption that women's pressure for equality results in their apparent increased representation in crime and court statistics has gone largely unchallenged.

Contemporary Canadian state policy, as reflected in official reports, describes the "special needs" of women offenders as largely psychological. Three of the factors cited as giving rise to special needs for women in custody are:

• low self-image, increased by society's strong condemnation of women offenders,

• weak family ties and few friends, making for a vulnerable situation of exploitation,

• tendency toward self-mutilation and self-deprecation instead of outward aggressive behaviour.[91]

Such assumptions stem largely from folklore about the inherent nature of women, rather than from scientific analysis. For instance, Widom identifies three factors (self-esteem, sex-role identity and feminism), thought to be important to female criminality, and illustrates that all three have been based on limited empirical research.[92] She argues that research dealing with low self-esteem is methodologically weak and "limited by the fact that most of these studies are. . . conducted *after* these women have been caught up in the criminal justice system." Hence, "any findings regarding self-esteem may be the *result* of a person's being labelled and incarcerated, instead of a causal factor in explaining a person's criminality" [emphasis in original].[93] Her research indicates that we cannot assume female offenders have low self-esteem.

In sum, I would argue that the sexist assumptions underlying much of criminology must not give way to feminist theory that treats *only* the question of gender. In Canada, we need look no further than the position of Native women to illustrate that issues of race and class are of equal significance.

As well, feminist criminology must avoid general, ahistorical explanations of women's crime. In our struggle to understand the intricate weave of law and crime into women's lives, the change over time in definitions and positions of law must be examined.

NOTES

1 See, among others, Dorie Klein, "The Etiology of Women's Crime: A Review of the Literature," *Issues in Criminology* 8 (Fall 1973): 3-30; Carol Smart, *Women, Crime and Criminology: A Feminist Critique* (London: Routledge & Kegan Paul, 1976); Susan Brownmiller, *Against Our Will: Men, Women and Rape* (New York: Bantam, 1975); Dorie Klein and June Kress, "Any Woman's Blues: A Critical Overview of Women, Crime and the Criminal Justice System," *Crime and Social Justice* 5 (Spring-Summer 1976): 34-39; Joseph G. Weis, "Liberation and Crime: The Invention of the New Female Criminal," *Crime and Social Justice* 6 (Fall-Winter 1976): 17-27; Jocelynne A. Scutt, "Debunking the Theory of the Female 'Masked Criminal,'" *Aust. & N.Z. Journal of Criminology* 11 (March 1978): 23-42; Jocelynne A. Scutt, "Sexism in Criminal Law," in *Women and Crime*, eds. S.K. Mukherjee and Jocelynne A. Scutt (Sydney: Aust. Inst. of Criminology/George Allen & Unwin, 1981), pp. 1-21; Carol Smart and Barry Smart, *Women, Sexuality and Social Control* (London: Routledge & Kegan Paul, 1978); Clarice Feinman, *Women in the Criminal Justice System* (New York: Praeger, 1980); Ann Jones, *Women Who Kill* (New York: Holt, Rinehart & Winston, 1980); and Susan Edwards, *Female Sexuality and the Law* (Oxford: Martin Robertson, 1981).

2 Meda Chesney-Lind, "Women and Crime: The Female Offender," *Signs* 12 (Autumn 1986): 78-96.

3 Ibid.

4 Cesare Lombroso and Enrico Ferrero, *The Female Offender* (New York: D. Appleton, 1900).

5 Weis, pp. 17-27.

6 Klein and Kress, pp. 34-49; Weis, pp. 17-27; Carol Smart, "The New Female Criminal: Reality or Myth?" *British Journal of Criminology* 19 (January 1979): 50-59; Meda Chesney-Lind, "Re-discovering Lilith: Misogyny and the New Female Criminal," in *The Female Offender: Selected Papers from an International Symposium*, eds. Curt Taylor Griffiths and Margit Nance (Vancouver: Criminology Research Centre, Simon Fraser Univ., 1980), pp. 1-37; and Allison Morris and Lorraine Gelsthorpe, "False Clues and Female Crime," in *Women and Crime* (Cropwood Conf. Series No. 13), eds. Allison Morris and Lorraine Gelsthorpe (Cambridge: Inst. of Criminology, 1981), pp. 49-70.

7 Freda Adler, *Sisters in Crime: The Rise of the New Female Criminal* (New York: McGraw-Hill, 1975).

8 Lombroso and Ferrero, pp. 2-3.

9 Ibid., p. 151. I am indebted to Meda Chesney-Lind, whose "Re-discovering Lilith: Misogyny and the New Female Criminal," drew this passage to my attention.

10 Lombroso and Ferrero, p. 153.

11 Edwards, op. cit.

12 Ibid., p. 50.

13 Ibid., p. 49. Others have noted similar images which have long pervaded the criminal law's theory and practice; see Feinman, for reference to the madonna/whore distinction; for discussion of the Lilith/Eve image, see Chesney-Lind, "Re-discovering Lilith."

14 Edwards, p. 55.

15 Ibid., p. 74.

16 See also Nigel Walker, *Crime and Insanity in England*, vol. 1: The Historical Perspective (Edinburgh: Edinburgh Univ. Press, 1968); and Scutt, "Sexism in Criminal Law."

17 Edwards, pp. 75-80.

18 Herschel Prins, *Offenders, Deviants, or Patients?* (London: Tavistock, 1980), pp. 316-317.

19 Otto Pollak, *The Criminality of Women* (New York: A.S. Barnes, 1961).

20 Ibid., p. 2.

21 *Toronto Star*, 14 April 1981. This article was followed by "Female

hormones head for the courts," *Toronto Star*, 18 April 1981. For other articles dealing with premenstrual syndrome, see "Women's violence blamed on period," *Toronto Star*, 25 August 1978 and "Menstrual stress a factor in crime?" *Toronto Star*, 14 April 1981.

22 Katharina Dalton, *Once a Month* (Glasgow: Fontana, 1978).

23 Prins, op. cit.

24 Pollak, op. cit.

25 Ibid., p. 161.

26 Ibid., p. 111.

27 Ibid., p. 3.

28 John M. Beattie, "The Criminality of Women in Eighteenth-Century England," *Journal of Social History* 8 (Summer 1974-75): 80-116.

29 Smart, *Women, Crime and Criminology*.

30 Scutt, "Debunking the Theory of the Female 'Masked Criminal'" pp. 23-42.

31 Pollak, p. 5.

32 Meda Chesney-Lind, "Chivalry Reexamined: Women and the Criminal Justice System," in *Women, Crime and the Criminal Justice System*, ed. Lee H. Bowker with contributions by Meda Chesney-Lind and Joy Pollack (Lexington: D.C. Heath, 1978), p. 207.

33 Feinman, p. 23.

34 Michele Barrett, *Women's Oppression Today: Problems in Marxist Feminist Analysis* (London: Verso & NLB. 1978), pp. 236-237.

35 Pollak, p. 154.

36 Ibid., p. 149.

37 Smart, *Women, Crime and Criminology*, p. 50.

38 Mary Eaton, "Mitigating Circumstances: Familiar Rhetoric," *International Journal of the Sociology of Law* 11 (November 1983): 385-400; "Documenting the Defendant: Placing Women in Social Inquiry Reports," in *Women in Law: Explorations in Law, Family and Sexuality*, eds. Julia Brophy and Carol Smart (London: Routledge & Kegan Paul, 1985).

39 Mary Eaton, "Documenting the Defendant," p. 138.

40 Mary Eaton, "Mitigating Circumstances," pp. 385-400.

41 Carol Smart, "Legal Subjects and Sexual Objects: Ideology, Law and Female Sexuality," in *Women in Law: Explorations in Law, Family and Sexuality*, eds. Julia Brophy and Carol Smart (London: Routledge & Kegan Paul, 1985).

42 Adler, p. 16.

43 Ibid., p. 24.

44 Smart, "The New Female Criminal," pp. 50-59; Morris and Gelsthorpe, pp. 49-70.

45 Morris and Gelsthorpe, p. 53.

46 Quoted in Weis, p. 17 and in Chesney-Lind "Re-discovering Lilith," p. 3.

47 Quoted in Chesney-Lind, "Re-discovering Lilith," p. 3.

48 Morris and Gelsthorpe, pp. 63-66, fn. 5.

49 *The Female Offender—Selected Statistics: Report of the National Advisory Committee on the Female Offender* (Ottawa: Solicitor General Canada, 1977), p. 7.

50 See Alison Hatch and Karlene Faith, "The Female Offender in Canada," paper presented at the Annual General Meeting of the American Society of Criminology, San Diego, CA, 13-17 November 1985, p. 9, table 3.

51 Morris and Gelsthorpe, p. 56.

52 Smart, "The New Female Criminal," p. 57.

53 Chesney-Lind, "Re-discovering Lilith," pp. 14-15.

54 Morris and Gelsthorpe, p. 57.

55 Smart, "The New Female Criminal," pp. 50-59.

56 Victoria Greenwood, "The Myths of Female Crime," in *Women and Crime* (Cropwood Conf. Series No. 13), eds. Allison Morris and Lorraine Gelsthorpe (Cambridge: Inst. of Criminology, 1981), pp. 73-84.

57 Morris and Gelsthorpe, "False Clues and Female Crime," pp. 49-70.

58 *Report of the National Advisory Committee on the Female Offender* (Ottawa: Solicitor General Canada, 1977), p. 16.

59 Weis, pp. 17-27.

60 Lombroso and Ferrero, pp. 3-35.

61 Cathy Spatz Widom "Perspectives of Female Criminality: A Critical Examination of Assumptions," in *Women and Crime* (Cropwood Conf. Series No. 13), eds. Allison Morris and Lorraine Gelsthorpe (Cambridge: Inst. of Criminology, 1981), pp. 33-44.

62 Ibid., p. 38.

63 Jeanne Gregory, "Sex, Class and Crime: Towards a Non-Sexist Criminology," in *The Political Economy of Crime: Readings for a Critical Criminology*, ed. Brian D. Maclean (Scarborough: Prentice-Hall, 1986), p. 320.

64 Smart, *Women, Crime and Criminology*.

65 Klein and Kress, p. 37.

66 Smart, *Women, Crime and Criminology,* pp. 77-107; Klein and Kress, pp. 38-42; and Nicole H. Rafter and Elena M. Natalizia, "Marxist Feminism: Implications for Criminal Justice," *Crime and Delinquency* 27 (January 1981): 83-87.

67 Mary McIntosh, "Review Symposium: 'Women, Crime and Criminology,'" *British Journal of Criminology* 17 (October 1977): 396.

68 Ibid., p. 396; Mark Cousins, "Mens Rea: Sexual Difference and the Criminal Law," in *Radical Issues in Criminology,* eds. Pat Carlen and Mike Collison (Oxford: Martin Robertson, 1980), p. 111; and Greenwood, pp. 73-74.

69 Greenwood, pp. 75-76.

70 Ibid.

71 Ibid., p. 79.

72 Ibid., p. 81.

73 Hatch and Faith, op cit.

74 Carol P. LaPrairie, "Selected Criminal Justice and Socio-Demographic Data on Native Women," *Canadian Journal of Criminology* 26 (April 1984).

75 Ibid., p. 162.

76 Ibid., p. 166

77 Greenwood, p. 82

78 Rafter and Natalizia, pp. 81-98.

79 See Linda MacLeod, *Wife Battering in Canada: The Vicious Circle* (Ottawa: Canadian Advisory Council on the Status of Women, 1980); and Ian Taylor, *Law and Order: Arguments for Socialism* (London: Macmillan, 1981).

80 McIntosh, p. 396.

81 Barrett, p. 240.

82 Persimmon Blackbridge and Sheila Gilhooly, *Still Sane* (Vancouver: Press Gang Publishers, 1986); P. Susan Penfold and Gillian Walker, *Women and the Psychiatric Paradox* (Montreal: Eden Press, 1983); Dorothy Smith and Sara David, eds., *Women Look at Psychiatry* (Vancouver: Press Gang Publishers, 1976).

83 In a recent Canadian case dealing with the law's attitude towards lesbian mothers, the judge decided custody in favour of the father when the mother resumed living with her lover in contradiction to her original custody order. In the original order, the mother got custody after telling the court that she had ceased living with her lesbian lover. *(Elliott vs. Elliott* (1987) B.C.D. Civ. 1528-01 — unreported).

84 Prins, op. cit.

85 *Report of the Royal Commission to Investigate the Penal System of Canada (Archambault Report)* (Ottawa: King's Printer, 1938).

86 Ibid., p. 145.

87 Ibid., p. 147

88 *Report of the Canadian Committee on Corrections (Ouimet Report)* (Ottawa: Queen's Printer, 1969).

89 Ibid., p. 389.

90 *Report of the National Advisory Committee on the Female Offender* (Ottawa: Solicitor General Canada, 1977), p. 15.

91 Ibid., p. 14.

92 Widom, op. cit.

93 Ibid., p. 34.

In Their Own Words

by Ellen Adelberg
& Claudia Currie

his article acquaints the reader with some of the women about whom this book is written. What follows are summarized accounts of the lives of seven women who have been in conflict with the law. In an effort to point out how those of us who are feminists can try to understand these dramas, we have added our own commentary in the final pages.

In our own work with convicted women, we became aware of the significance of women's life circumstances, including early childhood experiences, in understanding their involvement with crime. Yet rarely are these factors discussed in the academic or professional literature, particularly from the perspective of women offenders themselves.

The pages that follow reveal the stories of **Elaine**, a woman charged with three counts of aggravated assault; **Barbara**, who was convicted of manslaughter; **Anne-Marie** and **Francine**, who both served time for armed robberies; **Nicole**, convicted of importing narcotics; **Cindy**, who has an extensive history of drug and fraud convictions; and **June**, who is serving a life sentence for murder. Their names have been changed to protect their identity because as one woman told us, "we still feel the power that can be used against us, and the reactions of society ...you never stop paying your dues." When contacted, the interviewees were extremely helpful and supportive of our project. It was evident that these women were not often asked their point of view, but felt that they had a lot to share.[1]

All of these women were convicted of indictable offences, which are those considered most serious in law. While cautioning that these seven stories should not be interpreted as "every-woman's" story of her involvement in crime, our experience as workers with women offenders tells us that they mirror, in many ways, the reality of many women offenders' lives. The statistics presented earlier in this book provide evidence that the women interviewed represent an approximate cross-section of women serving federal sentences in relation to their age, marital status, and the types of offences committed. The women interviewed are not, however, representative of the ethnic backgrounds of women under federal sentence, due to the fact that only one is Native, and Native women can represent up to thirty per cent of the federal female prison population. Women who are sentenced to serve any time under two years in prison serve their sentences in provincial jails, usually for less serious offences than those committed by the women we interviewed.

In the stories that follow, poverty, child and wife battering, sexual assault, and women's conditioning to accept positions of submissiveness and dependency upon men are themes that recur frequently among these women. We suggest, as others have elsewhere,[2] that the response to different forms of oppression vary from woman to woman, depending upon the internal and external resources upon which each of them has to draw. The following stories are evidence of seven women's responses to such oppression. In our opinion, the serious crimes committed by these women do not represent bizarre manifestations of "unfeminine" women's instabilities (as traditional criminologists might have us believe), but rather they represent behaviour that makes some sense within the context of each one's life, and within the context of women's status in Canadian society.

ELAINE

The first woman you will meet, Elaine, tells a tragic yet far too common story which reveals the depths of deprivation that are possible in our patriarchal society. Her story illustrates graphically that women do not have the control they need to ensure their own and their children's safety, and that in certain cases this can lead to devastating consequences.

At the time she was interviewed, Elaine was awaiting trial for three counts of the aggravated assault of her children. Her co-accused was the man with whom she had been living at the time the charges were laid. While she was pleading guilty to lesser charges, he had already pleaded guilty, had been tried and was sentenced to six years in prison for the offences.

Elaine told us that a major event which affected the path of her life was a teenage pregnancy which resulted in her giving the child up for adoption.

I knew I should give [the baby] up because I was still a baby myself, I couldn't handle the responsibility and my parents felt I should give it up, but after I did I always wished I had kept the baby with me. I think I wanted to get married and have more kids right away to make up for having lost my baby.

When she was seventeen, Elaine met the man who eventually became her husband and within a short time they were travelling together across the country. Very quickly, she became pregnant.

At the hospital they wanted to give me an abortion but my husband said no way. He said "that's my child and you're not going to get an abortion or give it up or nothing, we're going to keep it." I was so happy. It was a baby that I could keep and I had somebody who cared.

She was married two months before the baby was born. For a while she had what she described as a "good relationship" with her husband, despite the fact that she discovered that he was wanted by the police for several offences involving fraud. By the time her first child was a year old, the relationship was crumbling. Even so, Elaine stayed with her husband for five more years. When she left him, she was the mother of three small children, ages five, three and two. She describes the reasons she left him:

He was fooling around with other women, he was on welfare, and going to the race track; he was an alcoholic. I don't know if he took drugs, but I know he was drinking and buying flowers for all his women and sending the bills to our place. And then he hit me once in a while and I couldn't stand it anymore and I just had to get out. I was fed up with having to knock on my neighbours' doors for peanut butter and bread to feed the kids.

Before she left her husband, Elaine had experienced her first conflict with the law. She was convicted of offences related to fraud and sentenced to two years probation.

I didn't have any money, and I wanted to get stuff for the kids, so I was willing to do almost anything. But I never got caught for drugs or drinking or beating people or anything. That wasn't my style, I wasn't raised that way.

After leaving her husband, Elaine very quickly hooked up with another man, who, as it turned out, had an even more disastrous effect on her life. The new man was to become her co-accused in the child assault charges.

Before those charges occurred, Elaine experienced a very difficult battle with her ex-husband for custody of her children. At one point he abducted and kept one of her daughters for almost two years. She was determined to regain possession of her children and her feelings for them are reflected in this passage, as she recounts the end to the abduction event.

I'll never forget the day I got Cathy back. When I had last seen her she was four and now she was six. She had gotten so big. We both just stared at each other and then she started yelling Mummy, Mummy and she ran right for me and she held me. She sat on my knee all the way home and most of the time we both just cried. I thought finally all three of my children and I were reunited, we could all live together.

Unfortunately though, Elaine's dreams were quickly shattered. Although her new boyfriend bought a house for her and the children to share with him, he offered only violence and intimidation instead of a safe refuge.

At first he started with just hitting and then he started to torture the children, like putting them upside down in hot showers and hitting all of us with a cattle prod. It got worse and worse and I never did nothing about it because I was afraid to. I had just got my children back and I didn't want anybody to take them. He told me if I said anything to anybody he would kill me and the children. I knew he had a gun, a 32.

After all that I had been through I didn't know what to do. I was in a state of mind where I wasn't insane, I knew what I was doing, but I was paralyzed. If I even went out of the house with makeup on John would beat the hell out of me because he thought another man would look at me. It was like I was in jail, I realize now that's what it was.

After charges were laid against her and her co-accused, Elaine experienced a harrowing five months of imprisonment. Even though she maintained throughout that she was not insane, Elaine was sent to a psychiatric hospital for observation and assessment. At the end of the thirty day psychiatric assessment, Elaine spent four months in prison in "protective custody," to remove her from harassment by other inmates who look down on suspected child abusers. Finally, she was transferred to a community residence for female offenders run by the Elizabeth Fry Society.

The day I got out and got to "Smith" House and I went to the store and bought a pack of cigarettes was like the first day of a new life. John wasn't there to beat me. I could look at someone and smile and they weren't going to beat me up, or think I'm drunk or a dope addict or a pervert, which I'm not. I've been working for ten of the eleven months since I've been here, at an answering service. It's good for me because I can't sit still right now. I'm too hyper. I've got to get up and go. It's a great feeling when you know you're working from nine to five, you come home, have supper, relax, take a shower and go to bed. It feels beautiful. Because at the end of the week you know you're going to do your shopping and it's yours, you don't have to steal for it because you worked for it and nobody can take it away from you.

While facing great uncertainty about her future, one thing has remained clear in Elaine's mind.

I can raise my kids. I can work for them, I know I can do it, I just need that chance. If I don't get that chance then there's no point in me even existing because I won't have my three children. I already lost one when I was young, I don't intend to lose my other three. . . .

That's why I'm working. I can't sleep at night. I have nightmares. I don't eat. If I eat, I feel sick. I will always have to live with having seen my kids beaten in front of me. As far as I'm concerned that is far more punishment than anything they could give me in court. I want the chance to make that up. I do feel guilty of neglect and I have to live with that. I did the best I could at home. What would another woman do in the same situation? Maybe kill the man. Who knows.

She also feels clear about her future relationship with men.

When I get my children back I will never live with another man. Ever. I'm seeing a man now. He's very nice. He knows everything. He's helping me to be strong. He gives me life, he makes me shine and I love him very much for it but I won't live with him. I can't do that to my children. It would go against my rights, my will. Can you imagine what it would do to my children's heads if I lived with another man? They'd say "wow Mummy, you're crazy". . . It's going to be hard, but I'll make it.

In fact Elaine is now in prison. For her part in the abuse of her children, she was found guilty of three counts of assault and sentenced to a prison term of four and a half years. The sentencing occurred shortly after our interview with her.

BARBARA

Barbara's first offence was manslaughter, committed at the age of thirty. As a child, Barbara lived in northern Ontario. She was exposed to violence early in life.

We moved a lot because my father couldn't pay for the homes we were in. My father's an alcoholic. He beat my mother quite a bit. When my father and mother separated, my brother and I lived in different homes and we were both molested there.

Barbara's natural mother died of cancer, and her father remarried. The abuse continued, at the hands of others as well as her natural parent.

My father used to beat my stepmother all the time and he used to travel out of town quite a bit so we were alone with her. It was never hidden that we weren't wanted. We had to stay in our rooms all the time. She called me a lot of names when I was young, like "stupid," "slut," things like that. She said I was going to go to hell like my real mother.

The first time I was ever raped was by the babysitter's boyfriend and I was eleven at the time. I was always running away from home and of course my father would find me and beat me.[3]

She then moved to Ottawa where she worked as a waitress and met her future husband, who was a rock and roll musician.

When I got married I was sixteen and he was twenty-four. It was a horrible marriage. . . . He was a very possessive, jealous person. He wouldn't allow me to go out alone, to go back to school. I used to go with him where he played but I'd have to sit at a different table because it was bad for his image. He also spent a lot of time calling me "stupid." It got worse and worse and although I wanted to get help, I was just so down. I was used to people treating me that way.

She left the marriage at age twenty, with a two-year old son. By the time she was twenty-one, she was in another relationship and had another child who died a few hours after birth.

[The doctor told me] beforehand that the baby was going to die. . .I went through a pretty hard time and eventually our relationship ended because of that. Again, I went back to school and again I couldn't make it. . .It was always financial reasons that I couldn't get through school.

Barbara started to work part-time to support her child, and moved frequently to find affordable housing. At the age of twenty-eight, she met a man with whom she became pregnant and had a daughter. She moved out west to be with this man, but when he deserted them, she returned to Ottawa.

At that time when I came back, the rent situation was really bad, so for five months we had no place to live. Our name went into emergency housing; we lived in hotels, apartments for a while, at friends' places; there were times when we were separated.

Barbara also suffered two sexual assaults by strangers after returning to Ottawa. She did not report the incidents, and she recounts how she felt at the time:

Along with everything else that had happened in the last few years, that really sent me down. The mistake I've made all through my life is never going for help. I was always afraid to go for help because I thought if they think I can't handle something, maybe I'll lose my kids. I was afraid of authority. I was afraid they were going to tell me I was crazy or something.

Finally Barbara was able to move into a subsidized housing project. Shortly thereafter she began dating a man who was a neighbour. At her interview she described him as being without ambition, a thief and a heavy drinker. Looking back on that relationship, she stated:

I started dating people who didn't really care because it was easier for me. . . I felt more a part of them; I never felt comfortable around people who were doing well anymore. I just started living a whole different lifestyle.

Her boyfriend became more physically and verbally abusive as the relationship progressed. One night, he broke into her house and raped her. She did not retaliate until the next day:

We got into a big argument. There was another adult there, my kids and his brother. From what I've been told, I was really hysterical, tried to get him to leave, asked people to call the police, and nobody would do anything. And I walked over to the drawer, took out a knife, and I walked over and stabbed him. I don't remember doing it at all.

He didn't die right away; he died about twelve hours later. . . I was charged with second degree murder and I pled guilty to manslaughter.

For the first eight months after the offence, she saw a psychiatrist three times a week, trying to deal with the awful event.

I just couldn't believe that it had happened. And I couldn't believe that I did it. It was not my intention for him to die. And of course I was pretty mad at him too for dying.

In court, Barbara received a two-year federal sentence followed by three years' probation.

The Crown Attorney wanted four years . . . I was willing to pay to some degree because I wanted to try to somehow be able to live with it. There's nothing you can do to change it and you really feel like you owe something. I felt I could live with it a little better if I went to jail for it.

But when the first person Barbara dated after the offence also tried to beat her up, she continued to blame herself.

I really started thinking that it must be something I'm doing in my life that this is always happening. Obviously I hadn't learned anything—here somebody was dead and the same things kept happening to me.

Barbara credits the assistance of counsellors in helping her remove herself from the cycle of violence and abuse. She obtained academic upgrading while in prison and is now taking college courses; she participates in a battered women's group and in a group for adult children of alcoholics. Barbara's perspective on her relationships with men has changed and she explained to us why she broke up with her last boyfriend.

He had hit me once and the chances are it would happen again. I just don't want to take that chance. I don't want to go back to the same life at all, or to anybody who abused me. And even though he has done a lot for me, it's not worth the price. I don't owe him. I never asked him to do any of those things. I guess people like making you feel obligated; that's how they keep you.

She has also discovered that she is not alone in her experiences.

I find, well, every halfway house resident, every inmate that I've come across has been abused emotionally or physically throughout their lives. And just about every woman in that federal penitentiary is there because of some guy they believed in while they were on drugs or whatever. Just totally abused. And to see them going back to it really bothers me . . .

The battered women's group I get really angry with too. I really think the problem there is that nobody seems to realize how fragile life is, the dangerous games they're involved in. These are serious games, where guys are shoving guns down their throats and machetes at their stomachs and it's only a matter of time before something will happen.

ANNE-MARIE

Anne-Marie was raised in a small town in Quebec until she was twelve. At that time she moved with her family to the east end of Montreal. She remembers her family life with warmth, describing her folks as "not having a lot of money, but surviving." At a very early age, though (seventeen), she married for the first time. From that point on, her relationships with men dominated her life, and that, plus her eventual involvement in drugs, played a monumental role in her later convictions for armed robbery.

After a short and disappointing first marriage to a man who had affairs with other women, Anne-Marie moved back home for a while. She soon met her second husband, the man with whom she eventually committed robberies. Even though her parents disapproved of him from the start, Anne-Marie describes her fatal attraction to him:

We met in a club in North Montreal and because he was big and maybe because he was crude, I don't know, I was attracted to him. I fell in love with him and when I'm in love with somebody, I'll do anything. If you tell me to go slap the person across the street, if I'm really in love I'll go and do it. And that was the problem, I had no judgement at all. So even though I knew it was wrong, I started helping him with his crimes. I thought I was being brave and gutsy. . .I certainly wasn't getting a future, or stability or security. But I was always hoping that one day he would change or love me enough that he would go straight. . .

Her second husband quickly introduced her to hard drugs, and Anne-Marie developed a liking for hashish and cocaine, but she never used heroin. Her husband however had a growing heroin habit. She describes the link between their drug usage and the crimes they committed:

It was a vicious circle. We didn't want to work because we couldn't earn enough money to buy the drugs. So we stole the money. If you steal the money, you don't mind using it for drugs because you don't really know the value of the money. And you want to keep doing the drugs, so you keep stealing so you'll have the money to pay for them. The irony is that I never really got much out of the robberies, maybe a few grams of coke. But most of the money was going to my husband's habit. By then he was *using a lot. It could cost $1,000 just in one evening.*

At times, Anne-Marie thought of leaving her husband, but fear of his violence kept her from taking any action.

I was scared. I stayed with him because I was scared of him killing me or doing something bad to me or my family. At the end I was in a love affair that had turned into a scary nightmare. He used to beat me up and that was another reason I liked to take drugs—it made me feel like everything was okay. Even when I was black and blue, if I was on drugs, I felt like it didn't matter.

After a few years of committing robberies with her husband and getting away with it, Anne-Marie got involved in a bank robbery planned by her husband and one of his friends. While her husband waited outside in the getaway car, Anne-Marie and the friend held up the bank. The operation failed though, and both she and the friend were shot by the police and ended up in hospital. Anne-Marie recalls how proud of herself she was at the time for not "ratting" on her husband.

I thought I was such a good person. I thought about how nice it would be if somebody would take my charge for me. I realize now my thinking was totally distorted. When you think like that it doesn't matter if you kill somebody or you're doing life, because you're doing it for HIM, but him, he's doing fuck-all for you.

While her husband carried on his life with other women, Anne-Marie spent four years of a six-year sentence in the Prison for Women. She recalls her helpless sense of frustration at the way her husband treated her at the time, and her reaction to this treatment.

When he came, [to visit at the prison] there was always a girl in the car with him, waiting while he had his visit with me. Once in a while though he would bring me some hash or some clothes or some money. And that was keeping me from telling him to go to hell. When you're inside, what you miss is the contact with humans. If you don't have lesbian relationships, you're by your-self. It was hard because in those days, I didn't have a relationship with a woman yet. So I depended on my husband and my family for all of my human contact.

When Anne-Marie was released on parole, she moved to a halfway house in Ottawa and attempted to make a fresh start in life. She enrolled in university and received a student loan. Her family was fully supportive.

It was not long though before her husband came looking for her and despite her family's protests, the couple re-united. Within months, she and her husband committed another robbery together. Again, Anne-Marie was caught and charged, while he escaped undetected.

This time, while she was in prison, Anne-Marie decided to separate legally from her husband. She credits the support of her family for helping her to follow through with her decision. Even so, she found the separation hard to accomplish.

I had thought about it before, in fact I even started the proceedings before, but I stopped when I realized that I had no clothes, I had just a pair of shoes, a pair of jeans, a sweater. . . after all those years. . . . This time it's hard too, not just because of losing the relationship, but losing my things. I had a lot of clothes when I lived with him and my books and some other things. We lived together for seven years, and we had lots of furniture and things. Now I've lost everything. I'm starting again at zero at my age. It's not easy.

At the time of the interview, Anne-Marie was feeling positive about her ability to get out and stay out of prison permanently. Her recent conversion to evangelical Christianity was giving her a new focus.

I've really changed the way I think, I've become a Jehovah's Witness. I've already been out on six passes so I could go to the Kingdom Hall here. When I get out I'll be able to do some door-to-door witnessing for the Church.

Religion has given me a support group. And I feel healthier, fatter but healthier. I've quit smoking because of the church, and swearing, and I wear a dress whenever I go to the Kingdom Hall. It's really given me a new personality.

This time when I get out, I won't have my husband looking for me and making me go back with him again. I've broken contact with him completely. . .

Last time when I got out of here, even with a wrong relationship, I stayed out for a year. This time I plan to stay out forever.

FRANCINE

Francine grew up in a large Quebecois family and is the only one of the family's seven children to have been in conflict with the law.

I cannot say my family wasn't a good family. It was really a good family and still is. My dad had a booze problem but he never put us in a bad situation. . .we always had three meals, and a roof over our heads, and everything we needed.

At the time of her interview, Francine was twenty-six years old. She had been released from federal penitentiary a year earlier and was serving the mandatory supervision segment of a four-year sentence for armed robbery. She was first charged with a criminal offence at the age of sixteen, although she had been involved in petty drug offences, store thefts, break-ins and acts of fraud since the age of twelve, largely as a consequence of a growing drug addiction.

I started on drugs really early because I didn't like booze and I had started on booze at about twelve years old. I remember I wanted to impress people around me and prove I don't know what, but that's where it started and I got involved with really strange people.

I can say that the gang I was hanging around with were influential, because I was really impressed. They could make a lot of money so easily, have drugs and booze so easily, and big cars. I thought it was great, and I wanted to do the same. Have cars and have money in my pocket all the time and get my own apartment, like I didn't need school anymore.

Francine did quit school at age fourteen and describes her teenage years as "hell."

I got involved so much in drugs slowly but deeply and I got involved in crime and connections and everything. . .I also had a kid at fifteen but my boyfriend and I couldn't handle the responsibility. We broke up and I just kept going downhill. I didn't think about the baby, I just thought about myself really, and I thought life wasn't worth it. I didn't want to face any responsibility; just party, get high and get drunk and not care about tomorrow.

Her parents cared for the baby and Francine eventually had to leave her parents' home due to her increasingly aggressive behaviour. As her drug addiction progressed, her property offences became more frequent and serious.

When I started with fraud and things like that it was to support my habit. My little habit at first, but I needed more and more money because I ended up doing coke every day. I never wanted to hurt anybody really, to pull a gun in front of anybody or scare anybody. That was not my nature; but it was the drugs—I needed the drugs. I couldn't think straight and I thought it was the only solution.

Francine was convicted of property offences a few times and was given terms of probation or very short sentences. Her living situation continued to deteriorate, as she describes here:

I got apartments with a girl who had a worse habit than me, and we'd have to leave the apartments because we'd spend the rent on booze and drugs. I was up to my head in debts because of coke...We ended up in skid row really. No place to go, no place to eat; we'd have to steal and everything. So anyway, I said "Well, let's go do an armed robbery." I thought we were Bonnie and Clyde.

She and her friend held up a small corner store and were arrested shortly thereafter. She received an eight-month sentence in a provincial prison.

I was always in segregation; I escaped; I was always on everybody's case, fighting and everything, so I did more time than I was supposed to at the beginning. I met some people in there and there were about five of us getting out at the same time. We all went to have a party in the Laurentians... That party kept going for about two weeks and we ended up the five of us in jail. For three armed robberies.

Francine was sentenced to two years, four months for those offences. She began serving her sentence in Quebec and escaped five times in five months.

When I was inside I built up more resentment and hate than you could believe. I didn't want nothing to do with anybody. I didn't think the armed robberies were my fault. I thought that people were just putting me in there and leaving me there. Nobody wanted anything to do with me but they wanted me to respect them in return. So I'd say to myself, "When I get out I'll be worse and it'll be your fault."

After her release on parole, Francine's cocaine addiction continued to progress and it wasn't long until she committed another armed robbery, her last.

We walked into the store and I had a gun. There was a little girl in there, and I was high, and it just froze me. I didn't want to hurt nobody. Her mother looked like she was going to have a heart attack and the little girl said, "Just give them the money, that's all they want." It froze me; I got the money and I got out and I felt really cheap. I felt disgusted with myself, like I was not worth a thing.

She and her accomplice were arrested and convicted. Francine was sent to the Prison for Women in Kingston because she was considered a high escape-risk. It was only after arriving at the federal penitentiary that she began to re-think her life.

I made up my mind about it. Like I was going to quit [committing crimes] and that was it. I had lost my family, everyone, anyway; I was all alone. So now it was up to me to do something. I started in school and I'd get good marks, good performance slips and I was really encouraged. My English was improving so people could understand me at least. I took a butchering course and it was great, really great. I was so proud of what I could do, like I never thought I could do any of these things.

It took a longer time for Francine to quit her drug habit and she did overdose once, after her release on parole to a halfway house.

I had a hard time coping with what was going on around me. But after that [the overdose] I had a lot of help at the house. They could have sent me back to Kingston but they didn't. I hated myself for about a month, but I kept going to school and everything, and finally I got back on my feet.

Francine graduated from her college course in meat cutting with excellent marks. She was the only woman in her program and has found a lot of discrimination in the working world. She has not been able to find consistent employment. As Francine described her work experience so far,

I was expecting that there was going to be discrimination, but not as much as I found in that trade. . . The first job that I went to I was doing everything but meat cutting, he was using me for clean-up after the butchers were done, and "go-fer" jobs. I didn't think that was really fair. . . I told him I was going to look for work where I can practice my trade and he said "Well, you're dreamin'." And, you know, every job I've had so far, that's four jobs, it's been the same thing everywhere.

So now I say, "What the hell, I've got my diploma anyway." I know that I did prove it to myself, that I can go and take courses and I can do it if I really want to. The main thing was to get back my self-confidence.

Francine is also involved in Alcoholics Anonymous and has not used drugs for a year. According to her, she has "turned a chapter" in her life and there is no going back.

NICOLE

Nicole was born in Quebec, thirty-one years ago. As a young child, she experienced the harsh conditions of a life of poverty. Nicole describes her later criminal activity as stemming not only from a need for money, but a strong desire for material goods, and a wish to achieve a financial status comparable to those around her.

She recalls the dramatic change in her family's economic situation that occurred when she was seven years old and the eldest of three children.

My father died suddenly. He didn't have insurance and there was no welfare or anything back then. All my mother had left when my father died was a dollar thirty. . . We were living four in one room. . . We got fed with lots of macaroni, bread and potatoes, things that weren't expensive.

The ensuing years were difficult and painful for Nicole as a child.

We had no money at all; we had to wear second-hand shoes and

old socks and stuff. I never had toys unless somebody wanted to get rid of them. It's hard on a kid. I was the only girl, and there was no-one to pass me clothes.

Nicole also remembers feeling the injustice of her situation and promising herself a different future.

People were always laughing at us because we didn't have money...When you're poor, people think you're shit. I was getting angry at everybody and nobody at the same time. Against society, I guess. I would say "Why are we poor? Why are they doing this to us. If my father was here, nobody would do this to us, nobody would say these things to us."

I always said in my childhood "One day I'll have money, one day everybody will pay me back."

Their financial position did not improve substantially over the next several years. Nicole's mother worked as a cleaning woman and they gradually moved into larger quarters. As a teenager, Nicole babysat for extra money. "But," she says, "I was always thinking: what can I do to make money? I was too chicken to do a robbery or anything, so I never really thought about it too seriously. I just hoped that one day I would have a nice job."

Nicole began working full time in clerical positions when she was eighteen and remained living at home until she married at the age of twenty. The marriage lasted only a few years, and it was during this time that she first became involved in criminal activity. Both Nicole and her husband began selling marijuana, but were never arrested. Nicole did it for only a brief period because, as she explains:

In three months, I had bought everything I wanted: a sewing machine, a reel-to-reel, a colour TV, and a down payment on a car...I was making money because I wasn't smoking the stuff myself. I thought that the people who were buying it were really crazy.

After her divorce, Nicole spent time in British Columbia being supported by a wealthy man. She eventually returned to Quebec at age twenty-six. It was after she returned to Quebec that she got involved in a scheme which resulted in her arrest, conviction and sentencing to seven years in prison for a drug importing charge.

I was working for minimum wage, then I was unemployed for a year. Nothing was going on and my unemployment [insurance] had run out. I was offered a trip to Jamaica. This guy was going to pay me $10,000 cash, plus expenses, and all I had to do was stay there for a month, get tanned and bring back some grass.

It was my dream to go down south for a month. . .it was just like "Fantasy Island." Instead, for a month in the sun, I got seven years in the shade.

Looking back on her decision to go, Nicole states:

I knew I was taking a risk, but I didn't know the sentence was seven years. I thought it would be a year or something. . . Anyway, I couldn't even see jail because the money looked so good. When you see that amount of money, you just do it. . .I wanted it badly and fast. I had this nice idea of buying a house that was next to my girlfriend's, and using the $10,000 as a down payment. My intention was to do that one thing and stop.

After her arrest, she was pressured by the authorities to reveal who had sent her on the trip.

The Crown Attorney wanted ten years. They were telling me if I named the guy, I'd be free after a year. I didn't know the criminal law or anything and they scared me, but I didn't talk. When you're inside they know if you're a rat. I'd rather do my time and when I come out be free. Now I can go outside and not be scared of anyone.

Nicole didn't serve the full seven years in prison, because of early release provisions in Quebec, where she was permitted to serve her time. She was paroled to a halfway house in Ottawa after approximately one year in prison and will remain on parole until the expiry of her sentence in 1991.

She considers herself lucky to have been released from prison when she was. The experience of imprisonment was enough to dissuade her from any further criminal activity.

If someone had told me what it was like in jail, I never would have done it. I never want to be surrounded by four walls again, or be without my freedom. Now, I'm scared to do anything against the law and I get worried when I see a policeman. The other day, our car had a flash that wasn't working and I said to my boyfriend "You better get that fixed right now."

Nicole hasn't lost the desire for more money and a better standard of living, although she has made a commitment to herself to earn it the "hard and slow way."

When you try to make easy money, you get the "side effects" as well and you do get caught some day. Right now, I'm working, it's not a big job or anything, but at least I get a pay every two weeks [about $400] and I'm out of trouble because I have my own money. My boyfriend and I would like to have a child. All I really want is to have a quiet life, you know.

CINDY

Cindy is a twenty-nine year old Native woman who has been in and out of the prison system for drug-related offences for most of her teen and adult life. From her earliest memories, loneliness and alienation from her own culture and the rest of the world were her companions. Her parents died when she was very young and after that her only family life was in her grandmother's house on an Indian reserve in British Columbia.

When I turned five I was sent to a residential school. It was run by Catholic nuns and priests and it was super strict. I would say it was even stricter than some of the [correctional] institutions that I've been in. We weren't allowed to speak our own language, or practise our own religion or culture. If we did, we would be struck for it.

Up until I was twelve, I went to the school and I came back to my grandmother's house for holidays. I never felt too protected there. One of my aunts used to beat me brutally and her husband was always trying to molest me. Because I was adopted, I felt a bit like Cinderella. I didn't have nobody to look after me. I didn't belong to anybody. I think I was abused a lot just for amusement and also so that the older ones wouldn't have to do any work. I got to be very tough.

At the age of twelve, Cindy left home and quit school. Since then, she has been on her own. She has had a small amount of contact, none of it very supportive, with members of her family. Her involvement with drugs started early.

By the time I left, my school didn't want nothing to do with me anyway because I was sniffing glue and drinking and smoking and just being a holy terror. . . . I was nine or ten when I started sniffing and drinking and smoking. It was when I was twelve though that I started doing everything and anything. Mostly chemicals. Just a few months before I turned thirteen, I became a heroin addict.

Cindy's first contact with the legal system came soon after.

By the time I was fourteen I was dealing heroin and hooking, and getting other girls on the streets with me to support my habit. . . . Sometimes I found sugar daddies who would support my habit for a while, usually I was just finding tricks. . . . My first charge was for "theft under" [then $200] and I lied about my age. I was using my aunt's I.D. so my grandmother was contacted and they found out I was really a juvenile so they took me to the Juvenile Detention Centre. My grandmother had me charged with "unmanageability."

The Children's Aid system played an ineffectual role in Cindy's life for two years.

. . . I was made a ward of the Court so I got sent to assessment homes and treatment homes. But I would never stay. I just stayed long enough to pick up my $16 allowance, or sometimes for a month or two so I could get a $200 clothing voucher. I would still continue my life but as soon as I got what I wanted I would leave. By the time I was fifteen I had gone through all of the Children's Aid resources.

The only formal attempt she made to kick her heroin habit when she was a teenager was the result of a decision Cindy made by herself to try a treatment program in Campbell River, B.C.

Me and another guy, this male junkie who I had just met, went on the program. They put us on Methadone, on massive dosages. . . . Finally, after about six months, I told them I wanted to be detoxed, that I felt like I could handle it. But they wouldn't do it. I told them "Look, if you don't detox me today, I ain't coming tomorrow." They didn't believe me so I went back to Vancouver and started dealing drugs again.

As soon as she turned eighteen, Cindy started doing time in the adult prison system.

The first time I was in I ended up serving about eighteen months altogether in the adult system for various charges of possession, selling to an undercover cop, failing to appear. At one point I escaped and so I lost all of my "good time." After that I was out for a while and then I got arrested for numerous fraud charges. All of the crimes that I've ever done have been related to supporting my habit. When I got out after the eighteen months I went back into dealing heavily, but I wasn't dealing on the street anymore. I was moving up, well, just one step up from the street. I had people middling for me plus other people putting out dope for me, or else I'd put out on my own.

Finally, in 1981, Cindy decided to get off heroin on her own, cold turkey, in a prison cell while she was awaiting sentencing for her most recent round of convictions. Since then, and since spending two years in the federal Prison for Women in Kingston, Cindy has been trying to get her life onto a different track. Her attempts have been frustrated though by her low level of education and skills, her confusion over where she fits in as a Native person in a white society, and the failure she has encountered in her attempts to find work. At the time of the interview she was facing new charges for possession of hashish and theft under $1,000.

When I got out of Kingston and moved to the "Y" in Ottawa, I was living on $8 a day. That's what they gave me for food money. Now a woman needs to buy Tampax, Kotex, toiletries and everything and I was not prepared for winter. I was starving. I was about 140 pounds when I got there and I went down to 108. My bones stuck out and I was too proud to ask for help and because of my lack of experience at work, the only skill I have is hairdressing from Kingston, I was not able to find work. I can read, but I still can't add arithmetic. I could not be a cashier or a waitress or anything like that where I got to add quickly, or hand out cash. I don't know any of the school stuff. I don't know algebra, I don't think I know how to do fractions. I really don't remember what I learned in school.

When she thinks about the future, Cindy knows what she

wants, and what she does not want, but she voices her own confusion about whether or not her dreams will be possible to attain.

I'm really lonely because I don't want to hang around with street people any more. I don't want none of them in my life. Everybody here seems so cut off and so conservative. I've been through a lot of crowds in this city and I've not been accepted anywhere. I'm too honest and too vulnerable. I have my own code that I learned on the street. It was instilled in me as a child. One thing I know is I'm working hard not to touch heroin again. I don't want to go near it. All those years I didn't feel no pain. I was numb. Now I have to deal with all of the junk that is inside me, all of the resentment I feel. It's hard. It's really hard.

I just want to have a normal life. I'd like to have my own place and maybe my own hairdressing shop. I'd like to take an advanced course in cutting and hairstyling, though I'd concentrate on cutting because I consider myself a cutter. I've applied to take a cosmetician and an esthetician's course. I have a lot of interests, there's a lot of courses I'd like to take.

Being Indian and living in Ottawa, Cindy feels that she has yet to find her way out of a virtual no-woman's land.

The problem is I felt like I didn't belong all the time when I was a kid and I still feel that way today. Like I'm an alien, an outsider. Because nobody's experienced what I've experienced, and I can't erase it or not talk about it. When I tell people the truth, they treat me like I have the plague or I'm a leper. Especially in Ottawa. I'm not white, but I don't feel Indian, and I don't feel accepted by the Indian people here either. I know I'm Indian by race and blood, but I don't know much about my culture. I've been away from it for so long. I'd like to practise my culture, though, I'd like to learn about it.

JUNE

When we interviewed June, she was approaching her thirty-third birthday. Fourteen years earlier, at the age of nineteen, she committed a murder, for which she received a life sentence. June has been on parole for about five years now.

Her early life experience was characterized by intense isolation and alienation, which persisted throughout her teens. June's story is an account of her attempts to deal with those psychologically destructive circumstances.

Born and raised in rural western Canada, June was one of seven children. She describes a home life made painful by her father's character.

I don't think my father liked children, and that was a problem. I was scared and angry with him a lot so I stayed away from him most of the time. When he was home, I lived in my bedroom or I'd be outside to be away from him. And in so doing I isolated myself from the rest of the family.

As an adolescent, June was required to maintain more contact with her father. This caused her a great deal of anxiety, which was not relieved by the existence or support of other relationships.

My mother started working during the week. My dad was drinking a lot and he'd come home at night and we'd all have to suffer his drunkenness. He mostly didn't want us around but because I was taking my mother's place I had to cook for him and do anything he wished to have done, so I couldn't escape him anymore.

My mother and I never really had that much to do with each other. She taught me how to cook so I could take care of the family and to clean and all that kind of thing about being a housewife. We never spoke. We had very little to do with each other. . . . I wasn't really having contact with anybody in any kind of sense.

June recalls how she dealt with these pressures and the overwhelming loneliness.

I guess to a good degree I didn't care about life itself even at a young age. I was attempting suicide from the age of eight in different ways. . . I started drinking when I was about fifteen. I wasn't drinking that bad at that point. It got worse when I was eighteen, nineteen. I was also given valium when I was eighteen years old because I was having a nervous breakdown.

During her teenage years, June's attempts to establish relationships outside of the family were short-lived. "When I was sixteen I started dating and, I don't know, as a consequence or whatever, but I ended up getting raped, and that ended dating." The rape resulted in a pregnancy, a miscarriage, and a further rejection by her parents, who were "disgraced" by June's behaviour. June's parents were unaware that a rape had caused the pregnancy.

I was threatened [by the rapist] that if I told anybody I'd be dead so I didn't tell a soul. So they believed that I just went out with a man and went to bed with him and I just let them believe that. I knew my dad would go after whoever it was and I knew he had a gun in the house at all times and I didn't want him taking after somebody with that so I just kept quiet.

June's reaction to these events within the existing conditions of her life was one of despair.

I started going backward in emotions. I was going back into being a child because I didn't like how I was feeling so I just started leaving reality a lot. I would visit graveyards, picking places like that to be away from people. I guess I quit wanting to make anything of myself at that point because to me I'd ruined my life. All my life had been ruined and there was really no sense anymore to anything.

Her suicide attempts increased in frequency between the ages of sixteen and nineteen. "I started trying to O.D. with pills when I was eighteen. Before that, I was jumping off cliffs, jumping off roofs, I tried to hang myself, that kind of stuff." At the end of these three years and after numerous unsuccessful efforts to kill herself, she committed murder.

June explains that her suicide attempts had been expressions of anger towards others that she had been directing at herself, but she had reached a point where

I couldn't injure myself no matter what I wanted to do . . . When I did it [the murder] I felt the same anger that I had when I tried to kill myself. . .

I was feeling very angry towards the world. It's like they disappointed me. I couldn't get anything out of life; I couldn't relate to people. I felt nobody wanted me around and that made me angry . . . I guess a lot of times I felt really rejected by people.

The victim was a four-year-old girl whom she was babysitting. Although it is still extremely difficult for June to talk about the incident, in the interview she shared with us her understanding of why it had taken place.

People ask me why it happened and I can't tell them it's just one thing; it's a whole lot of reasons all mixed up together. . . I was on welfare, I had no place to live, I wasn't able to see my family, my therapist wasn't available to see me anymore, I was feeling rejected.

June also recalls more specific factors which influenced her at the time of the murder.

She was always crying. She was a really sad child. I thought nobody deserved to be that sad and that this would make her happier, because the next world must be better than this one. . . . She also really looked like my younger sister, there were a lot of similarities. I had felt that way before towards my sister, like I had wanted to kill her, although I never did anything to her.

June was sentenced to life imprisonment and spent nine years in federal penitentiary, including one and a half years in a psychiatric institution. Since her release on parole, she has had a difficult time adjusting, and has attempted to overdose with pills on more than one occasion. June currently lives in a halfway house for ex-psychiatric patients and continues to be under psychiatric treatment.

She chose to re-establish herself in an entirely new community upon release from prison and maintains very little contact with her family. Despite the difficulties, she is hopeful.

I'm restricted in jobs at this point; I'm restricted in my lifestyle. I guess being in prison didn't give me a good outlook on life because everyone in there is basically down on life, because life has done them wrong. But when I was able to have some freedom on passes, I could see what life was like outside prison. I could see it in a better light than when I'd gone in. It started making me fight to want to enjoy life, to strive for a good living, a job, just to be happy.

June performs volunteer work in the community and has an active interest in the peace movement.

I guess what I mostly want is to give society myself, to try to give it all the qualities I have to make it better. Like trying to help stop wars and to make an acceptable world. With nuclear arms and stuff lately it gets kind of discouraging you know, because I feel that one day I'm going to feel really great; everything will be going fine and then two presidents will push the button and everyone will be annihilated. . . . But I try to keep a positive outlook on things.

CONCLUSIONS

The stories of these seven women are deeply moving; they are also illustrative of common threads that run through the lives of all women who are oppressed. Early socialization that child-bearing and childraising are women's most important tasks, emotional and financial dependency on men, even those who beat and rape women and children, and the inability to earn a decent living due to sex discrimination in the job market are significant factors in several of these stories. They are also key aspects of women's generally inferior social and economic status.

While the women in this article were convicted of serious offences and as such represent only a small minority of women in conflict with the law in Canada, their life circumstances may be shared by hundreds of others who are tried each year for petty offences such as shoplifting, minor thefts, and drug and alcohol infractions. Certainly, of the few hundred women charged with criminal offences with whom we have had personal contact, the majority have been poor, with few job skills to sell on the labour market, and at some point have suffered physical or sexual abuse by men.

Their crimes were vastly different, but Elaine, Barbara and Anne-Marie all suffered at the hands of men who battered and abused them. Of the three, Elaine's crime of permitting the torture of her children, is probably the most difficult for people to accept. How, we might ask, could she allow such brutal events to occur? No doubt that question haunts Elaine, who said during her interview that if she couldn't get her three children back, "then there's' no point in me even existing. . . . "

Susan Cole addresses the same question in an article she wrote on "child battery":

And what about a woman's hellish life within the family? Freedom to choose pregnancy does not entail only choosing when to cope with having a child and terminating the pregnancy when times demand it. Reproductive freedom is real when pregnant women have the self-determination to walk out the door of a battery situation and have the resources to keep their children and rear them. But these circumstances do not occur frequently, and women, whether battered or "just" controlled, find themselves locked into situations which they do not feel they can change.[4]

That sense of being locked in is voiced clearly by Elaine, Barbara and Anne-Marie. During the time she lived with the man who abused her and her children, Elaine says "I was paralyzed.... It was like I was in jail. I realize now that was what it was." Barbara and Anne-Marie also speak of their inability to help themselves, due to their depression or their fear of reprisals. In each situation, another woman may have been able to cope differently, and leave before she was implicated in any crimes. But as MacLeod demonstrated in her study of battered women in 1980, the psychology of fear and consequent inaction is common to thousands of women abused in this country, who find themselves unable to leave men, even when they are in desperate situations.[5]

Like most North American women in the '50s and '60s, the women we interviewed grew up immersed in the ideology that love, that is the love of a good man, was the highest goal to which a woman could aspire. Back in 1970, Shulamith Firestone described the way this prevailing ideology defined women's experiences:

> ... a woman needs love, first, for its natural enriching function, and second, for social and economic reasons which have nothing to do with love. To deny her need is to put herself in an extra-vulnerable spot socially and economically, as well as to destroy her emotional equilibrium...[6]

Firestone's conclusion was that men were "decidedly" not worth the destruction of women's emotional equilibrium. Her decision though, was (and is still) not shared by millions of women in North America.

The cases of Anne-Marie, Elaine and Barbara provide vivid examples of how the struggle by women to attain love, that is, love defined in a man's world, and on men's terms, compromises women's chances to live their own lives, and to live in a state of well-being. Firestone argues that women are socialized to need male love to maintain their psychological stability. Ironically, for these women and for many others who have come into conflict with the law, it was holding onto that ideal which led to their criminal involvement and later emotional breakdowns.

Both Elaine and Barbara spoke of another threat they faced: that if they left their abusive partners, or even if they went for help, child welfare authorities might suspect they were unfit parents and confiscate their children. In Elaine's case, she knew that regaining her children from foster homes was dependent on her ability to provide suitable living accommodation for them elsewhere. Even to this day, she expresses gratitude to the very man who tortured her family because he bought a house for them, and stood by her in confrontation with the Children's Aid Society.

Elaine and Barbara's stories provide stinging indictments of the Canadian welfare system, which on the one hand sets enforceable standards of proper parenting, and on the other, provides such miserly allowances to single mothers that their ability to provide decent homes for their children is severely reduced. When Elaine attempted to survive on welfare payments with her first husband, she turned to illegal action just to feed and clothe her children because the payments were so low.

It is impossible to know what Elaine might have chosen to do with her life had she not felt, at the age of fifteen, that the most important thing she could do was "get married and have more kids right away to make up for having lost [her] baby." Even in the face of her assault charges, she indicated that her children were the most important thing to her in the world. Her goals are not surprising given the strong socialization of most young girls and women to believe that childrearing is one of the few things that can give their lives meaning. Again Susan Cole's insights are relevant:

> What the researchers who examine the "breakdown of mothering" fail to note is that many women are in the home via the coercion of social conditioning and that, if this conditioning were not so effective, many women who have no desire to care for children would not be in positions to have them. In other words, sexism's excessive—and false—advertising for the value of the nuclear family and the relative roles within it has a great deal to do with creating the battered child syndrome.[7]

It may be added that the excessive and false advertising for the value of the nuclear family also has a great deal to do with the battered wife syndrome, and the "stand by your man" motto that has landed more than a few women in prison as accomplices in crimes planned by their husbands or lovers. Certainly Anne-Marie stayed with her husband longer than she knew was good for her because she hoped that one day he would love her enough to change his ways.

In her in-depth study of homicide by American women, Ann Jones concluded that their crimes are "a last resort, . . . most often occur[ring] when men simply will not quit."[8] Like the majority of women who have been convicted of murder or manslaughter, the person Barbara killed was a man who had abused her. Women who kill are usually victims themselves of rape, battering or previous child abuse. This direct relationship between a woman's violence and her own victimization has been documented in the United States and Britain.[9] Although Canadian study lags behind, similar observations have often been made by women involved in the criminal justice system here.

Francine's story is one of rebellion at a very early age against the proper roles that were identified for her in her middle-class family. The rebellious streak lasted in Francine throughout her teens and twenties, and combined with her drug abuse, resulted in a rough road through the courts and the prison system. When she finally decided to change the course of her life and become self-sufficient through legitimate means, she entered a non-traditional training program to become a butcher. However, her attempts to work in a predominantly male trade were met with derision from her employers, and at the time of her interview, she was seriously considering learning a more traditional female trade. Like many of the women we interviewed, Francine's overwhelming desire for the future is to have a "quiet, stable life" filled with activities such as "[raising] children, cooking meals and taking Sunday drives with the family." Those role prescriptions still represent social acceptance in our society.

Nicole's crime of importing drugs for which she received a seven-year sentence, was done for reasons which cannot be condoned, but they are easily understood. Raised in a brutally poor family, yet desirous of the same material goods that are held out to us by the media as necessities of everyday life, Nicole was easily tempted to earn money quickly and illegally by acting as a courier. Like many other women serving sentences for the same offence, Nicole was not the ring-leader of the drug importing operation in which she was involved. That role belonged to a man who was never caught or charged by the police, partly because Nicole refused to implicate him in any way. Even though the state offered her a reduced sentence if she testified against that man, she refused, out of fear for her future.

Between 1980 and 1986, forty-two women were sentenced in Canada to seven-year minimum terms for this crime.[10] Various proposals have been made during the past decade to eliminate the mandatory minimum sentence for drug importation, or to allow for a reduction of sentence length based on the circumstances of the offence. And in June 1987, the Supreme Court of Canada declared that the seven-year sentence applied to every convicted drug importer constituted "cruel and unusual punishment" and is therefore prohibited by the Charter of Rights and Freedoms. A change in the law is now quite likely, and it will no doubt reduce the inordinate punishments that are imposed on women who are used as dispensable fronts for drug importers. It could also alleviate some of their manipulation and intimidation within the criminal justice system after charges are laid.

Cindy, the only Native woman we interviewed, describes her life as one of alienation and impoverishment. Now living in a large urban centre, far from her roots in Native society and outside the mainstream of life in the white culture, she does not know where she fits in. As discussed later in this volume by Carol LaPrairie and as illustrated by the data provided in Holly Johnson's article, Cindy's lifestyle is shared by many other Native women in Canadian cities, particularly in the west.

The poverty and violence that marked Cindy's early life is experienced by many Native people whose balanced and nurturing lifestyle has been uprooted by the colonization process. It is only too typical that Native women, who are victims both of white economic oppression and Native male violence in the face of larger impotence in white society, turn their anger inwards by abusing drugs and alcohol. With an almost total lack of schooling and job market skills, Cindy and her many Native sisters who have also been in conflict with the law, have very few options to pursue which will provide economic or social security.

While June's tragic story reveals a number of experiences common to other women in this section, she also tells of her experiences as a psychiatric patient. Phyllis Chesler and others have described the neglect, the sedation, and the sexist treatment of women at the hand of the male-dominated psychiatric profession.[11] They suggest that for many women patients, the problems they are experiencing at the time they first see a counsellor remain unresolved in traditional forms of therapy. June, who was ultimately convicted of murdering a child, was no exception to this; the chemical solutions prescribed for her in the form of valium only compounded her inability to cope with her life circumstances.

As Edwin Schur pointed out in *Labeling Women Deviant*, "the prescribing of drugs is an integral part of the medicalization of women's life situations. . . it functions very effectively to 'cool' women out, [and] to support a depoliticizing and pathologizing of their dissatisfactions."[12]

June's offence is one that shocks and disturbs. We do not wish to condone the act or to minimize the tragedy, but we do wish to try to understand it by examining the circumstances within which it occurred. These crimes do not happen in isolation, and in cases such as June's, there are factors specific to women's subordinate status in society which help set the stage for these awful events: factors such as her father's abusive treatment, her sexual assault and subsequent rejection from her family, and the denial by others of her suffering.

These seven women are all very different, yet they are linked through their experiences in the prison system and they are trying, in their individual ways, to pick up and rebuild shattered lives. It is no easy task, as Francine explained during her interview:

A lot of women get out of prison, they feel so guilty and so empty, and they feel rejected. Maybe people should know that they're not a piece of garbage, that they're human. They've been in just a little more trouble than someone else but they shouldn't have the door closed on them. Because if I didn't have the help I had when I got out I would never have made it. People I didn't even know were so good to me; they didn't judge me or judge what I'd done. You know, I'd been judged once and that was enough. I think it was great that I had people telling me "You don't have to worry about your past, look forward now." Maybe if people were a little bit more openminded it would be easier for other women when they get out.

Their stories lead us to reconsider the definition of crime. Is it a crime to steal food and clothes for one's children as Elaine did—or rather, is it a crime that the welfare system provides such miserly allowances that mothers cannot afford to adequately feed and clothe their children? Is it a crime that a woman kills a man who rapes her? Yes, but is not the causal event the rape, which occurs because society tacitly condones the sexual abuse of women? Is it a crime that a woman takes part in her husband's armed robbery? Of course it is, but it is also a crime that her husband can beat her into obedience and into fearing for her life. Is it a crime that a Native woman sells drugs on the street? Certainly, but it is also "criminal" that the dominant white culture actively destroys Indian culture and economic self-sufficiency, and causes feelings of such alienation and anger that the drug sub-culture appears as a welcome alternative.

As we listen to these voices, we question not only the morality, but the practicality of maintaining an expensive criminal justice system, when far less expensive means of preventing women from committing crime are available. For instance, were our society to provide adequate financial and social support networks for single mothers; or were we to allow women full and safe control of reproduction; or were we to socialize and educate our children to assume equality exists between the sexes; or were we to stop medicalizing female rage and to confront the problems faced by women, our need for criminal justice services would be substantially reduced.

The interviews provided us with far more material than we could incorporate into this section. Several women's comments about their experiences of imprisonment could not be included. We were surprised to find that some women saw their incarceration as a positive experience. We were told by these women that the federal penitentiary was the first place they felt accepted as themselves and were given a chance to work towards personal goals without having to fend for their survival.

The interviews confirmed for us that the problems suffered by women offenders are similar to the problems suffered by many women in our society, only perhaps more acutely. It is this reality, as much as any other, that we hope feminists will note and incorporate into their efforts towards an egalitarian society.

NOTES

1 Our interviews took place during the fall/winter of 1985/86. See Appendix 1 for interview schedule used.

2 See Pat Carlen, ed., *Criminal Women* (Cambridge: Polity Press, 1985).

3 "The Village," now known as Yorkville, in Toronto, was a haven for "hippies" in the late sixties.

4 Susan Cole, "Child Battery," in *No Safe Place*, eds. Margie Wolfe and Connie Guberman (Toronto: The Women's Press, 1985), p. 31.

5 Linda MacLeod, *Wife Battering in Canada: The Vicious Circle* (Ottawa: Canadian Advisory Council on the Status of Women, 1980), p. 39.

6 Shulamith Firestone, *The Dialectic of Sex* (New York: Bantam Books, 1970), p. 145.

7 Cole, p. 30.

8 Ann Jones, *Women Who Kill* (New York: Fawcett Columbine, 1981), p. 298.

9 Jones; Carol Smart, *Women, Crime and Criminology: A Feminist Critique* (London: Routledge & Kegan Paul, 1976).

10 Solicitor General Canada, Correctional Services Canada, Offender Information System, December 12, 1986, unpublished data.

11 Phyllis Chesler, *Women and Madness* (New York: Doubleday & Co. Inc., 1972); Dorothy Smith and Sara David, eds., *Women Look at Psychiatry*, (Vancouver: Press Gang Publishers, 1975); Robert S. Mendelsohn, *Mal(e) Practice: How Doctors Manipulate Women* (Chicago: Contemporary Books, 1982); P. Susan Penfold and Gillian Walker, *Women and the Psychiatric Paradox* (Montreal: Eden Press, 1983).

12 Edwin Shur, *Labeling Women Deviant* (Philadelphia: Temple University Press, 1984), p. 195.

APPENDIX 1

INTERVIEW SCHEDULE

A. Introduction (to us and to the project).

B. I would like to start off with your early years, so this section of the interview will ask questions about your life at that time.

1 What is your birthdate?

2 What city or town were you born in?

3 What city or town did you spend your childhood in, up to age 12?

4 Who did you grow up with?
—family by birth
—relatives
—foster parents
—friends
—other

5 How many people were in this family or home?

6 Would you say that any of the following problems or pressures existed in the home you grew up in, up to age twelve?
—money problems
—employment problems
—illness or death
—divorce or separation
—psychiatric problems
—personality conflicts among family members
—other, e.g. addictions

7 If so, how would you describe the effect that each had on you, up to age twelve? (For example, having more responsibilities around the home, having fights with family members, avoiding people, being angry or withdrawn, etc.)

8 If not, how would you describe your childhood years? (Happy, fun, average, lots of love and attention, etc.)

9 Who had a big influence on you and on what you did as a child? This could be a positive or negative influence.

10 How would you describe that influence? In what ways did that person (those persons) have an impact on you?

11 Can you remember any events that happened when you were a child (up to age twelve) that had a big effect on you? These could be really happy events or else very difficult ones.

12 If so, how would you say this (these) event(s) affected you? (Changed your life, made you happy/sad/angry/confused, etc.)

C. Now I'd like to talk about your teenage years. For many people, this is when they started getting into trouble with the law. Whether or not this is true for you, I'd like to ask about the circumstances of your life as a teenager.

13 Where did you live as a teenager, from age twelve to eighteen?

14 With whom did you live? What kind of situation was that for you?

15 Was there anyone who had a big impact on your life at this time? What kind of influence did they have on you (positive, negative, why)?

16 Do you remember any events or things happening at this time of your life that had a big effect on you (deaths, divorce, family problems, romantic relationships, etc.)?

17 If so, how would you describe their impact on you?

18 How would you describe your teenage years overall (happy, sad, difficult, lonely, etc.)? Why?

19 Were you taking drugs as a teenager?

20 Did you ever appear in juvenile court?

21 If yes, for what offence(s)?

22 What sentences did you receive as a juvenile?

23 Did the juvenile court experience have any kind of impact on you? How?

24 What do you think were the reasons you became involved in the juvenile offence(s)? (for instance, the people or events that you mentioned earlier?)

D. This section is concerned with your adult life. I'd like to ask you questions about more recent circumstances and your point of view concerning them.

25 What is the most recent offence for which you have been convicted?

26 What was the sentence you received?

27 What stage are you at in serving the sentence?

28 Did you have any previous convictions to this, as an adult?

29 If yes, what were they?

30 What were the sentences you received?

31 Before your conviction, what was your life like? (in terms of jobs, family, friends, relationships, living situations, finances, drugs and alcohol, etc.)

32 What kind of impact did your sentences have on those situations?

33 What factors do you think contributed to your adult offences? (for example, any of the circumstances you just mentioned, circumstances that you described in your teen or childhood years, other.)

34 What are you doing now?/What do you think you will be doing when you get out?

35 What do you see for yourself in the long run?

36 Do you have anything to add that we haven't discussed?

37 Do you have any questions about our research?

Native Women
and Crime
in Canada:
A Theoretical
Model

 CAROL LaPRAIRIE*

Although statistics show that Native people and especially Native women are heavily over-represented in jails and prisons across this country, statistics on the criminal justice system in Canada do not generally distinguish between registered Indians and other Native people. For instance, in British Columbia, self-identified Native women comprise twenty per cent of all women incarcerated, but Native people comprise only about five per cent of the total British Columbia population. In Ontario the figures are seventeen percent and about two per cent, while the Newfoundland Correctional Centre for Women has virtually an entirely Native inmate population. In various "correctional centres" in the prairie provinces and Northwest Territories, Native women comprise anywhere from thirteen per cent to eighty per cent of the inmate population,[1] and in 1983 they accounted for thirty-one per cent of the inmate population of Kingston Prison for Women (P4W), the federal women's prison.[2]

The author is with the Research Division of the Secretariat, Programs Branch, Ministry of the Solicitor General of Canada. Views and interpretations expressed in this paper are those of the author and do not necessarily represent the views of the Ministry of the Solicitor General of Canada.

Compared to other offenders, Native women are charged more frequently for certain types of crime. For instance, in a Winnipeg study published in 1974 (the findings of which have not been replicated), Bienvenue and Latif found that Native women were charged with twice the number of offences against the person as were Native men.[3] Recent statistics reveal that Native women are being incarcerated for more violent crimes than are non-Native women.[4] In P4W, almost three quarters of Native women have been committed for violent offences (i.e. murder, attempted murder, wounding, assault, and manslaughter) and less than one quarter for property offences (i.e. theft, breaking and entering), while for non-Native women the comparable figures are thirty-two per cent and thirty-eight per cent.[5] At the provincial level, the differences are even more pronounced.

Native women are also more likely than non-Native women to be arrested and serve time for defaulting on payment of fines.[6] Compared to Native men, available data (from Ontario only) indicate Native women in prison are twice as likely to have had alcohol play a role in their offences.[7]

A profile of Native women in prison adds to this disturbing picture. A study by the Ontario Native Women's Association found that over a third (thirty-seven per cent) of the Native women interviewed in Ontario provincial correctional institutions were twenty years of age or younger; slightly over half (fifty-two per cent) were first arrested in their middle teenage years (ages fourteen to seventeen) and an additional eighteen per cent were even younger when first arrested. Forty per cent had been arrested fifteen times or more and fifty-five per cent had been incarcerated one to three times previously. Over one-fifth (twenty-one per cent) had seventeen prior incarcerations. These findings are perhaps the most significant to date in documenting the vulnerability of Native women to criminal justice processing.[8]

What are we to make of all this data showing what appears to be a disproportionately heavy involvement with the criminal justice system on the part of Native women and Native female youth (the term "what appears" is used because of the lack of comprehensive, comparative criminal justice data on Native and non-Native people in general, and on Native and non-Native women in particular). However, even if data were available, it would be necessary to keep in mind the possibility of discrimination against Native compared to non-Native people, particularly by the police and officials of the court.

The purpose of this article is to provide an explanation for the above findings, by considering both the position of Native women in the overall system of structural inequality in Canada, and the socio-cultural milieu from which Native women come into conflict with the law. Reference is often made to Native women, because that is the categorization used in compiling statistics, but the explanations are probably particularly suited to the situation of status Indian women and non-status Indian women.

AT THE BROADER LEVEL

The notion that Canada is a classless society has generally been dismissed as naive propaganda. Canadian society is highly structured along class lines, not only internally but also in the larger world economic system. Ours is a hinterland society, an economic colony which has a history of exploitation by foreign metropolitan centres like London, New York and Houston, and by domestic metropolises like Toronto and Montreal. Like a child's playing blocks, these big cities and hinterlands form a nested structure wherein each metropolis has its hinterland and that hinterland in turn is a metropolis to its hinterland. For example, Thunder Bay is a hinterland to Toronto, but northwestern Ontario is a hinterland to Thunder Bay and Toronto is a hinterland to larger urban centres such as New York. Native communities, especially Indian reserves, usually occupy the bottom rung of the ladder of hinterland-metropolis relationships.[9]

By explicit design, during the settling of Canada, many Indian communities were moved off highly productive land onto marginally productive land, and in this respect their local economies can be said to be not undeveloped, but rather underdeveloped, where the latter term implies deliberate economic subordination. Although many Indian communities were able to carve out a renewable resource harvesting economy (hunting, fishing, trapping and/or agriculture) adequate for subsistence, and were able to maintain that economy into the early part of the second half of the twentieth century, those economies in community after community succumbed as the corrosive influence of the welfare state and/or the dominant group's economic system reached into their lives with the post-war industrialization of Canada. The debilitating effects of welfare payments (e.g. welfare dependency, loss of self-esteem) and of the ensuing alcohol abuse and culture of poverty are only a few of the forces impelling many Native women to leave their home communities to migrate to the cities. There, ironically, they increase their exposure to another system of social control—the criminal justice system.

Prior to the 1985 amendments to the Indian Act, this problem was compounded for those women who lost their Indian status due to marrying a non-Indian, in that they lost all their rights on the reserve. Ineligible for band housing, if they were allowed to live on the reserve at all, they usually had to share crowded accommodation with relatives. When that proved unsatisfactory, they often had little choice but to migrate to urban areas.

AT THE INDIVIDUAL LEVEL

The contemporary situation of Native women vis-à-vis the criminal justive system, especially their incarceration for violent crimes, must also be understood from the perspective of the basic social unit in society, the family. In particular, it is important to consider the breakdown of traditional Native roles and values, and the loss of power and personal status experienced by Native people, especially Native men. This social disorganization is related to the aforementioned macro-level economic forces.

Within the traditional economy, the household was the basic unit of production and consumption. Men and women maintained fairly distinct roles and skills, although these differed from one tribe to another. These roles and skills were essential to the survival of the predominant extended family unit. Family solidarity, a sense of place and community, stability, tradition, egalitarianism, co-operation, non-assertiveness (domestically) and avoidance of in-group conflict were the over-riding values and characteristics of life.[10]

With the coming of the Europeans four centuries ago, Indian people were encouraged to abandon traditional economic activities such as hunting, in favour of trapping and barter—the prevalent economic activities requested by the transnational fur trading companies.[11] Not only did this shift set in motion a series of changes in the power relations between various tribal linguistic groups, but also it fundamentally altered the reliance of Indian people on traditional economic activities. With that demise of traditional economies came profound changes in family roles. Through a series of causal steps, these changes eventually brought Indian men and women into conflict with each other.

The residential school system, which took Indian children out of their home community, also had an adverse impact. Parental values were denigrated, parental options were discounted, and children lost parental role models by being removed from their parents at a young age. The teaching of European skills and knowledge was probably less destructive for girls than for boys, as the disparity between the traditional and the Eurocanadian lifestyles was greater for male roles than for female roles. Thus, women retained many traditional roles while men lost their traditional roles and were forced to resort to welfare or other western economic options.

As traditional economies failed, forcing more families into the cycle of welfare, the system itself assisted in the confusion of roles and resulting frictions between Native men and women. Women became primary breadwinners under the welfare system because they received more funds than men by virtue of raising children. As a result, men lost their status as providers in the family. This role reversal led to a growing sense of impotence and frustration on the part of Native men.

In non-matriarchal Indian societies in particular, the eventual effect of these attempts at assimilation was to distort traditional relations between Indian men and women and to introduce male-female alienation. Men came to lose their sense of purpose in their community and to feel useless and impotent.[12]

With the loss of Indian male roles and as a result of being reduced to a state of powerlessness and vulnerability which their own culture deemed highly inappropriate, Indian men came to experience severe role strain. The disparity between the desired traditional roles and the available or achievable roles was so great as to produce tension, anxiety, frustration, and anger, to which different men reacted in different ways. The literature in psychology identifies aggression, regression, withdrawal, or accommodative behaviour as common types of reaction to frustration. The following description of the aggression reaction captures many of the behaviours exhibited by Indian men:

> Aggression may be expressed in overt behaviour or verbally. It may be directed at the source of frustration or at a substitute target. The substitute target may bear a symbolic relationship to the source of frustration, or it may simply serve as a convenient scapegoat on which to displace aggression. If no scapegoat is available, aggression may be directed toward the members of one's own group.[13]

The satisfaction of power needs, denied in the roles made available to Indians in the larger society, may be found in exercising control over vulnerable others. Thus, rape, child sexual abuse, and wife battering are being reported with increasing frequency in Indian communities in recent years. For instance, a probation officer who has lived all her life on the Grassy Narrows Reserve north of Kenora, Ontario has been quoted in the press as saying that gang rapes occur almost every weekend on that reserve.[14] The Canadian Council on Social Development also finds indications of a high incidence of family violence, sexual assault, and incest in many Native communities.[15] The Native Counselling Service of Alberta has also asserted that a great many crimes in Native communities involve family members.[16] Heather Robertson has succinctly described the role and consequences of alcohol in this process:

> . . .[I]nternal tensions become explosive, and alcohol provided a release by destroying inhibitions. . . . Intoxicated, an Indian's repressed hate comes to the surface and is expressed physically and verbally. He hits out at his wife, his children, his friends. This violence, like the drinking itself, is strongly suicidal, and the victims are those persons nearest to the drunk man. He is hitting, indirectly, at himself.[17]

Jim Harding provides another perspective on the relationship between underdevelopment and alcohol abuse. He concludes that:

> . . . underdevelopment created enormous stresses and contradictions and alcohol is used as a means of managing alienation by assisting people to modify their moods and thereby escape their real life situations.[18]

Although research in this area is very limited, evidence is mounting that suggests a direct causal relationship between the conditions of Indian men, male violence against Indian women, and subsequent criminal activity by Indian women. To cite a concrete example, the operator of a home for Native women prisoners in Thunder Bay, Ontario, has been quoted in the press as saying that all the female prisoners with whom she deals have been sexually abused.[19]

The broader sociological literature does provide some limited scientific support for the hypothesized linkage between victimization and subsequent criminality. While this is not the place for a review of that literature, the notion that "violence breeds violence" is supported in the literature on battered children and juvenile delinquents. For instance, emotional or physical maltreatment during childhood is a common feature in the background on child-abusing parents and other violent offenders.[20]

The conflict of some Native women with the law may be linked in a variety of ways to the aforementioned role strain experienced by Indian men. First, Native women may retaliate in kind against physically abusive Native men. Secondly, Native women may escape from a violent or otherwise abusive situation at home and migrate to an urban area where discrimination by the larger society, combined with a usually low level of skills and education, may relegate them to the ranks of the unemployed or unemployable. That in turn increases the probability of resorting to alcohol or drug abuse, or to prostitution, all of which increase the probability of conflict with the law. Even without engaging in any of these activities, being in an urban area increases their exposure to police, some of whom may be biased in the way they exercise their discretionary judgement when deciding whether or not to arrest a Native person. Finally, having observed neglectful or abusive treatment of children among role models in her community, or having experienced such treatment herself, the Native woman may be predisposed to treating her children in like manner.

CONCLUSIONS

The preceding explanation of Native women's conflict with the law has both strengths and limitations. The most important limitations are the unsatisfactory data base, and the broad generalizations that do not take into account the great variation which exists between and within Native communities. For instance, the reader should not draw the inference from the above discussion that family violence and interpersonal abuse are the norm in

Native communities. Indeed, there is much that the dominant non-Native cultures could profitably adopt from traditional Native practices insofar as childrearing, respect for the Elders and extended family relationships are concerned.[21]

An important strength of the explanation is that it avoids the common mistake of "blaming the victim" (the Indian woman in conflict with the law). Instead, the approach takes into account the broader economic, socio-cultural, and legal factors which are associated with being both Native and female in a male-dominated, non-Native society, and which contribute to women coming into conflict with the law. It suggests that Native women offenders' violent behaviour is a product of socio-cultural, legal and economic forces, including the undermining of traditional Native roles and values, discriminatory provisions of the Indian Act (prior to 1985 amendments), and social class. Systematic research still needs to be conducted to determine how much causal weight should be attributed to these factors, or to others not brought into the explanation.

In spite of the limitations of the information available, it is obvious that many Native women are alienated from the mainstream of Canadian life. That alienation is not so much a product of individuals unable to cope as it is a product of social inequality, both in society as a whole as well as on a personal level. The work of social science research needs to take account of this fact, and of the fundamental disparities structured into the Canadian social system.

Perhaps most importantly, we must find the ways and means to tackle issues of structural inequality in Canada, to better address the question of why Native women are in conflict with the law.

NOTES

1 See Carol Pitcher LaPrairie, "Selected Criminal Justice and Socio-Demographic Data on Native Women," *Canadian Journal of Criminology* 26, (April 1984): 161-169. "Native" is used throughout the text in a generic way to denote women of aboriginal descent, whether status, non-status or Metis. The term "Indian" is normally used to denote those individuals who have status under the Indian Act.

2 Carol Pitcher LaPrairie, "Native Women and Crime," *Perception* 7, 4 (1984): 25-27.

3 Rita M. Bienvenue and A.H. Latif, "Arrests, Dispositions and Recidivism: A Comparison of Indians and Whites," *Canadian Journal of Criminology and Corrections* 16 (1984): 105-116.

4 This conclusion is drawn from an analysis of the offences for which women were incarcerated at the Prison for Women in 1982.

5 Information Services Branch, *Non-Native Population Profile Report and Native Population Profile Report* (Ottawa: Correctional Service of Canada, Ministry of the Solicitor General, March 1982).

6 Cindy Misch et al., *National Survey Concerning Female Inmates in Provincial and Territorial Institutions* (Ottawa: Canadian Association of Elizabeth Fry Societies, 1982). Default on fine payments is, no doubt, an indication of Native women's low economic status.

7 A.C. Birkenmeyer and Stan Jolly, *The Native Inmate in Ontario* (Toronto: Ontario Ministry of Correctional Services and the Ontario Native Council on Justice, 1981).

8 LaPrairie, "Native Women and Crime," p. 26-27; and Bernice Dubec, *Native Women and the Criminal Justice System: An Increasing Minority* (Thunder Bay, Ontario: Ontario Native Women's Association, 1982, mimeographed).

9 Gail Kellough, "From Colonialism to Imperialism: The Experience of Canadian Indians," in *Structured Inequality in Canada*, eds. John Harp and John R. Hofley (Scarborough, Ontario: Prentice-Hall, 1980), p. 349.

10 Peter J. Usher, "A Northern Perspective on the Informal Economy," *Perspectives*, 1980.

11 Victor Valentine, "Native People and Canadian Society: A Profile of Issues and Trends," in *Cultural Boundaries and the Cohesion of Canada*, eds. R. Breton, J. Reitz and V. Valentine (Montreal: Institute of Research on Public Policy, 1980), pp. 35-136.

12 Marilyn Van Bibber, "Term Paper," unpublished (Ottawa: Department of Sociology and Anthropology, Carleton University, 1985).

13 I. Wardell Walter, "The Reduction of Strain in a Marginal Social Role," in *Problems in Social Psychology*, eds. Carl W. Backman and Paul S. Secord (New York: McGraw-Hill, 1966), pp. 328-335. The passage quoted in the text is from p. 331.

14 *Winnipeg Free Press*, 23 September 1983.

15 *Native Crime Victims Research* (Ottawa: Canadian Council on Social Development, unpublished working paper, 1984), p. 7.

16 Native Counselling Services of Alberta, Submission to the Federal-Provincial Task Force on Victims of Crime, 1982, p. 18.

17 Heather Robertson, *Reservations are for Indians* (Toronto: James Lewis and Samuel, 1970), p. 283.

18 Jim Harding, "Unemployment, Racial Discrimination and Public Drunkenness in Regina," unpublished paper (Regina: Faculty of Social Work, University of Regina, 1984), pp. 13-14.

19 "Sexual Abuse Just One of the Problems Affecting Indian Issues," *The Montreal Gazette*, 12 November 1983.

20 Proceedings of the Senate of Canada, *Childhood Experiences as Causes of Criminal Behaviour* (Ottawa, Issue no. 7, 1978). It should be noted that one drawback of many studies in the literature is that data is not collected on comparison groups. For instance, a study that finds, say, sixty per cent of delinquent youth experienced physical or sexual abuse in the home may offer no data on what proportion of non-delinquent youth experienced such abuse in the home; for the non-delinquent group the proportion having experienced abuse could be even greater than for the delinquent group. Furthermore, as in other criminological studies of offenders, the offenders are those who got caught, and the non-offenders are not necessarily any less culpable.

21 G.S. Clark and Associates, *Native Victims in Canada: Issues in Providing Effective Assistance* (Ottawa: Ministry of the Solicitor General, User Report, 1986), p. 50.

Young Women in Conflict with the Law

by GLORIA GELLER

T he adolescent female offender is a victim of our society's
double standard of sexual behaviour. Throughout the
past century, delinquent young women have been treated differently from their brothers because of their sex and their potential
roles as mothers. In a stereotyped way, adolescent women's *sexual*
behaviour and adolescent men's *criminal* behaviour have been
treated harshly, while the sexual behaviour of young men and
the criminal behaviour of young women have been of less concern
to officials.[1]

This pattern of stereotyping has been in effect since the Juvenile
Delinquents Act (JDA) was passed in 1908. From 1908 to 1984,
the JDA gave the state the right to bring young people to court
for violations of federal statutes including the Criminal Code,
provincial statutes, municipal by-laws and "status offences."
Status offences included a wide range of behaviours which were
not crimes, but were seen as violations of parental or adult
authority. (Examples were truancy from school, running away,
sexual immorality and incorrigibility.)

In contrast, under the Young Offenders Act (YOA) which was
passed in 1982,[2] young people may only be charged with acts

for which adults can also be charged. As I will discuss later in this article, with the removal of status offences, it should be harder for police and judges to treat the sexes differently. However, stereotyped views in the criminal justice system are strongly entrenched.

This article examines the nature of young women's offences and the double standard of justice that has been meted out to girls compared to boys. It looks at the recent changes in juvenile justice legislation, and finally, it analyzes the potential for young women's prospects to improve under the YOA, with the help of the women's movement.

OFFENCES COMMITTED BY YOUNG WOMEN

Young women have been more frequently charged with status offences compared to young men. This is what official statistics (police data) show, as I present below. However, another type of data, based on self-report studies of young men and women, reveals a different picture. In the self-report studies, young people are surveyed and asked to respond anonymously to questions about their delinquent behaviour. This approach is considered to yield more comprehensive results than official data because it covers offences that may not be reported to the police, or for which charges are not eventually laid.

Below are some of the findings of self-report studies, in comparison to official data.[3]

• For every girl, about six boys reported committing a major theft (theft over [then] $200), yet in the same year (1983), twelve boys for every girl were charged with this offence.

• For every girl, 2.5 boys reported committed a break and enter, yet the official statistics show that twenty-six boys for every girl were charged with this offence.

• Regarding status offences, self-report studies show that young men report more sexual activity than young women, and that boys and girls are involved equally in alcohol and drug abuse, truancy and running away from home. But official data shows that girls are brought to court more frequently than are boys for these offences.

To summarize, the self-report data suggests that young men and women are involved in roughly equal amounts of minor criminal activity; that boys commit a greater number of serious offences than girls; and that both sexes engage in equivalent amounts of status offences, although boys are more active sexually. The official statistics show that considerably more boys than girls are charged with sexual assaults, breaking and entering, theft over $1,000, robbery and mischief. Ironically, girls were charged more often than boys under the JDA for sexual immorality and vice, yet the self-report studies indicate that boys are more sexually active.

The total number of charges against juveniles in Canadian courts in 1983 was 115,915. Of these, twelve per cent were charges against females and almost 900 were charges against males.[4] While girls were charged with eleven per cent of the Criminal Code charges, they accounted for one quarter of the status offence charges.[5] This suggests that the non-criminal behaviour of female youth is of greater concern to authorities than the non-criminal behaviour of male youth.

In the early 1970s, a study of the juvenile court in Hamilton, Ontario found that after a finding of delinquency, a greater proportion of girls than boys were sent to training school.[6] One girl for every six boys was brought to court, but one girl for every *three* boys was sent to training school. Furthermore, two thirds of the girls were sent to training schools for incorrigibility, but only one fifth of the boys were locked away for this reason. Another study demonstrated that, across Canada, about five boys were charged with offences under the JDA for every girl, but only two boys for every girl ended up in training schools.[7] Unfortunately, Canada-wide data on training schools is unavailable after 1973.

The research shows that although they reported significant amounts of Criminal Code violations, girls were much less likely than boys to be charged with these offences. And while they reported roughly equal amounts of status offences as boys, girls were twice as likely to be charged for them. As well, studies of training school populations indicate that the commission of status offences was the major reason for incarcerating female youth. This behaviour was not criminal, and was mostly overlooked when committed by boys.

In the next section, I look at these and other problems that arose for young women under the JDA—problems that were largely caused by the enforcement of society's double standard of sexual behaviour.

THE ERA OF THE JUVENILE DELINQUENTS ACT

STATUS OFFENCES AND THE COURT

When the Juvenile Delinquents Act was developed at the turn of the century, social reformers were concerned about the welfare of children in conflict with the law. The juvenile justice system was intended to deal with youth who did not fit into the education system, but were not yet prepared to enter the labour force. Child labour was no longer acceptable or legal. The intent of the Act was to protect young people from adverse influences in their neighbourhoods, as well as from themselves—if it was believed they were behaving in self destructive ways. The state was given the power to remove young people from their homes for indefinite periods of time if they were found delinquent, and place them in reformatories, training schools or other institutions. The finding of "delinquency" could result from a violation of the Criminal Code, other federal, provincial and municipal statutes, and from the commission of status offences under the JDA.

The JDA was largely based on the concept of the care and protection of the young person by society. It stemmed from the British system of *parens patriae*, in which the state acted as and for the parent. Young persons who committed offences were viewed as not responsible for their actions. Therefore, they were not subjected to the procedures of a court of law and the possibility of imprisonment. But the commission of offences, including status offences, could define a young person as a delinquent in need of supervision, care or protection.

This concern for the welfare of young persons, however, often translated into negative and harmful actions towards them. Those placed in reform and training schools for their "best interests" usually found themselves with more hardened young people who had committed criminal offences. Through association with the more street-wise youth, those in for status or first offences could learn a range of more serious, anti-social behaviour.

In addition, boys and girls received different treatment under this system — as the data presented earlier indicated. But it wasn't until the 1970s that researchers and civil libertarians began to note with concern that a disproportionately large number of young women, compared to young men, were brought to court and placed in detention centres and training schools for running away, incorrigibility, sexual immorality, use of drugs and alcohol, and truancy from school (all status offences).[8]

One study revealed that the proportion of delinquent girls sentenced to training school was higher than the proportion of *adult males* charged with criminal acts and later imprisoned.[9] Officials in the juvenile justice system maintained they incarcerated young women for status offences to protect them from harm and believed they were acting in the best interests of the young women.[10] Indeed, young women were considered to need protection more than young men, because of their vulnerability to others who may have caused them harm, have led them into harm, or because they needed protection from their own self-destructive acts.[11] In other words, because girls were victims or potential victims of sexual exploitation by men, girls were placed out of reach.

Many outside the system, such as civil libertarians, lawyers and feminists, became critical of the use of the JDA to control young women's behaviour. One criticism was that all status offenders (male and female) were treated unjustly compared to adults, since the offences for which they were accused were not included in the Criminal Code.[12] Furthermore, it was argued that adults had a right to a lawyer and to due process of law, but juvenile delinquents were not granted such rights.[13] Attention was also focussed on the unequal sentencing rationales used to punish young offenders and in the mid-70s, incorrigibility ceased to be a legitimate reason for placement in Canadian training schools.[14]

Now, under the Young Offenders Act, it is no longer possible to imprison young women for incorrigibility or any other status offence. Those behaviours previously defined as status offences are now dealt with by schools, child welfare authorities and other family or social services. In addition, the YOA emphasizes the use of diversionary and alternative measures to deal with minor infractions, instead of resorting to court appearances and sanctions involving custody. Such measures include counselling and preventative intervention programs, community service orders and direct compensation for victims.

YOUNG WOMEN AND SEXUALITY

The sexuality of young women who have come before the courts for much of this century has been identified as a significant reason, indeed the major reason, for which they have entered the juvenile justice system.[15] Previously, most experts on the female juvenile offender assumed that young women who were sexually active were delinquent. In their writing, they went into considerable detail about the pathological nature of sexually active adolescent female offenders. One of the texts which presents psychiatric descriptions of adolescent females and focusses on their sexual activities is by Otto Pollak and Alfred Friedman.[16] Girls' sexual behaviour is described as "unhealthy, antisocial or asocial" and as a symptom of illness. A promiscuous girl is said to be "psychologically maladjusted." The same experts ignored the sexual behaviour of male juvenile offenders.

While the experts on female delinquency focussed on young women's sexual behaviour, data from self-report studies (as discussed earlier) has shown that young men have reported more sexual activity than young women. But authorities in the justice system have accepted the double standard of sexual behaviour and ignored the effect of sexual activity on young men.

This has been an international phenomenon, as many studies have demonstrated.[17] In one of the earliest studies on this issue, Chesney-Lind revealed that girls admitted to Honolulu's family court during the 1950s were given physical examinations to determine whether they had had sexual contact, and the findings of these exams were often added to the charges against the young women, a practice to which males were not subjected.[18] In the midwestern U.S., it has been found more recently that runaway girls are more likely to be held in custody and subjected to venereal disease examinations than runaway boys.[19] Linda Hancock's 1981 analysis of police referrals in Australia revealed that forty per cent of the referrals of girls to court made specific mention of sexual and moral conduct, compared to only five per cent of the referrals of boys.[20]

If it has been acceptable for young men to be sexually involved with young women, why have their female partners been condemned for the same activity? Calling in the justice and child welfare authorities to control young women, while turning a blind eye to their male partners, has resulted in a travesty of justice. It is true that young women and girls have been, and continue to be vulnerable to sexual exploitation. Various studies, including the 1984 federal government report on sexual offences against children, have shown that both boys and girls are vulnerable to such exploitation.[21] But in order to protect young women from sexual exploitation, it has usually been the victim who has been brought to juvenile court and controlled rather than the abuser.

For poor young women, especially those belonging to minority groups, protection has meant they have been placed in training schools. In these cases, the victims have been held responsible for their own victimization, while the men who have exploited them have usually avoided blame or punishment.[22] Those who work with both youth and adult female offenders are aware that a substantial number of their clients are victims of both physical and sexual abuse.[23] By concentrating on controlling the behaviour of victims, authorities ignore the real causes of the problems that often lead to young women's conflict with the law.

Prospects for Young Women Under the Young Offenders Act

For young women, the YOA at first sight appears to be an improvement over the JDA. It is clearly positive that status offences have been removed from the Act and that, officially at least, young women may not be incarcerated for non-criminal offences such as out of control behaviour, running away, or truancy. However, I suspect there will be a move in both the young offenders system and the child welfare system to find measures to incarcerate young women who are considered out of control, as I discuss below.

Under the YOA, young people are subject to a process similar to that in place for adult offenders. Offences under the legislation include only the infractions of laws under the Criminal Code and other federal statutes. Provincial and municipal offences, like drinking and driving infractions, are dealt with under the same legislation as adults.

Truancy is now the concern of the school system and not a part of the YOA. In such cases, a school counsellor who is aware of a child being frequently absent without cause may apply to the family court for a hearing to address the problem, a hearing which the child and his/her parents may be ordered to attend.[24]

The YOA strongly emphasizes the use of alternative sanctions for young people involved in minor infractions, to keep them out of the court system. On the other hand, provisions are made for imprisoning young people who have committed major offences.

The YOA has only been in operation since 1984 for youth under sixteen, and since 1985 for sixteen and seventeen year olds. Therefore it is too early to evaluate its impact on the punishment of young women. But research in the United States shows that similar legislation has not halted punitive responses to status offences committed by adolescent females.[25] There, status offences are still punished indirectly.

Canadian law goes further in eliminating status offences than U.S. law. However, one route used there which may be used here is to charge a young person for a criminal offence, so that authorities can deal with her/his status behaviour. As well, child welfare, drug and alcohol and mental health legislation have been used to punish young people for status or out of control behaviour. It has been reported in the U.S. that a growing number of youth (the majority of whom are female) have been placed in mental health and chemical dependency institutions without the requirement of legal authority or individual consent.[26]

In direct contrast to the underlying philosophy of the JDA, the YOA suggests that young people, to a large measure, stand apart from the family and the community as independent individuals capable of and responsible for criminal acts.

Early evidence in Canada suggests the YOA is being used in a punitive way to bring more youth to court for minor as well as major offences. In the opinion of a Winnipeg radio talk show host, too many young people are being brought to court for minor offences. He cited statistics showing there was a 150 per cent increase in the use of custody in Manitoba after the YOA was introduced.[27]

It has also been reported that in Ontario, sixteen and seventeen year olds on an average served ninety-one days in custody during 1984-85 (before the YOA), but a year later they were held in custody on average for one hundred and seventy-seven days (under the YOA). The same report noted that in Newfoundland, in some cases, the average adult served thirty days in jail while youths received eleven to twelve month sentences for similar or even lesser crimes.[28]

As well, the alternative measures approach does not seem to be evenly applied across the country. This is indicated by comparisons of data from five city police forces across the country.[29] In four of the cities (Halifax, Toronto, Winnipeg and Edmonton) there was no appreciable difference in the rates of boys and girls charged before and after the YOA was introduced. However, in Regina the figures show that there was a greater tendency to charge female young offenders after the Act was introduced. I am concerned that due to the way it is being applied, the YOA is simply creating a young person's version of the adult criminal justice system. Young people who enter the juvenile justice system are generally poor and disadvantaged, not hardened criminals. Alternative measures to keep these young people from being caught up in the web of the police, courts and youth centres, and instead provide support and assistance, would be more beneficial to them than punitive measures. This was the original intention of the Act.

I am also concerned that the attitudes which existed under the JDA have not been swept away by the writing of a new Act. In the late 1970s, while conducting research on the differential treatment of males and females in the juvenile justice system, I noted numerous signs of the old, sexist approach to dealing with young women. These are attitudes which I am not convinced died with the introduction of the YOA, a few years later.

I noticed that judges referred young women more often than young men to clinics for psychiatric assessment if they had been truant from school or labelled as out of control. Clinicians frequently recommended that such young women be placed in group homes or treatment centres. The young women were also more likely than young men to be held in detention centres for being out of control.

Various officials in the juvenile justice system, including the judges, told me they found female juvenile offenders more difficult to work with than males. Female delinquents were commonly described as "self-destructive." One judge said: "[The female delinquent] is unmanageable or she's promiscuous, she's on drugs, she's suicidal, everything that could go wrong, she's got it — besides she's got VD. Boys are entirely different. Their offences are against property."[30]

His statement is a clear example of the double standard within the juvenile justice system which existed then (and which I fear has not died); females were seen as "sick" and almost written off as having any potential to change. On the other hand, male delinquents were generally not viewed as sick, but instead as trying to gain mastery over the world.

While more young women than men were labelled as out of control, official statistics and self-report studies did not note any appreciable difference between the degree to which young women ran away from home, compared to young men. But girls who ran away seemed to be of greater concern to officials than did boys.[31]

Running away from home marks the entry into prostitution or serious crime for some young people, but for many others, it is simply an escape from an abusive home situation, to a safer environment with friends or relatives. Nevertheless, young women who ran were labelled as out of control, and seemed to be considered more deviant than their male counterparts.

THE NEED FOR ADVOCACY

Removing status offences from the law does not solve the problems poor young women confront. Some will still be charged and brought to court for criminal offences, while others will run afoul of child welfare legislation because they have run away from home, or have been born to parents who beat them. These include young women who become pregnant early and keep their children; who drop out of school by the age of sixteen; who are on the streets as prostitutes.

Over the past decade, feminists have developed constructive approaches to the problems women encounter, particularly in such areas as violence against women, including sexual assault, battering and incest, and economic and educational discrimination. In these instances there have been major changes in our approaches to working with women, and in women's views of our experiences. But little has been done on behalf of young women, particularly disadvantaged young women.

Yet young women from backgrounds of poverty are vulnerable to social, economic and political forces over which they have no control. They are victims of an oppressive socio-economic system and of a patriarchal system which devalues them as women, and as members of a minority group. Understanding the complex nature of these structures which have direct impact on their lives, helps us to appreciate their efforts to survive under such difficult circumstances.

There is little evidence that programs and services with a feminist philosophy have been developed in Canada for young female offenders. While there are numerous programs for young people in conflict with the law and those involved in child welfare systems, few, if any, seem to espouse goals of feminism such as sexual equality and overcoming sexual stereotypes and victimization.

At recent conferences where these issues should have been addressed, the absence of discussion in this area was noticeable. For instance, a symposium on street youth was held in 1986 in Toronto. While several of the keynote speakers were well-known feminists, there was little discussion on the issue of gender.[32] A 1985 international conference in Quebec on the status of girls addressed many young women's concerns, but it did not focus on poor and minority young women involved with juvenile justice and child welfare systems.[33]

The needs of young women offenders do not differ from the needs of any young person for a caring, supportive home environment, educational opportunities, job opportunities, good health care, and so on. Young women who lack a caring home environment may need assistance in gaining a sense of their own self-worth. If they have been on the street, on the run, involved in prostitution, survivors of incest, or are young mothers, they may need a great deal of assistance to establish a positive life.

Some may choose to continue living on the street, as prostitutes, or in other exploitative relationships. However, there should be help available to those who require it and for those who want to change, and that help should be supportive and non-judgmental.

Those who take part in administering the YOA must throw off traditional sexist notions of the proper behaviour and treatment of young women if they are to become truly helpful to those caught up in the juvenile justice and child welfare systems.

NOTES

1 Gloria Geller, "Streaming of Males and Females in the Juvenile Justice System" (PhD dissertation, University of Toronto, 1981).

2 The YOA was passed in 1982 but not put into effect until 1984 for young people between the ages of twelve and fifteen, and until 1985 for those aged sixteen and seventeen.

3 Official data sources used in this section are: Statistics Canada, *Juvenile Delinquents*, 1983; and Ian M. Gomme et al., "Rates, Types and Patterns of Male and Female Delinquency in an Ontario County," *Canadian Journal of Criminology*, 26 (July 1984). Self-report data sources are: Gordon West, *Young Offenders and the State: A Canadian Perspective on Delinquency*, (Toronto: Butterworth, 1984); Rosemary G. Sarri, *Crime and Delinquency* 29 (July 1983): 381-397; Josephina Figueira-Mcdonough, "Are Girls Different? Gender Discrepancies Between Delinquent Behaviour and Control," *Child Welfare* LXIV (May/June 1985): 273-289.

4 Statistics Canada, *Juvenile Delinquents*, 1983.

5 Ibid.

6 Barbara Nease, "Measuring Juvenile Delinquents in Hamilton," in *Deviant Behaviour and Societal Reaction*, eds. Craig L. Boydall et al. (Toronto: Holt, Rinehart and Winston of Canada, Ltd., 1972), pp. 190-193.

7 Geller, pp. 38-39.

8 Heather Berkely et al., *Children's Rights: Legal and Educational Issues*, (Toronto: Ontario Institute for Studies in Education Press, 1978); Meda Chesney-Lind, "Judicial Enforcement of the Female Sex Role, the Family Court and the Female Delinquent," *Issues in Criminology* 8 (Fall 1973): 51-70; Karen Weiler, "Unmanageable Children and Section 8," *Interchange* 8 (1977-78).

9 Geller, p. 3.

10 Geller, pp. 38-48.

11 Ibid.

12 Berkely et al., op cit.; and Weiler, op. cit.

13 Berkely, et al., op. cit.

14 Weiler, op. cit.

15 Nathan W. Ackerman, "Sexual Delinquency and Middle-Class Girls," in *Family Dynamics and Female Sexual Delinquency*, eds. Otto Pollak and Alfred Friedman (Palo Alto, California: Science and Behaviour Books, Inc., 1969), p. 47; Herbert H. Herskovitz, "A Psychodynamic View of Sexual Promiscuity," in *Family Dynamics and Female Sexual Delinquency*, p. 100; Seymour L. Halleck, *Psychiatry and the Dilemma of Crime* (New York: Harper and Row, Hollier Medical Books, 1967), p. 139.

16 Pollak and Friedman, eds., op. cit.

17 For a recent overview of related international research findings, see Meda Chesney-Lind, "Sexist Juvenile Justice: A Continuing International Problem," *Resources for Feminist Research* 13 (December/January 1985-6): 7-9.

18 Meda Chesney-Lind, "Judicial Enforcement," op. cit.

19 As reported in Chesney-Lind, "Sexist Juvenile Justice," p. 9.

20 Ibid., p. 8.

21 Report of the Committee on Sexual Offences Against Children and Youth, *Sexual Offences Against Children*, Vols. 1 and 2 (Ottawa: Minister of Justice and Attorney General of Canada and the Minister of National Health and Welfare, 1984).

22 See William Ryan, *Blaming the Victim* (New York: Vintage Books, 1976) for a discussion of this phenomenon.

23 Meda Chesney-Lind, "Sexist Juvenile Justice," p. 7. See also the articles in this book by LaPrairie and Adelberg and Currie which testify to this assertion.

24 *Young Offenders*, pamphlet published by Ontario Ministry of Community and Social Services and Ontario Ministry of Correctional Services, Toronto, 1984.

25 Anne Larason Schneider, et al., "Divesture of Court Jurisdictions Over Status Offences," in *An Assessment of Juvenile Justice System Reform in Washington State* (Institute of Policy Analysis, Eugene, Oregon and Urban Policy Research, Seattle, Washington, March 1983); Meda Chesney-Lind, "Girls and De-Institutionalization: Is Sexism a Dead Issue?", paper presented at the Annual Meeting of the American Society of Criminology, San Diego, California, November 13-16, 1985.

26 Chesney-Lind, "Sexist Juvenile Justice," p. 5.

27 Jack London, CBC Radio Morning Show, Winnipeg, 14 May 1986.

28 *The Ottawa Citizen*, 16 July 1986.

29 *Annual Report*, Metropolitan Toronto Police Force, Youth Bureau, Appendices A and B, 1983-85; *Juvenile and Young Offenders Statistical Report*, Edmonton Police Department, 1983-85; *Juvenile and Youth Court Yearly Report*, Halifax Police Department, 1983-85.

30 Geller, pp. 234-243.

31 Ibid., pp. 287-297.

32 *The Street is No Place for a Kid: A Symposium on Street Youth*, Symposium Proceedings, Toronto, Covenant House 1986.

33 Le temps d'y voir, Conference Internationale sur la situation des filles (1985), Montreal, Guerin, 1986.

The Evolution
of the Federal
Women's Prison

by SHEELAGH (DUNN) COOPER

A look at the treatment and punishment of the female offender in Canada since the earliest days reveals a fascinating mixture of neglect, outright barbarism, and well-meaning paternalism. Because of their small numbers and the insignificance attached to their crimes, women offenders have been housed wherever and in whatever manner suited the needs of the larger male offender population.

Early attempts to understand the female criminal generated a range of theories to explain an apparently bizarre kind of deviation from the socially defined female role.[1] The criminological literature, the perceptions of correctional administrators, and general public opinion have reflected a series of contradictory images and myths over the years. Early socio-biological theories of women's criminality, when coupled with the prevailing protectionist public attitude towards women, clashed sharply with the predominantly punitive correctional practices geared to the male majority. The female offender has been portrayed as "poor and unfortunate" on the one hand, and "lazy and worthless" on the other. She needs protection, yet can be a very destructive and scheming temptress. She has been said to require special and more delicate care, and yet she has also been considered far more difficult to confine than her male counterparts.[2]

The 1981 ruling by the Canadian Human Rights Commission that found the Correctional Service of Canada guilty of discriminating against women offenders[3] was the culmination of a long history of bureaucratic decision-making based on factors that had more to do with political expediency than with the welfare of the women in their charge. This historical review explores the evolution of this kind of practice and describes the way women have been imprisoned. As well, it provides an account of the controversy surrounding the unsuccessful attempts that spanned over fifty years to close Canada's only federal penitentiary for women. It illustrates the forces that have neutralized each other so that little which has been recommended in the best interests of the female offender has ever been implemented.

THE EARLY YEARS OF PUNISHMENT (1640-1912)

The first person to be officially condemned to death in Canada in 1640 was female. She was a sixteen year old French girl convicted of theft. A male criminal being tried at the same time escaped death by acting as her executioner.[4] From that time on, the death penalty was regularly invoked for theft and burglary. By 1810, there were over 100 more offences punishable in Canada by execution.

Corporal punishment, in its various forms, provided the only alternative to the death penalty. For example, in the Eastern Township District of Upper Canada on April 24, 1800, the sentence given the offender Mary Myers was that "you be taken from the place of confinement to the place of punishment and be stript and then tied to a post fixed for that purpose, and that you may be then and there whipped with small rods until your body be bloody."[5] The nature of the charge against Mary Myers is unclear. However, it is reported in the records of the Assize Court in the District of York in Upper Canada in 1804, that Elizabeth Ellis, for "being a nuisance," was pilloried opposite the market house for two hours on two different days.[6] The pillory consisted of a wooden frame into which the ankles and wrists (and sometimes the neck) were imprisoned and held fast for a stated period of time, usually from sun-up to sun-down. It was positioned in the marketplace where anyone with a sadistic turn of character could add to the punishment by spitting, jeering or pelting the offender with rotten vegetables or eggs (stones were not permitted). The hangman supervised the carrying out of such sentences along with his other punitive duties.

These forms of punishment were gradually replaced by periods of imprisonment in the early part of the nineteenth century. Penitentiaries began to be used in order to reform criminals through seclusion and penitence.[7] After the building of the Provincial Penitentiary (for Men) in Kingston in 1835, the first two women were sentenced to periods of imprisonment there. Mary Ingram from the Home District (Toronto) was sentenced to one year on a charge of accessory to larceny, and Mary Anne Lane arrived from Midland later in the year to serve a one year term for grand larceny.[8] These women were kept closely confined in a small temporary location directly above the mess table of the male convicts. In 1836, John McCauley, President of the Penitentiary Board of Inspectors, noted that

> It is to be observed that the sentencing of females to the penitentiary causes some inconvenience . . . and though their labour as seamstresses can always be turned to good account, they cannot be effectually subjected to the peculiar discipline of the prison until the separate place of confinement suggested for them by the plans and report of the recent Commissioner shall have been prepared for their reception.[9]

It was clear from the beginning that, because of their small numbers, women would be confined wherever and in whatever manner best served the administration of the larger male population. McCauley's quote also refers to the primary task of women prisoners in those early days, which was to make and mend the bedding and clothing of the male inmates.

Public concern during the early years of the Provincial Penitentiary at Kingston centred around the brutal treatment of the women and children confined there. The public perception of women and children as victims of a system designed for and appropriate only for men runs through the nineteenth century. Yet women in prison were often considered by correctional administrators to be far more difficult to manage than men, as revealed by one of the first wardens of the Kingston Penitentiary:

"A few of the worst of the female convicts are absolutely more turbulent than those of the male sex, and I may with great safety state the "cats" would make a very wholesome change with some of the worthless of them and not by any means endanger their health."[10] (The use of these leather, knotted whips, or "cats" on women prisoners was banned in 1848 following a recommendation of the Brown Commission).

A duality of images held of the female offender was quite evident among the correctional staff in the nineteenth century. When both the warden of the Kingston Penitentiary and the prison matron argued in favour of new facilities for the women, the nature of their pleas reflects the divergent views held of the female offender and of the objectives of her treatment. The warden characterized the women as

> Poor unfortunate creatures, who are sent here, generally of the unfortunate classes. They are taught the usefulness of labour, and those well disposed, are allowed to learn the working of the sewing machine, so that on their release, they may obtain a livelihood.[11]

His plea for larger accommodation was based on a positive characterization of the work that had been accomplished by the women. He wrote:

> A larger number of women have been employed in making articles of wearing apparel for persons living in the city and country, and have given so much satisfaction by their work, that the number of applicants to have work done, has become very great.[12]

On the other hand, the prison matron presented a very different image of the women in her charge, and she offered quite another rationale for additional space requirements.

> There were serious drawbacks for the want of proper cells, where lazy, worthless characters would be isolated and their day's work extracted from them. Such a system, I believe, would tend much more to subduing and reforming them than the present way I am forced to adopt—putting them in a dark cell on bread and water, where they can sleep all day, and in the night, sing and hammer, so as to disturb the whole establishment.[13]

Thus, there was little agreement among prison officials on how best to rehabilitate women prisoners, and the conflicting views tended to neutralize efforts to change the conditions of women offenders' confinement during the nineteenth century.

In 1843, Mary Douglas from Newcastle, convicted of murder, became the first female to receive a life sentence. She joined other women still confined in the original temporary location. The warden, complaining that this location was required for male convicts as part of an addition to the men's dining hall, described the women's unit as "inconvenient."[14] The welfare of the women prisoners was considered secondary to the space requirements of the men and in 1846, cells were temporarily fashioned for the women from rooms in another part of the building. Now numbering twenty-six, the women inmates were confined in cells measuring eight feet four inches long, seven feet six inches high and thirty inches wide.[15]

Criticism levelled at the Provincial Penitentiary in the 1840s, including a public outcry against the flogging of women, led to the appointment of an investigative royal commission in 1848. The Brown Commission, as this inquiry was popularly named, revealed a range of abuses, many of which related specifically to the treatment of female inmates, and to the lack of accountability enjoyed by their keepers.

The Commission discovered that girls as young as twelve and fourteen were being lashed with rawhide. Twelve-year old Elizabeth Breen, for example, was lashed six times on six separate occasions during one year.[16] Although the nature of her misconducts is not known, the Commission revealed a wide use of corporal punishment for such behaviours as bad language, refusing to wear shoes, and insulting staff members.

A strong recommendation was made by the Brown Commission to construct a new, separate unit for the women, in part because of the evidence it heard regarding their living conditions.

> The sleeping cells were frightfully over-run with bugs, especially in the spring of 1846; the women used to sweep them out with a broom. It was so very bad, that on one occasions it was suggested to the warden to let the women sleep in the day room and [the matron] would sit up all night with them, and be responsible for them; the warden would not consent. The women suffered very much, their bodies were blistered with the bugs; and they often tore themselves with scratching.[17]

But it was not only these conditions which spurred the recommendation.

The portion of the north wing which the female convicts now occupy, is not adapted in any way to carry out the penitentiary discipline; nor does it seem even to be attempted . . . The labour department has been as inefficiently conducted as every other part of the discipline. Female labour can scarcely be expected to prove a source of pecuniary to a penitentiary; but we believe that occupation might easily be found which would be conducive to the maintenance of order in the prison, at the same time repay, in part, the cost of supporting the prisoners. A suitable building must, however, be erected before any reform can be attempted with success.[18]

In general, the recommendations of the Brown Commission provided a central thrust toward change in the decade that followed. Penitentiary legislation in 1851 introduced a number of new features in harmony with the Report, including a reduction and regulation of the severity of punishment, and the removal of mentally ill women to the lunatic asylum of Upper Canada. However, the major recommendation, which proposed a suitable building for the women, was not implemented. This resulted in their persistent re-shuffling from one inadequate location to the next, inside the walls of the men's prison.

The year after Confederation, there were sixty-seven women sentenced to penitentiary. Of these, sixty-three were housed in Kingston, one in St. John's and three in Halifax.[19] Those at Kingston were still housed in the "temporary" location and in the small cells that were set up in 1846 for a female population numbering less than thirty. By 1868, the increased numbers of women had rendered the location far too cramped.

This prompted the warden to make an impassioned plea to the Superintendent of Penitentiaries, strongly urging "the building of a proper female prison outside the walls of the Provincial Penitentiary."[20] The following year, similar pleas were made both by the warden and the matron, but apparently to no avail.[21]

After the death of the matron in 1870, the atmosphere within the facility appears to have improved. In 1872 the new matron reported:

I am happy to state that everything in connection with the female department is progressing in a most satisfactory manner. The conduct of the female prisoners has been very good during the year. The system of granting remission of sentence and money gratuity for good conduct and industry has had the most beneficial effect. All the female convicts who could neither read nor write when received here, are being taught by myself and assistants, and I am happy to say, are making fair progress.[22]

The warden also observed:

The good order and cheerful industry maintained in the female prison is very creditable to the matron and her assistants, and the zealous and gratuitous labour of those Protestant and Catholic ladies who now visit the prison regularly to impart religious instruction have, I sincerely believe, produced good fruits.[23]

THE WINDS OF CHANGE (1913-1933)

In 1913, after sixty-five years of recommendations for adequate accommodation for the women, the female prison was finally erected in a new location within the penitentiary walls. The prison was now located in the northwest corner of the general enclosure, which was surrounded on two sides by an inner stone wall.

When public pressure again prompted a re-examination of the entire penal system in 1914, another royal commission recommended that the women be housed closer to their homes in provincial jurisdictions. Their report stated that "the interests of all concerned would be best served if these few inmates were transferred [and]. . . arrangements. . . made with the provincial authority for the custody of all female offenders."[24]

The relinquishing of federal female offenders to provincial jurisdictions was viewed by correctional administrators of the day as a retrogressive step largely because new facilities had just been provided for the women in the men's grounds. The recommendation, however, has plagued correctional planners to this day. Since 1914, scores of government and private sector reports have been published reiterating that recommendation, primarily because of the severe geographic and social displacement suffered by women under the centralized system of federal imprisonment.

In 1921, the Hon. W.F. Nickle was appointed to investigate the state of management of the female prison. This investigation appears to have been prompted by allegations concerning undue sexual familiarity between the male deputy warden of the institution and the female inmates,[25] although these suspicions were not later substantiated in Nickle's Report.

Nevertheless, the report represents a landmark in the history of the treatment of women offenders in Canada. To begin with, it was the first inquiry commissioned to look exclusively at the situation of the female offender. Perhaps even more importantly, the kind of insight offered by Nickle, not just about women convicts, but about corrections in general, represents a marked departure from past approaches. Although in some respects his perceptions of women were very much in keeping with the fallacies of the day concerning women criminals, many of his observations and some of his recommendations clearly reflected a desire to improve the status of female prisoners.

Nickle recommended that the women's pay should be increased to provide an incentive for the work they did. He referred to the labour in the laundry as "hard work that does not improve the worker."[26] The laundry equipment was antiquated (two or three stationary tubs, a poor ringer, a broken mangle, and out-of-date drying kilns), and Nickle recommended that these be replaced by modern electric washing equipment.

He objected strongly to the fact that the inmates were forced to do the personal laundry of the staff, and he recorded:

At times these washings are very foul and it is surprising that self-respecting people would send such soiled clothes to a public place to be cleaned, more particularly when it is known that the women do the washing by hand.[27]

He reported that the women bitterly resented the indignity and considered themselves degraded by what they were compelled to do. Nickle strongly recommended that this practice be stopped. He offered the following:

It is useless to contend that there is satisfaction with the work that has to be done or the tasks allotted . . . behind all is the fault of the system that ignores the principles of human nature; that work must be productive and reward for labour wrought.[28]

In addition, Nickle expressed concern over a range of other problems at the prison, including the cold concrete floor, the walls in need of paint, and the fact that women were being released with only five or ten dollars and in black gowns that were easily identifiable as prison-release garments. He further complained that the women were locked in their cells for too long, that they should have their own library, that they should spend their evenings receiving instructions in reading, and that they should have their own garden plots.

Reverting to a more popular view, Nickle perceived the women prisoners to be sexually aberrant. As Shelley Gavigan notes in her article, correctional practices of the day were informed by early criminological theory which emphasized that women who were criminal were sexually maladjusted, and that their deviance originated in their sexuality. Nickle's perceptions are therefore not surprising:

> Without doubt the women, more particularly at certain periods, are thrown into a violent state of sexual excitement by the mere sight of men. . . and my attention was called to one instance of this group of cases where a sedative had to be given to soothe desire. . . as a matter of fact, today the male staff, from the warden down, view with apprehension the administration of the female prison. . . any decent officers are fearful, knowing that a few designing, crafty women might ruin a well-earned reputation.[29]

In spite of such lingering views, conditions in the female section of the penitentiary appear to have improved considerably as a result of Nickle's report. The women were allowed to have their own garden plots; they were referred to by name instead of number; and the conditions within the work areas improved.

Unfortunately, one of the issues Nickle failed to recognize was the value of proximity to one's home community as part of the reintegration process upon release from prison. The 1914 Commission of Inquiry had suggested the return of the women to their home provinces but Nickle chose not to support that suggestion. His recommendation to build a new facility outside the walls of the male penitentiary was historically important since it was on the strength of this recommendation that the present Kingston Prison for Women was built.

A rather uplifting account of conditions in the female unit a few years after the Nickle Report was provided by a Mrs. Vera Cherry.[30] Cherry arrived at the women's unit of the Kingston Penitentiary in 1923 as an "industrial guard housekeeper." As her title suggests, she was employed in virtually every capacity in which staff assistance was required. She assisted the inmates in the preparation of the meals, supervised the work areas, tutored inmates who wished to learn to write, gave out medicine (she was a nurse by profession), and generally saw her role as that of "house mother."

Cherry lived with the other staff in an apartment adjacent to the unit. She would rise at 5:30 in the morning to let the inmate cook into the kitchen to light the stove and prepare breakfast, and her day finished at 9:00 in the evening when the lights were turned out.

Her description of the prison environment suggests an atmosphere more akin to that of a group home than that of a penitentiary in the early 1900s. Cherry reflected, for example, on the preparation for her wedding as being very much a family affair with the prisoners; the female inmates made her entire trousseau for her.

She recalled that during the early twenties, before a final decision was made to construct the new prison outside the walls, some brief discussion centred around the possibility of returning women to provincial jurisdictions so that they could serve their sentences closer to home. Cherry indicated that the only time this possibility was seriously considered was when the matrons requested a raise in pay. It was then they were informed that the unit would be closed and the inmates sent to the provinces if the matrons persisted with their requests for increased wages.

While some positive changes were occurring within the walls, other aspects of women's correctional treatment had not progressed at all. The notes of the then Secretary of the Parole Commission, Alfred E. Lavell, reveal that in the 1920s the approach of the Parole Board towards women still relied heavily on myths concerning deviant women:

> The women prisoners in Ontario are subnormal and immoral. . . I might add that the Board would rather deal with men's cases any day than the women's, and only sees women as a matter of duty and justice to them.[31]

THE NEW PRISON FOR WOMEN (1934-1986)

The acceptance of the Nickle Report meant that the 1914 recommendation to return women prisoners to their home provinces would be disregarded. Construction of the new women's penitentiary began in May 1925 and was completed in January 1934. It was located across the road from the male penitentiary, and it was surrounded by a sixteen foot wall topped with ten feet of woven wire fabric and barbed wire. The only thing that distinguished its appearance from a typical male institution was the absence of guard towers.

The prisoners were all confined in cells, and they no longer had outside windows as had been the case in the old prison. There was no recreation ground within the enclosure, no provision for outdoor exercise or recreation of any kind, and no educational facilities for the female prisoners.[32]

Although the women now had their own institution, its operation was not independent. Rather, the inmates retained their "afterthought" status under a system in which the management of the prison continued to be one of the tasks of the warden of the Kingston Penitentiary. The doctor and two chaplains performed their respective duties for the women's prison as well. Both staff and inmates were reluctant to move to the new facility; it was described by one of the matrons who made the move as a "great big barrack. . . cold and empty."[33]

Throughout the century that preceded the building of the new prison, women had been housed for periods of time in penitentiaries in St. John's, Newfoundland; Halifax, Nova Scotia; Dorchester, Saskatchewan; and Edmonton, Alberta. With the opening of the new prison, all federal female offenders were gathered in Kingston in order to increase the cost-effectiveness of the operation. This meant that a system which had once allowed for a modicum of decentralization was now obsolete.

In 1938, a royal commission investigating the penal system (the Archambault Commission) was appalled at the inferior conditions of the new institution, stating "the Women's Prison presents a marked contrast to any other institution. . . visited anywhere in this or any other country, whether for men, women or children."[34]

Although it was only four years after the prison's opening, this royal commission concluded that the prison should be closed. It reiterated the 1914 recommendation that the women be returned to their home provinces:

> Your Commissioners are strongly of the opinion that the number of female prisoners confined in Kingston Penitentiary did not justify the erection of the new women's prison and that further continuance is unjustified, particularly if arrangements can be made with the

provincial authorities to provide custody and maintenance for such prisoners in their respective provinces. Enquiries . . . lead us to believe that there would be no great difficulty in making such arrangements. This would have the advantage of eliminating the expense of transporting prisoners from eastern and western provinces. At the present the female prisoners brought from a distance seldom see any relatives during the period of their incarceration. There are no compensating advantages, only the heavy operating expenses already referred to.[35]

As the Commission suggested, the population profile that preceded the decision to build the prison justified neither the size nor the maximum security design. In the fifteen years prior to its construction, the female inmate population fluctuated from twenty in 1910 to twenty-seven in 1925, reaching a low of eight in 1912 and a high of forty in 1919.[36] The average population during that period was twenty-five inmates—a number which did not call for the building of a 100-bed facility.

In terms of their dangerousness, the women were characterized by the Archambault Commission as being "of the occasional or accidental offender class, carried away by the overmastering impulse of the moment, often the outbreak of long pent-up emotion. They are not a custodial problem. . . ."[37] the view that the majority of federal female inmates are not dangerous has been repeated often in studies and reports since the Archambault Commission. It is discussed further in the article in this book by Liz Elliot and Ruth Morris, who raise the issue of whether imprisonment is appropriate at all for most women offenders.

Following the Commission's recommendations for decentralized housing, the Minister of Justice approached the provinces to discuss returning federal women to their jurisdictions. The responses of the provinces, while generally positive, were accompanied by requests for additional financial assistance. It appears that because of what were considered to be rather substantial short-term savings, the decision was made by the federal government to continue to house their women inmates on a centralized basis in the Prison for Women.

In 1956, another government-appointed committee[38] reiterated the Archambault position and recommended the closure of the prison. This prompted the Minister of Justice, that same year, to rekindle discussions with the provinces. The majority of provinces again responded positively, providing funds were made available.

And once more it seemed financially more appealing in the short-term to maintain the status quo.

The prison operated at a limited capacity (never more than seventy-five per cent full) until the late 1940s. But the 1950s saw a significant increase in the number of inmates, due to the incarceration of Doukhobor protesters from British Columbia as well as drug offenders entering the system in record numbers. By 1959, the overcrowding had reached such a state that, with a population of 116 inmates, the women were being housed in the matron's quarters.[39] Rather than increasing the push towards decentralization, the over-population problem resulted in the expansion of the institution by fifty beds in 1960.

A review of the records indicates a remarkable similarity between the Archambault recommendations of 1938 for decen-tralized housing and the renewed series of reports that began to emerge thirty years later. Since 1968, no less than thirteen government studies, investigations and private sector reports have been produced which reiterate that the Prison for Women should be closed and decentralized facilities made available.[40]

One of these, the 1977 *Report to Parliament by the Sub-Committee on the Penitentiary System in Canada*, quoted a witness who described the Kingston Prison for Women as "unfit for bears, much less women."[41] The report continued:

> One area in which women have equality in Canada—without trying— is in the national system of punishment. The nominal equality translates itself into injustice. But, lest the injustice fail to be absolute, the equality ends and reverts to outright discrimination when it comes to providing constructive positives—recreation, programs, basic facilities and space—for women.... In light of today's advanced sociological knowledge, the institution is obsolete in every respect— in design, in programs, and in the handling of the people sent there... there seems to be remarkable indifference to a casual neglect of women's needs by both region[al] and [national] headquarters.[42]

The Parliamentary Sub-Committee Report joined those numer-ous voices that had been raised over many years in an effort to improve the status of women offenders. The culmination of all these efforts was the finding in 1981 by the Canadian Human Rights Commission that federal female offenders were discrimin-ated against on the basis of sex, and that in virtually all program and facility areas, the treatment of federal women inmates was inferior to that of men.[43]

CONCLUSIONS

The historical record of federal corrections tells us that the small female population has always been housed wherever and in whatever manner best suited the interests of the larger male population. For almost a century (from 1835 to 1934), the majority of women offenders were housed within the walls of the Kingston Penitentiary for Men. During this period, they occupied at least three separate locations within the walls, each of these, until 1913, considered "temporary;" and, in each case, the moves were made because the location was required for the male inmates.

It is evident that a move in 1914 to the decentralized options provided by provincial facilities would, in the long term, have cut the human and fiscal costs considerably. Despite the ensuing sixty years of recommendations that federal female offenders be housed in their home provinces; despite the ruling by the Canadian Human Rights Commission that centralized housing at the Prison for Women constituted discriminatory practice; and despite continued pressure from outside organizations in this direction, the Kingston Prison for Women continues to house the majority of federal women and houses them in conditions inferior to the vast majority of institutions for men.

The costs to the federal government of maintaining the status quo are enormous. In 1986, the Correctional Service of Canada reported that the 1984-85 annual cost per federal female inmate was $56,713.00, while for a maximum security male inmate it was $49,792.00.[44] Journalist Brian Johnson has commented on an additional expense incurred in 1980 by the Correctional Service of Canada:

> Erected. . . to replace a crumbling limestone wall, the new barrier, two feet higher than the old, cost $1.4 million and took two years to build. Eighteen feet high and almost half a mile long, it consists of 400 slabs of reinforced concrete, each weighing 16 tons, bolted 13 feet into solid bedrock. Its sole purpose is to contain the energies of about 100 women.[45]

A dominant theme throughout the history of the treatment of the female offender is the juxtaposition of neglect and paternalism. Both are the result of politically motivated bureaucratic decision-making based on expediency. The duality of neglect and paternalism has been rationalized using a whole host of uncontested assumptions, stereotypes and myths about the woman offenders' inherent nature. In the absence of sound data and informed criminological theory, the fate of the female offender continues to rest at the mercy of this cycle.

This historical review shows that public opinion can have a profound effect upon correctional services for women. The bureaucratic response is most often to commission report after report to diffuse public pressure at the outset, which has been a very effective delaying tactic. (It delayed the construction of the Prison for Women for sixty years.) However, history has also shown that at the point at which it becomes more expedient to accede to public demand than to continue to evade it, even an issue as "insignificant" as the imprisonment of a small group of women can command sufficient attention to force substantive change. This said, even the 1981 Human Rights Commission ruling that federal female offenders are victims of discrimination did not substantially change the status quo.

Dogged, collective and continuous pressure from a broad political base can be an effective catalyst for change. The key seems to be a smokescreen of bureaucratic reports and piecemeal reforms to divert the intensity or persistence of public pressure. A sound data base is also needed to demystify stereotypes and myths used to justify the status quo.

NOTES

1 See Shelley Gavigan's article, "Women's Crime: New Perspectives and Old Theories" in this book for a description and discussion of these theories.

2 The co-existence of conflicting images runs through the various Annual Reports published by the Minister of Justice, but is nowhere more cogently expressed than in the Annual Report of 1868 wherein the warden of the Kingston Penitentiary described the women in his charge as "poor...unfortunate creatures" and the matron described them as "lazy, worthless characters;" *Annual Report of the Directors of Penitentiaries* 1868, p. 22.

3 See "The Diaries of Two Change Agents" by Lorraine Berzins and Brigid Hayes in this book for a detailed account of this case brought before the Canadian Human Rights Commission.

4 Christina M. Hill, "Women in the Canadian Economy," in *The Political*

Economy of Dependency, ed. Robert Laxer (Toronto: McClelland and Stewart, 1973), p. 43.

5 Alfred E. Lavell, "The History of the Prisons of Upper Canada," Kingston, Queen's University, 1948 (pages not numbered).

6 Ibid.

7 John W. Ekstedt and Curt T. Griffiths, *Corrections in Canada: Policy and Practice* (Toronto: Butterworths, 1984), pp. 29-30.

8 Upper Canada, *Journals of the House of Assembly,* Vol. 1 App. 19, 1836, p. 2

9 Upper Canada, *Journals of the House of Assembly,* App. 10, 1836-37, p. 4.

10 Canada, *Annual Report of the Superintendent of Penitentiaries,* 1864, p. 7.

11 Canada, *Annual Report of the Directors of Penitentiaries,* 1868, p. 22.

12 Ibid.

13 Ibid.

14 Canada, *Legislative Assembly Journals,* App. GG, 1843 (pages not numbered).

15 Canada, *Legislative Assembly Journals,* App. 2G-AA, 1846 (pages not numbered).

16 *Report of the Royal Commission to Inquire and then Report upon the Conduct, Economy, Discipline and Management of the Provincial Penitentiary* (the Brown Commission Report), 1849, p. 49.

17 Ibid., p. 34.

18 Ibid., p. 74.

19 Canada, *Annual Report of the Director of Penitentiaries,* 1868, pp. 14, 45, 54.

20 Canada, *Annual Report of the Superintendent of Penitentiaries,* 1867, p. 14.

21 Canada, *Annual Report of the Directors of Penitentiaries,* 1868, p. 22.

22 Canada, *Annual Report of the Directors of Penitentiaries,* 1872, p. 20.

23 Ibid., p. 12.

24 Canada, *Report of the Royal Commission on Penitentiaries,* 1914, p. 8.

25 Memos from 1921 relating to the establishment of the Nickle Commission, National Archives, RG 73, Vol. 105.

26 Canada, *Report on the State and Management of the Female Prison* (the Nickle Report), 1921, p. 6.

27 Ibid.

28 Ibid., p. 7.

29 Ibid., p. 5-6.

30 Interview with Vera Cherry, 1979.

31 Lavell, op. cit.

32 Canada, *Report of the Royal Commission to Investigate the Penal System of Canada* (Archambault Report), 1938, pp. 314-315.

33 Interview with Cherry, op. cit.

34 The Archambault Report, p. 314.

35 Ibid., p. 315.

36 Canada, *Annual Report of the Minister of Justice as to Penitentiaries in Canada*, 1910-1913; *Annual Reports of Inspectors of Penitentiaries*, 1914-1918; *Annual Reports of the Superintendent of Penitentiaries*, 1919-1925.

37 The Archambault Report, p. 315.

38 The Committee Appointed to Inquire into the Principles and Procedures Followed in the Remission Service of the Department of Justice of Canada (The Fauteux Committee), 1956.

39 Canada, *Annual Report of the Department of Justice*, 1959.

40 These include: *Brief on the Woman Offender* (Ottawa: Canadian Corrections Association, 1968); *Report of the Canadian Committee on Corrections* (Ottawa: Queen's Printer, 1969); *Report of the Royal Commission on the Status of Women* (Ottawa: Information Canada, 1970); *Report of the National Advisory Committee on the Female Offender* (Ottawa: Solicitor General Canada, 1976); *Report to Parliament by the Sub-Committee on the Penitentiary System in Canada* (Ottawa: Supply and Services, 1977); "Brief on the Female Offender" (Ottawa: Canadian Association of Elizabeth Fry Societies, 1978); "Brief to the Solicitor General" (Ottawa: Civil Liberties Association of Canada, 1978); *Report of the National Planning Committee on the Female Offender* (Ottawa: Solicitor General Canada, 1978); "Brief on the Woman Offender," Montreal: Canadian Federation of University Women, 1978); *Report of the Joint Committee to Study Alternatives for the Housing of the Federal Female Offender* (Ottawa: Solicitor General Canada, 1978); *Progress Report on the Federal Female Offender Program* (Ottawa: Canadian Corrections Service, 1978); *Ten Years*

Later (Ottawa: Canadian Advisory Council on the Status of Women, 1979); "Brief to the Canadian Human Rights Commission" (Ottawa: Women for Justice, 1980).

41 *The Report to Parliament by the Sub-Committee on the Penitentiary System in Canada* (Ottawa: Supply and Services, 1977), p. 135.

42 Ibid., pp. 134-137.

43 Lorraine Berzins and Brigid Hayes' article in this book provides a detailed account of this case and its aftermath.

44 *Basic Facts About Corrections in Canada* (Ottawa: The Correctional Service of Canada, 1986), p. 30. The average cost per inmate includes those costs associated with the running of the institution only and does not include parole-related costs, staff training or headquarters costs.

45 Brian D. Johnson, "Women Behind Bars," *Equinox*, March/April 1984, p. 52.

Behind
Prison Doors

by LIZ ELLIOT
& RUTH MORRIS

O n my first night in jail, an elderly woman was dumped, screaming, crying and groaning, into a neighbouring cell. She was given no blanket since she had been arrested on a drunk charge after a fight in her home. This apparently meant there was some danger of attempted suicide. As soon as the guards had slammed the door and left, we noticed her taking off her stockings and proceeding to hang herself on the cross bar of her cell door.

We pounded on our cell door, and yelled, "Help! Police! Guard!" In a few minutes three of them came running in. They had to go back and look for scissors. Eventually they cut her down, bounced her around a bit until she started screaming again, dumped her on the cot, and left.

My experience was that all inmates, including those who might be expected to be most hardened by their experience in life, were depressed by the fact that any vestige of control over their own destinies had been taken from them. Most felt isolated and forgotten by those close to them, since they couldn't communicate with them. The response of the authorities was to remove any obvious means of committing suicide. . . [1]

This brief excerpt from a longer account by a woman in prison vividly describes the pathological interaction of women and prisons. When women are imprisoned they are deprived of traditional measures of social success, such as care of their children, and of more traditionally male forms of status achievement, such as the chance to succeed in the job market. Women often enter prisons for violating codes of female behaviour, but unlike their male counterparts, most react self-destructively instead of striking out at others. The prison system, instead of restoring any of the means of communication or sense of self-worth which might remove the temptation to commit suicide, further disempowers women by trying to remove the means of self-destruction. And so the vicious cycle spins.

This article focusses on women's experience of federal imprisonment. The conditions of women's imprisonment are described generally, and a diagnosis is provided of problems specific to women prisoners caged in a patriarchal system of punishment. Finally, a prescription for change is offered with roots in feminist theory.

The reality of prison conditions for women must be recognized as a status of women issue. Feminist studies have already exposed the fact that the socio-economic status of women as a group is significantly worse than that of men. To feminists providing services to women in conflict with the law, it is painfully obvious that women in prison generally function at the bottom end of this diminished status prior to their incarceration.[2] It is equally obvious that the stamp of prison leads to an even more hopeless situation and status after release.

For most feminists, the facts brought to light in recent years on the socio-economic status of women have merely confirmed what had long been suspected. Over two-thirds of single poor people in Canada are women, and almost half of all female-headed families live in poverty.[3] As well, legal sanctions against violence towards women are largely unenforced, and services for victimized women are poorly funded.[4] By 1990 the socio-economic status of women may well suffer a further setback when nearly one million more women in traditional support occupations will face unemployment due to the growing use of microelectronics.[5] Confronted with obstacles such as these, women ex-prisoners must negotiate a still more formidable hurdle: the additional burden of a criminal record. While searching for jobs, seeking child custody, or looking for a place to live, female ex-prisoners must deal with their label and the resulting discrimination, as well as their lack of economic security.

WOMEN'S OPPRESSION AND IMPRISONMENT

Incarcerated women have deeply experienced the global oppression of women in general. Few of them have been successful in meeting the criteria of the "ideal woman" set by the media and advertising world, and most have been economically and socially dependent on coercive relationships with husbands, common-law partners, siblings, guardians or employers.[6] A large proportion of them are incest survivors who left home at an early age to escape abusive familial relationships.[7]

Many mainstream criminologists have pointed out that the rate of female incarceration is low compared to that of men. This observation is indeed true, but the reasons are disturbing. For one, women who fail to adjust to their socially defined status are more likely to be institutionalized in psychiatric facilities.[8] When there, women are twice as likely as men to be subjected to electroshock "treatments."[9] Or, quite commonly, they become addicted to sedatives prescribed by a medical profession which has historically been eager to help women overcome what appears to be diagnosed as a gender-inherent valium deficiency.[10]

As well, women's relatively impressive track record in avoiding high rates of incarceration is due to the patriarchal values which have long shaped our social beliefs. Women have traditionally been viewed as naturally passive, emotionally expressive, affectionate, nurturing and concerned about interpersonal relationships.[11] These qualities are in direct conflict with the aggression, emotional detachment, violence and poor interpersonal relationships which criminologists attribute to the traditional (that is, male) criminal. Women prisoners who show signs of emotional detachment, violence and poor interpersonal skills may be perceived as even more deviant than their male counterparts.

Women who go to prison, then, are deviant both as citizens and as women. Once they are in, they are caught up in a prison sub-culture which is strongly influenced by the street sub-culture and demeans women's status further. As one woman ex-prisoner put it:

> Being a woman in the system is ten times—no a hundred times more devasting—because the fact is it's a man's world in and out of the system. Women even in the so-called criminal subculture are considered second rate. In fact especially in the subculture, women are very demeaned. You are to be used sexually, passed around, abused; there is no respect, no understanding. I was the only one that used to break the code. I broke the code in *both* cultures. . . .[12]

Women in conflict with the law who eventually receive sentences of imprisonment arrive at the gates burdened by sentencing rationales beset by sexist discrimination. One argument for committing women to longer sentences is that women are "psychologically different" from men, therefore they are "more susceptible to rehabilitation."[13] Aside from the undocumented sexist basis of this assumption, there is another equally unfounded assumption that prisons are rehabilitative, rather that destructive.

A woman's success in parenting is also often considered in sentencing. If her children are already in the care of the state, or she is otherwise evaluated as a poor mother, her sentencing prospects may be bleak,[14] for a crucial redeeming quality of her womanhood (her ability to parent) is in question. Moreover, there is a great deal of circular, self-fulfilling prophecy in the assumptions of authorities who make decisions on these matters. As one woman prisoner who spent much of her childhood first in Children's Aid care and then in training school explained:

> They have one more control over me than they do over men—my kids. Children's Aid considers that because I was a Children's Aid child, . . . I won't know how to parent them because I didn't have proper parenting and training in how to parent. I used to tell them: "not once did I ever accept you as my parents. So I am certainly not going to use what you gave me as an example. I will use it to measure what I *won't* do. . . ." They just couldn't understand that logic. Because most women whom they condition into violence, abuse, and all that, do react that way because that is all they know. . . .[15]

The resulting situation is startling. A social institution in effect acknowledges its own care of children is so inadequate that these children will grow up to be poor parents. It then demands to take responsibility for the care of their children. Generation after

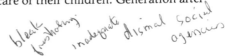

148

generation falls into its care, precisely *because* it is acknowledged to be inadequate. The same convoluted logic lies behind the chronic institutionalization of women in prisons and mental hospitals and prevents society from breaking this vicious closed circle.

It is hardly surprising that this method of evaluating women before incarceration is reflected in the conditions that await them when they enter a prison. Dr. Nancy Shaw has described these conditions frankly:

> Jails are punitive, not helping institutions . . . female prisoners are demeaned; infantilized. Meanwhile, they are expected to behave in accord with traditional female sex-role patterns, which include pleasant submission to these inequalities and indignities. In contrast to this expectation is the fact that many jailed women are locked up precisely because they have refused to accept their designated lots. Most have been willing to break laws and take chances. As women and as mothers, they have fought against difficult odds and survived.[16]

THE FEDERAL PRISON FOR WOMEN

Women's incarceration in Canada back to the nineteenth century has been an exercise characterized by after-thought planning and "temporary" arrangements.[17] Through it all, women have suffered what a recent Correctional Service of Canada researcher baldly described as "more official indifference than official contempt."[18] In 1934, the first and only federal Prison for Women was built in Kingston, Ontario. Its 1986 population hovers at around one hundred and forty, with about eighty other women serving federal sentences in provincial prisons by virtue of a transfer agreement between the federal and provincial governments. This transfer agreement was struck in 1973 to accommodate the concerns of critics who had long claimed that distant geographical separation of women from their families and community supports risked the destruction of these important relationships.

While this agreement is still used, the overcrowded status of provincial prisons and the ongoing disputes over funding between the two levels of government ensure that most women serving federal time will eventually do so in Kingston, whether their home is in Gander, Newfoundland or Whitehorse, Yukon Territory. The Maison Tanguay prison in Montreal, Quebec is the only provincial jail which keeps most of its federal prisoners in the province, sending only very long term inmates or prisoners considered escape risks to the Prison for Women. Despite the advantage of being closer to home, women in Maison Tanguay serving federal sentences continue to face "hard time" in an institution with inadequate programming and facilities.[19]

In the Prison for Women, the prisoners are as varied as the crimes they have committed. As writer Brian Johnson notes, the prisoners' histories illuminate their current status:

> There are teenage girls who took to the streets at 13, selling their bodies and buying drugs. . . There are middle class women who tried to pay debts by peddling drugs. There are working class women who waited in the car while boyfriends robbed banks and shot cops. There is a woman who killed her baby to stop the crying. . . Before becoming aggressors, most of them were victims of sexual or physical abuse from fathers, stepfathers, husbands, or strangers. Their crimes tend to be acts of passion, desperation, and intoxication.[20]

In 1985, there were forty-nine women in Canada serving life sentences, representing over one-fifth of the total population of federal women offenders.[21]

Despite the seriousness of their crimes, only fifteen per cent of federal women prisoners are considered dangerous by prison security staff.[22] However, because the rate of women's imprisonment is so low, the Prison for Women must accommodate all women, whether they are classified as maximum, medium or minimum security. In order to maximize the safety of women prisoners, women in need of protection are held in a separate, segregated unit. In effect, they serve their sentences in a prison within a prison.

In this protective custody unit, women have less access to prison programs and activities than those in the general prison population. They can enter the institutional workshops two afternoons per week, compared to daily access (excluding these afternoons) afforded the other women. Visits by outsiders are allowed daily for most of the women, but are only available one afternoon per week and on occasional noon hours to those in protective custody. The small number of prisoners in protective custody have access to the library one afternoon per week, compared to its daily availability to prisoners in the general population. They also have comparatively limited opportunity to use the institutional beauty parlour and canteen.[23]

The more flexible economy afforded by the larger male prisoner population results in a different system for men. Men are incarcerated in institutions where everyone is classified at the same security level. Relaxed security measures applied accordingly allow for a gradual increase in programs. Men requiring protective custody in federal prisons are incarcerated in one of two prisons which are structured exclusively to accommodate them, allowing greater freedom of movement and program access than the protective custody unit within the Prison for Women.

WHAT'S WRONG WITH THE SYSTEM?

In 1986, the typical federal female prisoner was between twenty and thirty-four years of age, serving the first eighteen months of her first term, which was likely to be under five years. She was probably unmarried, and serving a sentence for manslaughter or robbery. Although the crimes sound serious, often the surrounding circumstances were those that would occur only once in a woman's lifetime. In fact, it is doubtful she would be dangerous in any other situation. The average annual cost for incarcerating each of these women in 1986 was $56,713.[24]

These statistics beg obvious questions. Why do we spend so much money to lock up women of whom eighty-five per cent are not considered dangerous while, as the women's community contends, programs and services for women outside are chronically underfunded? Those services, which include rape crisis centres, battered women's shelters and employment assistance programs, are desperately needed to help women survive and champion their diminished status before they need to commit crimes.

It is estimated that between thirty to fifty per cent of incarcerated women in Canada's federal and provincial institutions have children in their care prior to imprisonment.[25]

Why are so many women of child-bearing age incarcerated and separated from the children they already have? Moreover, why do women in general accept and submit to a patriarchal "criminal justice" system that not only is reluctant to protect the best interests and political priorities of women, but imposes male-defined punishments based on values entrenched in our man-created laws? This process of submissiveness training is described in the following statement made by one woman, much more resistant than most:

> They always told you "Little girls don't do that." And the more they said that, the more I would do it. I'd say, "Well, *this* little girl does." But eventually what happened was I got involved with a man who beat me. My friends would say, "You used to take on six training school guards, how come you let him do that to you?"[26]

The reason was that even this indomitable woman had begun to learn part of her sex-ascribed lesson, from both the authorities and her similarly afflicted peers.

Clearly women in prison suffer greatly from oppression, yet the issue has only recently been addressed by the feminist movement in Canada. Kingston Penitentiary for Women was described in 1978 by a former Commissioner of Penitentiaries as "unfit for bears, much less women."[27] In the Lakeside Women's unit of British Columbia's Oakalla provincial prison, the punitive segregation was so physically decrepit in 1977, that its sight caused a visiting lawyer to issue a telegram to the B.C. Attorney General, stating:

> We represent T.B., presently held along with 3 other women in cell underneath old cow barn. These small cells have wet concrete floors and walls, no sanitation facilities, are infested and smell of manure. Client is kept in these conditions 24 hours a day with only mattress on floor, a bucket, and a blanket at night.[28]

Despite reports such as these, we have heard many people protest that the living conditions of women are generally better than those of men prisoners. They cite examples such as greater internal inmate movement in the P4W, the privilege of receiving limited parcel packages, and the opportunity for dormitory-style living for some women.

Compared to their male counterparts, women prisoners are more peaceful co-inhabitants. While the violence in men's prisons is usually overt, much of the violence in women's prisons is self-inflicted; it commonly takes the form of slashing.[29] To disturbed prison authorities, this self-mutilation is perceived as a way of "acting out," and the action is followed by punishment. One woman vividly described the logic of self-mutilation when she told of her first incarceration at age eleven:

They charged me with threatening and assault. For me it was the first time in a jail. All I remember is the feeling I had when they made you go in this little cell—it had a toilet. First they deloused you. They check your body in places where at 11 years old I have never done anything with boys yet. So I felt pretty degraded. This big, hairy, masculine, aggressive matron body-searched me. She was not sensitive at all—we were bad children. So they put me in this little 6 x 8 cell, and all I remember is a little toilet and a steel bed—it looked exactly like Metro West [detention centre] today. They shut that door with keys that clanged, and I thought again and again, "You must be really bad or you wouldn't be here. . ." So I unravelled a tube of toothpaste and the edge was razor sharp. My mother had been suicidal. I hurt so bad and I felt so bad. I felt, "You are terrible, you are terribly bad—look at you, you are terrible." I didn't want to kill myself. My thought was I was so bad I wanted to hurt myself. So I just started digging at my wrists. . .[30]

This brief description condenses the overwhelming sense of social rejection, its internalization, and the girl's desire to carry out what she felt was society's message to her by attacking herself. In this case the irony was complete, for the judge concluded that she was a danger to herself. Consequently he sent her for her first term to an institution for longer term juvenile offenders.

To Brian Johnson, the concern of prison authorities to "protect" inmates was disturbing in a different way: "The warden is not known for his sensitivity. As he went on about the financial distress caused by slashing, I began to wonder if prisons do not confine the keepers as well as the caged."[31] And indeed, prison staff members who feel inclined to assist women on release to the community because they've developed a positive working relationship with them during incarceration are discouraged by employment regulations which officially limit contact. The rationale for these regulations is that contact between prison staff and ex-prisoners, when planned and not accidental, may result in further conflicts of interest.

Women prisoners are expected to accept the physical conditions of their incarceration with submission. Their reduced status is reinforced by the general sexist attitudes of the system. For example, women in prison are referred to and treated as "girls," although they range anywhere from eighteen to sixty-five years, and are often mothers.[32] This is a common way society treats groups labelled inferior. It is similar to the widespread calling of all black men "boys" throughout the U.S., especially in the south.

The misnomer of girls applied to women in prison vividly accentuates the meaning of their imprisonment. Women have little opportunity inside prison walls to move towards gender equality, or to assert the strength of their womanhood. No apologies are made for this by prison officials. Relatively powerless in free society, women prisoners are further burdened by the patriarchal definitions of their gender role that dominate the prison regime.

These traditional expectations are reflected in institutional attitudes and programming for women in prison. As seen earlier, women prisoners are considered bad mothers and/or wives, often by virtue of their incarceration and with little regard for their parenting opportunities before they entered prison. One prisoner, incarcerated in Lakeside Correctional Centre in British Columbia, lamented on her release, "I only knew that 'Welfare' was going to prove that I was an unfit mother. I'd never had a chance to *be* a mother, so how were they going to know if I was unfit or not? I was in jail."[33] Given this ex-prisoner's place of residence during her child's custody hearing, she had little chance to win the battle.

It is a monumental challenge for prison officials to reform these "deviant" women to an acceptable level of stereotypical womanhood, but this has not prevented their trying to do so. Skill training for women prisoners is restricted usually to traditional female occupations such as housekeeping or clerical work. British, Scottish, and American feminists working with female criminals report the same phenomenon—that regimes in penal institutions for female offenders typically reinforce the traditional sex roles of women as a class.[34]

In Canada, reports of training for women prisoners are littered with similar criticisms. In Lakeside, for example, it was noted that ". . . programs for women fitted the traditional stereotypes: laundry, kitchen, hairdressing."[35] In the Prison for Women, employment and training programs are dominated by cleaning, laundry, hairdressing, cooking, sewing, and clerical work. While authorities insist that great changes have been made with the provision of non-traditional skills training such as carpentry, auto-mechanics and microfilming for women prisoners, some of these programs are located in men's prisons, and are therefore available to very few women in prison.

The widespread apathy of those responsible for implementing change is rooted in a patriarchal rationale all too familiar to feminists.[36] Apart from the obvious fact that it is easier to run an institution when its prisoners are submissive, women are still not seen as primary breadwinners or in need of meaningful employment.[37] Women reformers have repeatedly argued for an increase in the *quantity* of programs. but historically these were designed to integrate them better into the domestic, female sphere.[38]

FEMINIST ATTEMPTS TO RESPOND

Due to the growing visibility of feminism, the challenge to expand training opportunities in women's prisons has broadened in support.[39] Yet the challenge remains largely unheeded, and we still have a great distance to travel. One ex-prisoner observed, "They're [prison officials] simply more concerned with training men to get jobs, and not at all worried about training women to get jobs, although they must be fully aware of the fact that women who go to jail, because of their records are, by the social standards in this country, unacceptable as wives."[40]

The individual progress of women prisoners towards "rehabilitation" is generally assessed on the basis of a woman's potential as a wife and mother only; that is, upon her ability to act in traditional feminine roles. According to one American warden at a world conference on prison health care, the success of a newly-implemented co-correctional program (where men and women were incarcerated together) could be seen in the "better attitude" of women who now paid closer attention to their physical appearance by wearing makeup, ironing their clothes, and fixing their hair. How this better prepared women to deal with the economic realities of life after prison was not clear.

In Canadian prisons for women, the feminist message to prisoners is not easily tolerated, and occasionally silenced outright. In 1983, many prisoners eagerly anticipated a songwriting workshop at Kingston Prison for Women by Arlene Mantle, a popular feminist performer, but it was abruptly cancelled when reports by staff on the performer's show for prisoners the previous night claimed that the singer was "anti-authoritarian, flippant and promoted lesbianism."[41]

Although the efforts to train women to fit the stereotypical mould are not usually successful in prisons, financial rationalizations are offered instead of attempts to change existing programs. Due to the small number of women incarcerated compared to men, equality in women's programming is deemed to be too costly. Recidivists especially are seen as being "without family, sociability, femininity and adulthood. Consequently, too, they are also seen as being beyond the help of the legal and caring profession."[42] While these quotes are taken from work concerning British jails, Canadian jails too "reflect in good part the assumptions inherent in the work of several criminologists . . . namely that women and girls who commit offences are abnormal either biologically or psychologically."[43]

The prison administrators we have encountered pay polite lip service to suggestions for change made by feminist critics, while quietly continuing to believe that their clients are largely beyond the hope of traditional standards of acceptable womanhood and personhood.

A PRESCRIPTION FOR CHANGE

Radical feminists of the late twentieth century have stated they would prefer to end the imprisonment of women.[44] A strong argument can be made that incarceration itself should be abolished, in the light of its absolute failure to address properly the problem of crime. Until that goal is achieved, we believe feminists working in prisons should attempt to initiate a personal empowering process for women that would promote self-confidence and opportunity for personal choice.

The treatment and counselling programs in women's prisons, where they exist, are generally rooted in patriarchal definitions of normal, appropriate behaviour for women. They are also rooted in a belief in the inherent worthlessness and sinfulness of people in prisons. One woman prisoner described her own therapeutic role in women's prisons:

> I saw them take advantage of young kids. It was mainly these kids who would get caught in the system. They wouldn't have the emotional stability to deal with the system. And they would abuse them mentally. They would keep pounding on their head "You're no

good—you're worthless—you're useless." And I would say, "No, you're not—these guys are fucked up—they don't know what they are talking about..."[45]

There is both great irony and great realism in the sentence, "They wouldn't have the emotional stability to deal with the system," for it required a lot of emotional durability to survive the treatment offered in these rehabilitative institutions.

It is imperative that the women's movement challenge the existing definitions of deviance and "rehabilitation" by ensuring that a feminist philosophy is used in practice and in the evaluation of services to incarcerated women.[46] Initially, the challenge for feminists is to raise the political consciousness of women in prison, who often have little or no understanding of the structural causes of their incarceration.[47] Such consciousness-raising is altogether foreign to penal philosophy. As one ex-prisoner articulated:

> Prisoners haven't really been able to make themselves aware of what's being done to them. There's no political consciousness... There's no possibility of getting women's liberation literature, civil rights literature. The magazine section is mostly middle-class type, McCall's and Maclean's and Chatelaine and Good Housekeeping.[48]

The lack of feminist consciousness in women's jails and prisons is exacerbated by traditional assumptions about women generally—an a priori assumption that they are "irrational, compulsive, and slightly neurotic."[49] In a system based on patriarchal values and judgements, it is simple to see why women who steal or kill are considered incomprehensible. It is the task of feminists to challenge these assumptions both in theory and in practice. Prisons for women hold a multitude of needy consumers of feminist counselling.

Lacking resources to help restore a sense of self-worth and purpose in life, many women prisoners go under. One ex-prisoner described the problem this way,

> Of all the women I went through the system with, and I am only 24, about a third are caught in the adult system, a third are dead, and a third are in mental institutions. Of all of them *only four* have made it, and three of those four only made it because they married some guy that beat them.[50]

Did those three of the last four really "make it"? In effect, they seemed only to exchange one prison for another. Later in the same interview, she identified three choices for women prisoners:

"Either you do drugs, or you latch onto some guy and give him a free fling once in awhile, and he gives you a little bit of comfort in return, or you fight. I fought, but I would never recommend it . . ."[51] The option of fighting from a feminist base, with the backing of the women's movement, is not visible to many women prisoners. The tools to assist these women are, however, available to feminist counsellors, who should be employed in the prisons. Feminist therapy resources, such as those found in the work of Jean Baker Miller[52] and Edna Rawlings and Diane Carter[53] embrace objectives such as physical/sexual/emotional frankness; proper care and growth of all people; private and public sexual equality; and creativity in life. In fact these resources should be used to work with men as well as women so that we do not merely maintain and perpetuate misogyny towards women.

Counsellors (who are often male) now working with women in prison focus on developing behaviour changes palatable to the system, but what is needed is a healing and educational process conducive to women's needs. Women prisoners should be encouraged to share their experience and struggles with each other and the world outside. They need to demystify their "pathologies" and develop support networks within the closed prison community, which would replace existing efforts by prison officials to divide and conquer. Counsellors with a feminist approach are needed to encourage prisoners to become full, functional, self-reliant and empowered members of society, and to lobby prison officials to expedite this process.

It is obvious to feminists currently working with women in conflict with the law that practiced feminism will not be easily tolerated, much less accepted, in a prison setting. Such changes must be given the full support of the feminist movement in general, which must openly challenge the current attempts to perpetuate the oppressed status of women while they are incarcerated. Feminists need to recognize that our sisters in prison are women like ourselves, driven to alternative lifestyles and practices as a result of the limiting expectations placed on us in a patriarchal society.

CONCLUSIONS

> Eliminate societal racism and sexism, allow economic and sexual autonomy for all women, and women's prisons will no longer be necessary.[54]

Our criticism of women's prison conditions must be constant and unflagging. Actions by feminist groups in the past, notably the Women for Justice appeal to the Canadian Human Rights Commission regarding the inequality of opportunity for women prisoners as compared to men, may lead to short term cosmetic changes. Yet in the long term, the system consistently reverts back to its patriarchal philosophy.

It is exactly this philosophy that needs to be challenged in the criminal justice system, as it is being politically challenged elsewhere by feminist groups. While the wheels of change grind slowly, we must demand the right to practice as feminists in women's prisons. We must act as constant watchdogs, to ensure that our successful lobbies for change are in fact implemented in the spirit of feminism. We need to give a voice to imprisoned women in both traditional and feminist discourses. Stronger pressure must be exerted to improve the lot of women as a whole, thus reducing the need for women to seek solutions that contravene existing laws. As feminists, we need to change a social structure based on profits and power, to one that speaks to human development and shared dignity.

NOTES

1 Joanne Young, "Confessions of a Jail Bird," *Arthur*, 23 March 1983.

2 Christie Jefferson, "The Female Offender: A Status of Women Issue," *Canadian Association of Elizabeth Fry Societies Newsletter* 10 (March 1984), p. 3.

3 *The Shocking Pink Paper* (Ottawa: The Canadian Advisory Council on the Status of Women, 1984).

4 Lisa Freedman, "Wife Assault," in *No Safe Place*, eds. Connie Guberman and Margie Wolfe (Toronto: The Women's Press, 1985), pp. 55-58; and Toronto Rape Crisis Centre, "Rape," in *No Safe Place*, pp. 68-80.

5 *The Shocking Pink Paper.*

6 Ellen Adelberg, *A Forgotten Minority: Women in Conflict with the*

Law (Ottawa: The Canadian Association of Elizabeth Fry Societies, 1985), p. 9. See also the article in this book by Ellen Adelberg and Claudia Currie wherein women offenders speak of their own experiences and those of women they know.

7 F. Hawthorn, L. Elliot, L. Snyder and A. Welch, *Report to the Fraser Committee from the Elizabeth Fry Society of Kingston* (Kingston, Ont.: Elizabeth Fry Society, 1984), p. 6.

8 Interview with Dr. Bonnie Burstow by Liz Elliot, February 1986.

9 Ibid.

10 Robert S. Mendelsohn, *Mal(e) Practice: How Doctors Manipulate Women* (Chicago: Contemporary Books, Inc., 1981), p. 14.

11 Z.W. Henriques, *Imprisoned Mothers and Their Children* (New York: University Press of America, 1982), p. 17.

12 Interview with "Nancy," an anonymous woman ex-prisoner, by Ruth Morris, March 1986.

13 Ann Jones, *Women Who Kill* (New York: Fawcett Columbine, 1980), p. 9.

14 Pat Carlen, *Women's Imprisonment: A Study in Social Control* (London: Routledge & Kegan Paul, 1983), pp. 69-70.

15 Interview with "Nancy."

16 Nancy S. Shaw, "The Female Offender," in *Judge, Lawyer, Victim, Thief*, eds. Nicole H. Rafter and Elizabeth A. Stanko (Boston: Northeastern University Press, 1982), pp. 265-266.

17 Lorraine Berzins and Sheelagh Cooper, "The Political Economy of Correctional Planning for Women: The Case of the Bankrupt Bureaucracy," *The Canadian Journal of Criminology* 24 (October 1982).

18 Correctional Service of Canada, "History of Crime and Punishment in Canada," *Crime and Punishment Journal* 10 (August 15 1985): 6-7.

19 Programs at Maison Tanguay are limited, with preference for employment and skills training offered to women serving shorter, provincial sentences rather than to women serving longer federal sentences.

20 Brian Johnson, "Women Behind Bars," *Equinox*, March/April 1984 p. 53.

21 See Holly Johnson's article, "Getting the Facts Straight: A Statistical Overview" in this book.

22 Johnson, p. 53.

23 Discussion with Karen Howe, Co-ordinator of Community Programs, The Elizabeth Fry Society of Kingston, May 1986.

24 *Basic Facts About Corrections in Canada* (Ottawa: The Correctional Service of Canada, 1986).

25 Linda MacLeod, *Sentenced to Separation: An Exploration of the Needs and Problems of Mothers Who Are Offenders and Their Children* (Ottawa: Solicitor General Canada, User Report No. 1986-25), pp. 11-12.

26 Interview with "Nancy."

27 Gerard McNeil and Sharon Vance, *Cruel and Unusual* (Toronto: Deneau & Greenberg, 1978), p. 75.

28 Claire Culhane, *Barred from Prison* (Vancouver: Pulp Press, 1979), pp. 171-172.

29 Johnson, p. 61.

30 Interview with "Nancy."

31 Johnson, p. 61.

32 V. Rosenbluth, "Women in Prison" in *Women in Canada* ed. M. Stephenson (Don Mills, Ont.: General Publishing Co., 1977), p. 213.

33 Ibid., p. 223.

34 Carol Smart, *Women, Crime and Criminology: A Feminist Critique* (London: Routledge & Kegan Paul, 1976), p. 140; Carlen, pp. 71-73; Shaw, p. 266.

35 Culhane, p. 172.

36 Canadian Association of Elizabeth Fry Societies, "Brief to Solicitor-General," 1979.

37 Smart, p. 141.

38 Estelle B. Freedman, *Their Sisters' Keepers* (Ann Arbor: University of Michigan Press, 1981), p. 2.

39 As Lorraine Berzins and Brigid Hayes document in their article in this book, Women for Justice—an Ottawa feminist lobby group—won a Canadian Human Rights complaint which argued that women in prison did not have the same program opportunities as male prisoners.

40 Rosenbluth, p. 221.

41 Personal experience of Liz Elliott.

42 Carlen, p. 199.

43 Smart, p. 144.

44 Freedman, p. 155.

45 Interview with "Nancy."

46 Helen Levine, "Feminist Counselling: Approach or Technique?" in *Perspectives on Women in the 1980s*, eds. J. Turner and L. Emery (Winnipeg: University of Manitoba Press, 1983), pp. 75-86.

47 Male prisoners who come mainly from low socio-economic and minority groups, also tend to lack this kind of political consciousness.

48 Rosenbluth, p. 219.

49 Smart, p. 111.

50 Interview with "Nancy."

51 Ibid.

52 Jean B. Miller, *Toward a New Psychology of Women* (Boston: Beacon Press, 1976).

53 Edna Rawlings and Diane Carter, eds. *Psychotherapy for Women: Treatment Towards Equality* (Springfield, Ill.: Charles C. Thomas, 1977).

54 Freedman, p. 156.

The Diaries of
Two Change
Agents

by Lorraine Berzins
& Brigid Hayes

This article documents some of the individual and collective struggles to change the way women are treated in Canadian prisons. It describes the experiences of two women who dedicated several years of their lives to challenging, both from within and without, the stale and debilitating imprisonment policies of the Canadian government. Their experiences reveal that change comes slowly, if at all, and only at great personal sacrifice. In one case, it cost the change agent her job, and her chances of advancement in the government bureaucracy.

Lorraine Berzins presents her experiences as a social worker and a bureaucrat, when she struggled to identify and effect changes to meet the needs of imprisoned women. As one of the first women to enter the traditionally male-dominated field of corrections, she takes us from the dynamics of the prison setting to the intricacies of national policy development.[1]

Brigid Hayes provides the story of Women for Justice, an independent lobby group, which submitted a successful complaint to the Canadian Human Rights Commission. She was the group's spokeswoman for four years, the duration of its involvement with the complaint. The Commission upheld the group's charges against the Correctional Service of Canada of discrimination against female offenders.[2]

As both the women's experiences reveal, pressure brought to bear on the government for reforms to penal policy is only effective if it comes from outside, as a result of sustained and widespread lobbying, and if it garners support inside.

LORRAINE BERZINS
DATELINE: 1970
STRATEGY: FRONT LINE WORKER

My first job in the criminal justice system was in 1969, as a social worker at a medium security penitentiary for men. There I witnessed suffering, hardness and despair, yet the busy-ness of the place seemed to offer hope. There were programs, activities, categories and slots for us to offer to the inmates.

By way of comparison, in 1970, when I became the social services director at the only federal penitentiary for women (the Prison for Women—P4W—in Kingston, Ontario), I found no illusion of purpose or hope. Since I started working in the correctional system seventeen years ago, I have come to realize that a whole dimension of human need is not met through this system, for men or women. But this awareness was most acute when I tried to apply correctional theory I had been taught to the female offender.

After a year in a larger male institution, the casual informality of P4W seemed like sheer chaos. I found practically nothing with which to work; there were virtually no programs. Many women were too far from their homes to maintain community contacts for visits, support or planning. Several lost custody of their children for this reason. Some gave birth during their sentence and were removed from their infants after four days, making it painful to bond, impossible to breast-feed and difficult to build the relationship.

Removal from their home provinces also made it difficult for the women to get legal aid or to enter mental health facilities because the various jurisdictions battled about accountability for these "living bodies"—to quote the legal documents that accompanied them to prison. The women, no longer residents in their home provinces, were apparently only "accidentally" residents in Ontario, according to the government.

Gathered together in one facility were women from Newfoundland, British Columbia and the North West Territories. The highly educated were mixed with the illiterate. Two all-American college girls found with hashish at the border and serving mandatory seven-year sentences for importation were alongside the homeless Newfoundlander sentenced to two years for public mischief. (She had broken a store window and waited for the police to get her. The authorities sent her to Kingston because they had no facilities appropriate for her in Newfoundland.)

The sophisticated government official who had used her position to fraudulently obtain hundreds of thousands of dollars was alongside the woman born into a career criminal family who got caught smuggling a gun into jail so that her lover and her brother could escape. The nineteen-year old who killed the man who raped her was alongside women who made their livings out of "rolling their tricks." Women who helped their boyfriends rob banks or sexually abuse other women and children, were mixed with countless others deeply addicted to drugs and alcohol.

They were all together, with different needs and different abilities, far from home, in one place, waiting it out.

My staff and I tried to find some purpose for their time: group therapy, interest groups and recreational activities, opportunities to work, study or just visit outside the prison, a self-help drop-in centre in the community as an option to the bar rooms—the best from the grab bag of correctional programs designed for men. But ultimately, no matter what we did, we didn't touch the real problems that festered there. A few exceptions benefitted from a few exceptional alternatives, but, for the most part, other forces to neutralized the well-intentioned but superficial programs.

Many of the women came from backgrounds of deeply entrenched low self-esteem. They had been victims of incest and poverty, they had learned to use sex, manipulation, emotions and violence as their only means of survival and self-expression. Their fear of failure was great, they saw no real hope of a more positive self image.

Our time was consumed by impressive looking "Initial Assessment" and "Parole Preparation" reports that led to the same old options: the laundry, the kitchen, the occasional hairdressing or school program, and getting out as soon as possible to earn quick money cleaning local motel rooms. We were busied with details, and had very little time for the people underneath. Faced with the futility of our best efforts, we felt demoralized and confused.

To the rest of the system and to the community, the female offender was a low priority: those two hundred women were no trouble compared to the ten thousand men serving prison sentences. We had to fight for anything new; the criteria were cost and convenience. The authorities argued there was never enough money, and never enough female offenders to make reform as inexpensive per capita as it was for the men. It seemed no one cared if we were effective, as long as we kept the lid on.

I am now shocked at how quickly I became an instrument of repression. I quite self righteously played "cops and robbers" with the inmates suspected, for example, of bringing drugs in on passes, until one day I found myself making two women vomit the contents of their stomachs.

The shame, that I could have come to think that this was right.

DATELINE: 1976
STRATEGY: NATIONAL
CO-ORDINATOR

After two years I left P4W with great relief. But the stories of these women had touched me deeply in mind and heart. The problems seemed insoluble, but I could never cease to be haunted by the burning memory of hopeless lives in the stark penitentiary. Some would be in and out of there for the rest of their days, for that was all they had. Others would never be back, but would forever be marked, like me, by the experience. As one of the American college girls wrote in a letter to me much later:

> Part of who I am has been shaped by the incredible and wasted strength of those women, the screams echoing through the cell block, the scars from acting out, the devastating kindness of the damaged. I still have dreams about going back, finding the people still there and wanting to scream, "leave them alone, leave them alone, can't you see you've hurt them enough?"

When an opportunity came in 1976 to plan national policy for the female offender, I vigourously set out to improve services for women. The Ministry of the Solicitor General was favourably disposed to this: P4W had been a controversial thorn in its side for many years. Its closure had been called for repeatedly almost since its inception, because of its archaic design (which even in the 1930s was considered inappropriate for women), and because it was so far from many of the women's homes.

In response to a growing lobby by concerned women's groups, a national consultation committee comprised of provincial and federal corrections experts had been struck to advise the ministry.[3] I was assigned to follow up on its recommendations. This marked the first time someone was hired to work exclusively on the needs of women.

The committee had stressed the importance of joint federal-provincial planning for women. Therefore I developed a master plan to sensitize bureaucrats to women's needs. The intent was to re-organize services for federal female inmates, which would include locating them in provincial prisons or new, small, community-centred facilities as close to their homes as possible. This would help them to maintain family contacts, develop new skills and re-settle after serving prison terms.

But there was a problem. Although no one denied it would be nicer to improve services for the female offender, there was no political will to do anything about it. Federal and provincial officials who were supposed to follow up on the advisory committee's recommendations saw little reason to probe more deeply into the specific needs of the women or to wrestle with complex factors that were blocking access to existing services for men. A common response to our proposals was "the men need that too, so when we're ready to develop a mechanism to address this issue for men, we'll make it available to interested women as well."

It was becoming clear to me that the standard working tools of corrections could not solve the problems of the female offender. And female offenders were too insignificant in number to warrant the time to even find out why, let alone justify the development of more suitable alternatives. The provinces saw little benefit in collaborative efforts and chose to define the issue as a federal problem.

By 1978, no progress had been made towards solving the plight of women at P4W, but enough work had been generated due to the nation-wide attention to the issue to warrant expansion of staff for the Female Offender Program. Up until now, I had been working alone. At this point, I was joined by another woman, Sheelagh (Dunn) Cooper. Our task continued to be the development of improved services and programs for women offenders, and the decentralization of prison facilities.

We understood we were to develop these plans in co-operation with the provinces and that the federal government would take this opportunity to re-consider the ways in which it spent money on the female offender. Areas such as research, staff training, decentralized services and specialized programs were to be examined.

But instead of seeing our efforts bear fruit in the form of new ways of treating female offenders, we found our work stymied at every turn. When we produced a review of existing programs which did not meet the commissioner of corrections' approval, it was banned from distribution[4] (afterwards it was made available upon request). The report provided for the first time, an accurate and detailed review of the inmates in the Prison for Women, regarding issues such as their level of danger to others, their skills and education and their family status.

It demonstrated clearly that, contrary to the existing assumptions, even the most dangerous women did not require maximum security, and the existing programs in the prison far from met the needs of the women for rehabilitation. It also suggested specific improvements that could be made if the women were re-located in regional or provincial institutions. In particular, issues such as maintenance of contact with children and other family members, skills training and personal development were addressed.

However, after the report was released by mistake (before it had been approved by senior officials), its content became the focus of the commissioner of corrections' wrath. Our participation in decision-making was gradually eroded, our contact with senior federal and provincial officials was virtually eliminated and our roles were reduced to an advisory capacity. Underlying all of this was the fact, at that point hidden, that the commissioner of corrections had no interest in seeing any major changes in the treatment of female offenders.

DATELINE: 1979
THE DISMISSAL CRISIS

Finally, in 1979, we were fired. (See Appendix 1 in this article for a copy of the memo of dismissal.) The reason given was that we had responded inappropriately to an outside consultant's proposal to re-organize female offender programs. When we asked for a more detailed explanation of the cause for dismissal, the commissioner of corrections told us our response to the consultant's proposal was emotional, irrational and therefore unprofessional. We lobbied for an inquiry into the dismissal, but while our firing was discussed by the House of Commons Justice and Legal Affairs Committee, and the motives of the commissioner in dismissing us were questioned, no action was ever ordered to re-instate us.[5]

This experience marked a major turning point for me. I realized it was impossible to reform the system from within, without major pressure brought to bear from without.[6] My colleague and I discovered that the task of planning adequately for the needs of women in conflict with the law quite simply couldn't be done within the prevailing constraints. The tools the correctional system provided (bars and fences, security classifications, assignment to available program slots and economic criteria), could not be properly fitted to the women's real needs. We realized it was impossible to deal with the hurt and violence of human persons in a framework based strictly on economics.

Finally, we had put our finger on the crux of the problem that had been stalemating the planning process for years: to plan adequately for the female offender was going to require more change than the bureaucracy had bargained for and this was too much to expect for such a small group of women. My colleague and I became caught up in a complex web of forces that sought to neutralize our effectiveness in the very mandate we had been hired to carry out. In retrospect, it appears that a powerful system which did not hesitate to compromise the interests of women in its charge for convenience's sake, also dealt unscrupulously with women hired to correct those inequities.

We believe we were dismissed because our findings did not assist the government in preserving the appearance, with two women in the figurehead role, of actively attempting but in fact doing nothing to promote the best interests of female offenders. As members of the same powerless sex whose interests we had been hired to represent, we were vulnerable to the same discrimination that had allowed these concerns to be disregarded for generations by the correctional system and society. Despite our credible record in other areas of correctional management, our views were not taken seriously.[7]

The organization created our positions for political reasons, and slowly but inevitably divested the positions of power. As incumbents who resisted being used as mere figureheads, we were particularly susceptible to retaliation.

Stated political objectives are often lost within large, well-established bureaucracies if they go against the vested interests of the most powerful bureaucrats. In this case, the political decisions to create the position of co-ordinator of the female offender program and to close the Prison for Women, were actively undermined by the senior program managers and the senior prison administrators. This resulted in an informal erosion of the co-ordinator's power, and an equally effective undermining of attempts to close P4W.

The perception of our comments as emotional was based on a particular stereotyped view of women in the work force. The only grounds for the interpretation of emotionality were an overall perspective which typifies women as more emotional than men and too emotional in the work force. Had the same memo been authored by two men, we believe such an interpretation would not have been made. Another justification for the dismissals would have had to be found. This one happened to be particularly believable of two women working on a women's issue.

If the bureaucracy is allowed to discard inconvenient recommendations as irrational each time they are made, then two more discriminatory features of our society are, like P4W, likely to be with us for years to come. Token women will be allowed to pass through public service positions without hope of ever having any significant influence on the development of our social institutions, structures and organizations. And federal female offenders will continue to be processed through a system designed to meet the needs of a large number of men, without any regard for the adjustments required to meet in an equal manner the needs of this small number of women.

BRIGID HAYES
DATELINE: 1980
STRATEGY: WOMEN FOR JUSTICE

In the spring of 1980, a small conference in Ottawa brought together women working in the criminal justice system. They spoke of their conflict as women dealing with a system designed by and for men. Shortly afterwards, some of the participants formed Women for Justice, a lobby group which grew to include women from other fields. After hearing a speech by Inger Hansen, former correctional investigator and then privacy commissioner, we decided to lay a complaint with the Canadian Human Rights Commission. Women for Justice became a political action group.

Our major concerns were conditions at the Prison for Women, the lack of options available to the female offender, and in turn, to any woman who came into conflict with the law. We believed the conditions in the Prison for Women reflected systemic discrimination in a correctional system which designed its activities to meet the needs of men, and considered women as an after-thought. Our complaint to the Commission alleged sexual discrimination on the part of the Correctional Service of Canada in its treatment of women sentenced to penitentiary.

We realized a human rights complaint was of limited value in resolving the issue. While it could force changes in the way female inmates were treated, those changes would only bring female inmates to the same level as male inmates. It would not bring about fundamental change in the treatment of women offenders. However, any change for the better seemed worth the attempt. Naively, we expected a speedy decision on our complaint, and that the process would not take too much time or energy for our small group.

We knew that many of the inmates in P4W had fears about changes that would mean they were transferred to even less adequate provincial prisons, so we informed the inmate committee of our plans, and received support from many of its members. But we made it clear in our complaint that we were filing on behalf of all women—because all of us were intrinsically affected by any discrimination in the treatment of female offenders.

Our complaint consisted of eleven separate charges which we

hoped would force the Commission to examine every aspect of the Correctional Services' policies and programs for women serving federal sentences. Briefly, the charges were:

• lack of education, vocational, social and recreational programs;

• lack of employment and pay opportunities;

• no range of security classification and only one institution for women;

• poor facilities, especially segregation;

• inadequate medical and psychiatric services; and

• the over-representation of male prison administrators and senior managers.

We heard little from the Human Rights Commission in the first few months after laying the complaint but we kept busy analyzing and disseminating information. We alerted women's groups and the media, and the *Globe and Mail* ran a full page spread on our issue.[8]. A vital piece of knowledge had been moved from our private experience into the national headlines.

The investigation lasted seventeen months and revealed a myriad of problems in substantiating the claim, finding a remedy, and achieving our objective. Counting became the name of the game—counting programs, counting institutional options, counting employment opportunities. We recoiled at this process, because none of us believed that the system for male inmates was an ideal to be achieved. The process began to smack of equality meaning sameness, not equal value—in the sense of developing equally useful programs for women in prison which would likely be different from those available to men. We had a strong inclination that women needed innovative programs (such as assertiveness training and overcoming math anxiety), but even before the case was heard, we realized our suggestions of establishing an outside monitoring group, and of hiring people with expertise to develop acceptable remedies, would not be heeded.

Finally the Commission brought down a ruling that upheld all but two of our eleven charges. One was considered outside its jurisdiction (the fact that few senior policy makers within the Correctional System were women), and the complaint that administrators were male was dismissed—although it was noted that the majority of them were men. A decision was made not to order remedies. Instead, the case was sent to conciliation, so that Women for Justice and the Correctional Service (CSC) could negotiate remedial action.

We were jubilant! The *Toronto Star* and the *Globe and Mail* praised the decision on their editorial pages and called for closure of the prison. Even the Solicitor General noted there was some substance in our complaint.

Our enthusiasm waned considerably, however, when we entered into the conciliation process that the Commission had ordered. We had already outlined our own objectives and determined what we would accept as a solution to the complaint. We knew we were looking for major changes in programs and housing facilities for women serving federal sentences.

The CSC conducted interviews with every inmate asking for her needs in education, vocational and counselling programs, but there was little follow-up. A new activities building was opened, but it was under-used. Word processors were brought in, but to teach keyboarding, not programming. And to bring things into line with the men, the women were told to remove personal possessions from the walls.

After ten months, we requested a detailed outline from the CSC of its activities in response to the substantiated cases of discrimination. Almost four months later, we received a two inch sheaf of paper containing a disjointed collection of memos, minutes of meetings, and a job description for an equal opportunity officer.

The worst part of the conciliation process was that we felt the onus for ending the discrimination had been placed on us, not on the guilty party. At the only meeting arranged by the Human Rights Commission with prison officials during the conciliation process, we were asked to propose suitable remedies, which we had carefully broken down into short and long term objectives, benchmarks and proposed methods to achieve them. The CSC's responses were sketchy and non-committal. Ideas were shared, but there was little agreement. We wanted to see long term changes and new tools developed to work with women, while the CSC only seemed interested in cosmetic alterations.

The Human Rights Commission wanted an agreement. It

appeared to be much better able to deal with cases where job reinstatement or monetary compensation were the remedies—the kind of cases that could be monitored relatively easily. Well over three years after we laid our complaint, we were asked to sign a conciliation agreement. We refused. We would and could not agree to cosmetic changes to the treatment of federal female inmates, and we could not continue to be involved in a process which placed the onus for resolution on us, without providing any support.

We asked the Human Rights Commission to re-evaluate its ability to respond to and challenge systemic discrimination. We also suggested that in the future it consider the following: providing complainants with independent expertise; advocating on behalf of the complainant for resolution of the problems once conciliation has been ordered; and requiring the discriminator to propose remedies and provide sufficient information for evaluation.

The chief commissioner responded by saying that while he believed broad sexual reforms may be needed in the Canadian penal system, they cannot "be achieved solely via the conciliation of a complaint of discrimination. Public debate and political lobbying have been the traditional routes used to elicit basic reforms of our institutions."

Conciliation had failed to bring about the settlement of our complaint, and Women for Justice accepted the futility of further attempts. In June of 1984, the chief commissioner closed the case, writing ". . . considering the Correctional Service has, if not fully, at least substantially, addressed the issues, the Commission has decided to consider the complaint partially redressed."[9]

DATELINE: 1986
THE AFTERMATH

We won some important victories. The Human Rights Commission did uphold our charges, and we managed to turn the public's attention to the issue of female offenders. Similar complaints have since been lodged regarding provincial inmates. In Quebec, the provincial human rights commission ordered its staff to investigate the Maison Tanguay prison for women and sought expert advice. And a case is before the courts in 1987 alleging that a sentence to the Prison for Women infringes upon fundamental rights guaranteed by the Charter of Rights.

The Women for Justice complaint may have been the first few rumblings of the mouse that roared. There is no doubt that it has altered the way female inmates are treated more than any other process used before it. Some positive changes have been made at the Prison for Women, and the case is still being used as a rationale for more programming and funds.

For instance, in February, 1984, the Solicitor General announced that the federal government had approved a funding program to stimulate and support the voluntary sector's involvement in expanding and improving services and facilities for women in conflict with the law.[10] His public statements on that occasion marked the first time some of the insights of the female offender program co-ordinators and Women for Justice were integrated into official policy. Providing new services is no longer simply "a nice thing to do if we could," it is the law.

But we cannot claim true victory. The changes at the prison are cosmetic. The issues of distances from home for inmates, security classification and segregation facilities have not been addressed. There have been no fundamental changes in the attitudes of bureaucrats either in the front lines or at headquarters. Feminist approaches have not been accepted into the prison's programs.

Nevertheless, we feel the process we went through was worthwhile. We forced at least minor improvements in the treatment of female offenders, and we forced the CSC to question some of its actions. We also feel at least partly responsible for the development of new government funding programs targetted towards female offenders.

Women for Justice has since gone on to successfully challenge another dimension of discrimination in the justice system against women— the "man in the house rule" in the Ontario Family Benefits Act that said single parents forfeited their rights to benefits if they had live-in companions. In 1986, the Ontario government announced its intent to abolish the "man in the house" provision. The fight against this rule also took many years (about five), but again, the results seemed worth the effort.

Our work has taught us that we cannot expect government officials to find solutions to problems in the system—they lack motivation, tools and interest to do so.[11] In 1982 for example, the commissioner of corrections said:

> In my view, no one has ever been able to identify anything that some of the women [at P4W] are in any way interested in doing. . . I think the final result will still be that there will be a number of women who will not be participating in very much. But when you look back over their life history, there's a limit to what we can do and what can be expected of CSC with regards to this residual group. That's 250 women in all of Canada: now to me that's not a very large number.[12]

This is precisely the kind of attitude Women for Justice wanted to see challenged. Expertise on women's needs is available and must be brought into the prison system. Our experience is that women in prison have a great deal in common with others who are disadvantaged, such as histories of physical and sexual abuse. Such was the finding, for example, of Maude Barlow, a consultant on women's issues, when she conducted a pilot workshop on career readiness and life skills with a small group of inmates at P4W.

> By the time they're in prison, they feel there's nothing out there in the world for them. Their self-esteem is so low that they're not in a position, because of their socialization, to see themselves able or ready to take advantage of the usual type of programs. The same could be said of many men in prison, but women are doubly disadvantaged because they live in a society that discriminates against them. . . .[13]

Barlow is confident these women can be helped to a point where they see some hope. "But it takes years of work and special measures to assist the disadvantaged to take advantage of opportunities once they have been made more equitable."[14]

There are many people in government who think, as we do, that changes are needed, but they cannot make these changes happen until the community clearly indicates its political support. We have come to the conclusion that the only worthwhile changes are those which come from community pressure, and that women have a particularly important role in bringing them about.

The biggest breakthrough we made came from realizing that the women's movement offered valuable models for planning new services, such as peer counselling and assertiveness training, for female offenders. Even more importantly, we realized a feminist approach to working with women in prison was needed to help them break their dependency on men who abused them, and who often led to their imprisonment.

But we have not yet been successful in bringing other women to recognize those in conflict with the law as their sisters, with similar problems and needs that call for solidarity, networking and empowerment. The Toronto Elizabeth Fry Society has a button which reads "Women inside need friends outside." Women prisoners need friends in the feminist community who will advocate on their behalf for better living conditions, and spend time with them so they can see the possibilities for more independent living are real, and not just fantasies lived by other women they have never met.

Women in conflict with the law lose all rights to any power—according to society they have proved they can't handle it and don't deserve it. Incarceration is a totally disempowering experience. And at what price to inmates do we begin to encourage them to start claiming power, in a system that will not allow it? Caseworkers are still somewhat loathe to encourage networking among consumers of criminal justice services, as is the trend among consumers of other services. For women in conflict with the law, networking is not of much value if they are united only in their isolation from other women and from the mainstream of society.

The starting point in improving the situation for women offenders is to think about what occurs, every day, in the courts and the prisons. Who is being dealt assembly line justice? Who is helping the victims to cope with their feelings and questions? Who is going to prison? For what? For how long? How far are they sent away from home? Who is helping their families in the meantime? Are they doing anything to make amends to the victims of their crime? Are they doing anything to take responsibility for themselves and their dependents?

If we can't answer these questions about our own communities, we can't get started on strategies for change. We must all come to understand and accept female offenders as full fledged persons and stop isolating and ignoring them.

NOTES

1 The story of Lorraine Berzins' confrontation with the Correctional Service of Canada is shared by Sheelagh (Dunn) Cooper, and we gratefully acknowledge her contribution to the understanding and analysis of events.

2 The story of Women for Justice was made possible by the determination and courage of its members.

3 The committee was called the National Advisory Committee on the Female Offender (also known as the Clark Committee).

4 *Progress Report on the Federal Female Offender Program*, (Ottawa: Correctional Service of Canada, Ministry of the Solicitor General, 1978).

5 Government of Canada, House of Commons, *Minutes of Proceedings and Evidence of the Standing Committee on Justice and Legal Affairs* (Dec. 6, 1979), pp. 13:9-13:10.

6 A longer analysis of these experiences is found in Lorraine Berzins and Sheelagh (Dunn) Cooper, "The Political Economy of Correctional Planning for Women: The Case of the Bankrupt Bureaucracy," *Canadian Journal of Criminology*, 24 (1982): 399-416.

7 One of the editors of this book, Claudia Currie, faced a similar hostile reaction to a feminist approach to understanding the female offender. In 1986, when she presented findings of a study she had been contracted to carry out on appropriate research methodologies pertaining to women offenders, the research department of the Solicitor General was less than receptive. Much of its criticism was aimed at the "feminist bias" of the contractor. Some members of the department wrote they saw no relevance of feminist theory to understanding the needs of female offenders.

8 The *Globe and Mail*, Toronto, 17 December 1980.

9 Letters to Women for Justice from Gordon Fairweather, 19 March 1984 and 21 June 1984.

10 Speech by Solicitor General Robert Kaplan to the Canadian Association of Elizabeth Fry Societies, Ottawa, 17 February 1984.

11 In 1981, while the Solicitor General was still publicly proclaiming his intention to close P4W, his parliamentary secretary announced that it really may be in the greater interest of the female offenders to improve services at the Prison for Women. Suggestions made by the Canadian Association of Elizabeth Fry Societies to that end, however, were all rejected as "unfeasible, impractical, unnecessary, unrealistic, too costly or unwanted."

12 "Women in Prison: The Human Rights Connection," *Liaison* 8 (1982): 19-21.

13 Ibid., p. 20.

14 Ibid., p. 21.

APPENDIX 1

October 22, 1979

CONFIDENTIAL

Dear Mrs. Berzins:

It is with regret that I must inform you of the termination of your contract with the Correctional Service of Canada, effective two weeks from this date.

The overriding factor that led to this decision is the manner in which you took action to express your views on the whole issue of CSC plans to relocate the offenders at the Prison for Women. I refer to the memo you co-authored with Miss Dunn.

In addition, the incumbent Coordinator of the Female Offender program is mandated to devote full time attention to all matters related to female offenders, so that the development of the IPP process and community resources becomes a major part of her responsibilities.

I wish to assure you that the decision to terminate your contract was arrived at only after thorough assessment and careful consideration of these matters.

Many thanks, Lorraine, for the general services you have rendered and for your specific contribution toward the female offender program. Good luck in the future.

Yours truly,

L.M.W. Pisapio

Media,
Myths and
Masculinization:
Images of Women
in Prison

by KARLENE FAITH*

T his article focusses on the distorted and destructive images of women in prison presented in film and television. The media perpetrate mythical and masculinized images of criminal women. These images are rooted in nineteenth century criminological models and in the tendency of both scholars and media producers to assume female prisoners and prisons are like their male counterparts. As an exploratory discussion, this article considers images of the female offender in the contexts of the media, traditional academic theories and the actual prison environment.

* This article is adapted from a longer unpublished paper by Karlene Faith, ©1987. From 1972-1982 Faith taught and co-ordinated programs for women in prison in California.[2] In 1982 she returned to Canada, her home country, where she has continued to teach and do research in this area. This article draws on her work and research in women's prisons in Canada and the U.S.[3]

MEDIA FABRICATION

Most women who are sent to prison are not "career" criminals; that is, they have not purposefully developed devious skills so as to support themselves through intentionally illegal activity. On the contrary, one can generalize that most women are at first traumatized by the experience of being labeled a criminal. They often hold to conventional stereotypes about "criminal" women and they are discomfited by the stigma associated with this label. Those who enter prison generally come to recognize their commonalities with other prisoners—not only in terms of their present circumstances, but also often in terms of shared background factors (such as poverty, racism, single-parenthood, abusive spouses, alcoholism and so on) which may have contributed to their illegal behaviours.

It is difficult in prison to sustain individuality; as "criminal women" they share an institutional identity yet commonly resist being labeled or categorized. To illustrate this point, the following is an excerpt from my 1972 journal notes, describing an informal conversation that took place in prison among women who were critical of research for which they had been interviewed:

Today a group lingered after class to talk about sex. We didn't actually talk about sex; we talked about people who talk about sex.

It's not that these women aren't interested in sex. They say that they just don't want to be categorized as "butches" and "femmes" by sociologists who write about prison role-playing as an adaptive form of behaviour, and they don't want to be subjects for deprivation theories.

The women were saying that men who have come to the prison to interview them have been obsessed with sex. Bobbie said, "These research guys would bring us in, one at a time, and ask us, 'How do you do it? How often? With how many different women?'". . . and then she added, "Isn't that sick? Isn't that lewd and perverted?"

They were irked by social scientists who objectify them with negative sex-related characterizations, and also by Hollywood images of women in prison which play on these themes. To continue with my journal excerpt:

They protest that their lives are mocked by B-grade movies about women's prisons which feature male-oriented sex-and-violence plots complete with predatory characters who prey on young, innocent types who somehow got to prison by mistake. These movies almost invariably include stock characters: a cold, "masculine" female warden; sadistic lackey guards who stalk vulnerable prisoners; tough-broad convicts who inflict torture on their prison mates; and, goody-goody snitches who get everybody in trouble. The violence in these movies typically connects with sex, and the attackers are portrayed as sleazy and very masculine lesbians. These films give the impression that women's prisons are inhabited by brutal dykes who rape and corrupt the normal criminals; female prisoners are then stereotyped in the public eye on the basis of these fictionalized movie/TV characters.

These women were critical not just of the slander against their identity, but also of the political implications. As one woman put it: "It's this kind of media jive that helps politicians convince voters that more money is needed to build more prisons to protect society from criminal beasts." In a discussion of female imagery in the media, Lisa Steele raises the problem as follows: "For women concerned with the images of women, the question becomes, How do we rescue our images from their virtual control by the mass media?... How can we replace the homogenized stereotypes with our own individual and group portraits?"[4]

As will be discussed in this paper, Hollywood filmmakers have indeed been guilty of generating monstrous images of women in prison, beginning in the 1950s when construction of segregated women's institutions accelerated. One such film that made an impression on me as a teenager was *So Young, So Bad*, (1950) starring Anne Francis as the pretty blonde who didn't deserve to be there (unlike the other grotesque women with whom she was imprisoned) and who was tormented by masculine female guards and convicts. In one particularly memorable scene, the women were knocked to the floor with the force of a powerful water hose, all of them screaming in agony while the sadistic guard watched with glee.

Such films are as insulting to the women who work in prisons as to those who are locked in them. Guards are almost invariably portrayed as the enemy. And whereas many prison guards are indeed contemptuous and cruel toward those over whom they wield physical (and often psychological) control, I have also known and observed many guards who are humane and even respectful toward women in their charge, and prisoners commonly credit caring staff members with providing them with needed encouragement and practical support. Given the institutional context, the punitive function of prisons, and the status differential between prisoners and guards, it is reasonable to assume an adversarial climate of distrust, but it is no more realistic to portray guards as predators than it is to portray prisoners in this light.[5]

THE FILMS

This article focusses on women's prison films as distinct from films based on the lives of notorious individuals who are in big trouble with the law. The latter films tend to glorify or study the character of the anomalous offending woman, who is portrayed in sharp relief against blurred backgrounds. She isn't intended to represent criminal women, only herself. Examples of this genre would include *I Want to Live* (1958), starring Susan Hayward who received an Academy Award for her portrayal of Barbara Graham, who was executed in the California gas chamber. *The Badlands* (1973), with Martin Sheen and Sissy Spacek, was based on the story of Caril Ann Fugate who, at age fourteen, went on a killing spree with Charles Starkweather, her nineteen year old boyfriend. Bonnie Parker and Clyde Barrow, 1930s outlaws, were portrayed in the 1937 *You Only Live Once*, produced by Fritz Lang, with Sylvia Sidney and Henry Fonda; another version of this story was produced in 1967, *Bonnie and Clyde*, with Faye Dunaway and Warren Beatty.

More recently there have been films such as the television docu-drama *The Burning Bed*, starring Farrah Fawcett in the story of a battered woman who kills her husband. Such films are of interest in that they offer vivid indicators of social attitudes toward women who commit crimes of violence, but with rare exception, they individualize these women out of context.

Also very different from the women in prison genre are those films with fictional characters whose crimes are fun and amusing: for example, Jane Fonda's role in *Fun with Dick and Jane*(1977) or Whoopi Goldberg, in *Burglar*(1986). These films, and others of this genre, are refreshing in that they don't denigrate the female protagonist; they do not, however, accurately represent women who come into conflict with the law.

Two recent films do take seriously the conditions of ordinary women's lives: the Dutch film *A Question of Silence*(1983), directed by Marleen Gorris, is a fictionalized story of three unacquainted women who spontaneously murder a store proprietor (male) who caught one of them shoplifting; their crime is not at all realistic, but the background for their action surely is. The film *Working Girls* (1986), produced by Lizzie Borden in New York, is a graphically accurate and even matter-of-fact portrayal of bawdy house prostitution. This is an important film but, again, it steers away from depicting the lives of the vast majority of prostitutes, who work the street.

All of these films offer substantially more texture, dimension and human quality than the typical B-grade movies about women in prison, but they do not (nor are they intended to) convey a realistic understanding of the motivations or social conditions behind conventional female crime.

Following are summaries of two women's prison films, the first of which is a Hollywood classic, titled *Caged*, which was produced in 1950 featuring two respected actors—Eleanor Parker and Agnes Moorehead. This film was a prototype of the genre— it established the stereotypes. The second is *Turning to Stone*, a 1986 television feature movie produced in Canada by John Kastner in a departure from his work as a documentary filmmaker. To my knowledge, this is the only Canadian fictionalized film about women in prison, and it is much more reflective of the U.S. women's prison film genre than it is of the actual experience of women in prison in either Canada or the U.S.

CAGED

The theme of the sympathetic character whose crime is not her fault, which sets her apart from "real" criminal women, perhaps first occurred with the 1945 film *I'll Be Seeing You*, starring Ginger Rogers as a woman doing a prison sentence for killing a man in defence of her honour. The story, however, takes place not in the prison but during a good-behaviour furlough with her relatives. It wasn't until 1950, with the release of *Caged*, that the prototype of the good-girl-unjustly imprisoned was fully developed, as follows:

Marie Allen, age nineteen, was waiting in the car while her young unemployed husband robbed a gas station of $40 to buy food for his pregnant wife. He was killed in the act and Marie was convicted, with no prior record, on an accessory charge. Her father is dead and her poor, sick mother is not in a position to help her.

Marie (played by Eleanor Parker) has terror on her very pretty face as the police van approaches the gothic structure of the institution, with the words PRISON FOR WOMEN carved in granite at the portal. Inside, Marie timidly asks for a comb to straighten her hair before her mug shot is taken. (The viewer is given to understand that she is a very feminine woman who cares about her appearance.)

The warden of the prison (played by Agnes Moorehead) calls Marie into her office to help orient her to the institution. She is like the wardens of most later films in this genre in that she has a "masculine" demeanor. However, she is a kind person—very efficient and reassuring as she tells Marie, "I'd like to be your friend . . . you weren't sent here to be punished; just being here is punishment enough." (This film was produced at the outset of the construction of treatment facilities based on the medical model—in which rehabilitation and not punishment is the purported purpose of the institution.) The corrupt matron (Hope Emerson), whose masculinity is overbearing, attempts to gain Marie's attentions by offering her candy or even drugs: "I like to do a good turn for my girls . . . maybe you got a little habit . . . ? I could get you whatever you needed."

We quickly learn that it is not the good warden but rather the evil matron who is in charge. Having rebuffed her overtures, Marie is assigned to floor duty—that is, she scrubs floors all day over her protestations that the doctor has warned her against strenuous physical exercise. The matron slaps her hard, shoves her to the floor, and she goes to work. Meanwhile we are introduced to the other women, for whom violence is part of the daily routine. A snitch is held by one woman while others beat her up. Not all of the women are violent: some are simply insane. Kitty, an older prisoner who recruits "new fish" for her crime ring, takes a liking to Marie, and instructs her: "You see kid, in this cage you get tough or you get killed."

Marie does have one good friend but one day she discovers this woman dead in her cell by hanging. Soon afterward Marie delivers her premature baby. Since she doesn't have any blood relatives who can take care of it, the baby is taken away by the state and placed for adoption. Marie's innocence begins to erode into cynicism as she suffers this heartbreak. She continues to evade the matron's overtures and the angry matron confronts the warden with the need for greater discipline; she says that in the old days if women didn't behave they were hosed down, their heads were shaven and they were treated like "animals in a cage—like they should be."

At her parole hearing, after one year, Marie pleads with the three men on the panel to release her—assuring them that if they'll let her out she'll get a job. "What could you do?" they ask her. She says, "I could be a salesgirl, or wait tables, or do laundry. . ." but they turn her down because, they say, she's still too young to take care of herself. Her bitterness shows but she continues on bravely, and adopts a contraband kitten. When the evil matron attempts to take it from her she refuses to relinquish it and the other (violent) women assist her by starting a riot. Marie's punishment is that she is taken by the matron into a private room where she is tied up and her head is shaven, her screams stifled with a towel. She is then thrown into dark solitary confinement where, after pleading unsuccessfully with God to release her, she finally becomes hardened like her prison-mates. In a subsequent riot in the feeding unit, a tough older prisoner plunges a fork into the matron's chest while Marie chants "Kill her, kill her. . . ."

When Marie is finally released on parole she is no longer innocent, and she tells the still-kindly warden: "From now on what's in it for me is all that matters." For the $40 her husband attempted to steal, she says, "I got myself an education." As she exits, the warden's assistant inquires, "What shall I do with her file?" "Keep it active," says the warden; "she'll be back."[6]

When this film was produced, not long after the Great Depression in North America, it was not a dishonour to be poor because so many people were, and audiences could identify with the plight faced by Marie and her husband. The primary message, however, with the warden and the matron representing the polar views, is that custody-oriented prisons have exacerbated prisoners' violent and criminal tendencies and have corrupted people who work in them; prisons, instead, should be for the purpose of rehabilitation. In effect, the film advocated the actual trend in the 1950s, when the field of psychology was taking hold, from prisons and penitentiaries to "correctional facilities."

The more insidious message of *Caged* is that most women in prison are hideous, scary or pathetic and decidedly unfeminine. Marie's appeal, as The Innocent, is in her comforting femininity — at a post-war time when women were being strongly encouraged to resume full time domestic-dependency functions. Even though Marie would have to be employed to survive, following her release, she appropriately anticipates a female occupation: "sales girl, wait tables, do laundry.... " She abides by society's gender imperatives in demeanour, appearance, attitudes and values; she's self-effacing, pretty and eager to please — until she is finally hardened by the evil surrounding her.

TURNING TO STONE

In the tradition established by *Caged*, Hollywood continued to produce low-budget pictures which exploited the theme of the innocent central character who is corrupted by the prison and the criminal monsters with whom she is imprisoned.[7] None of these films, however, surpassed the misogynist imagery which is presented in the 1986 drama *Turning to Stone*, produced by John Kastner for Canadian national television (aired on CBC February 25) and written by a (female) playwright who had never been inside a prison.[8]

Allison is a middle-class "girl" in her early twenties who, on return from a holiday, is set up by her boyfriend at the airport; he gives her his drug stash to hold while he gets away and the customs officials arrest her. En route to the prison in the van she is treated kindly by Dunk, a large black woman who is being returned to prison and who, we are given to believe, has ulterior motives in her overtures of friendship.

At first Allison remains hopeful that she will obtain a successful appeal and when her worried father visits (her mother is dead) she reassures him that being in prison is "just like boarding school." He advises her that she should "do your own time," and not get mixed up with the other women. His point is well taken, since the other prisoners soon take every opportunity to slap her around until two of them—Dunk and her rival, Lena—begin to vie for her attentions. Both of them are characterized as masculine lesbians (though Lena is apparently latent); Dunk's prison girl-friend begins casting threatening jealous glances in Allison's direction. Allison, however, is a mature young woman and she spurns offered protections by insisting "I gotta do it my own way."

The woman who occupies the cell next to Allison is also apparently crazy, but more pathetic than frightening. Like Allison, she is a target of hostile, violent energy and in one of the film's turning points, Allison unwittingly colludes with the monsters by distracting the guard while this woman is fiercely beaten up by a mob in a shower stall. Subsequently this same woman violently attacks herself, slashing her arms with a razor blade; the camera zooms in on her bloodied arm dangling through the bars of her cell.

Allison is stalked in a prison tunnel by Dunk, who keeps pornographic pictures of women on her cell walls. Lena, the prison's illicit drug-dealer who is Dunk's rival for Allison's loyalties, threatens Allison with violence if her good but naive father refuses to bring drugs into the prison. During a tense visit with her father, Allison warns him that, if he doesn't cooperate, she will be badly harmed. Despite her pleas, he insists that the authorities wouldn't allow such a thing to happen. (The authorities in this film are simply not present: we never see the warden, and the guards are innocuous and in the background.)

Having been terrorized throughout the film by masculine women who hit her, or threaten her with much worse, Allison's comeuppance finally occurs full force when she is stripped naked and raped, with a (phallic) knife at her throat, by Dunk's vicious, jealous girlfriend at Lena's bidding and with the collusion of Lena's violent gang of lackeys. This scene is horrifying beyond words, graphically depicting the sadistic violation of the only human symbol of innocence in the film. As the film ends, Allison has snitched and is being escorted to solitary confinement, for protection.

The horror of this film was exacerbated by the advance publi-city which suggested that the film would be true to the reality of life at the Prison for Women (P4W), and the exterior shots of the prison erroneously implied that it was filmed within the institution. Having gained the impression prior to viewing the film that it would be an accurate representation, I had encouraged students to watch it. To my chagrin, a number of male students thought it was "really good," "very realistic," or "just what you'd expect." The female students, however, did not find it believable. Women who are locked in the prison were predictably distressed over the hideousness of the drama and concerned that their friends and families across Canada would assume that such terrifying brutality was a normal part of the prison routine.[9]

Unlike the typical Hollywood version of women in prison, the guards and the warden were not implicated in the violence in *Turning to Stone*. Instead, they were portrayed as simply passive and apparently unaware of, or unable to do anything about, the atrocities occurring all around them. The onus here was strictly on the prisoners, characterized as animalistic subhumans in keeping with the Hollywood formula and consistent with nineteenth century criminological mythology. (This film is discussed further in later sections of this article.)

ACADEMIC MYTH-MAKERS

Many of the fictional media stereotypes of female criminals which have been perpetrated by movies and television are reflective of the assumptions of positivist criminologists, beginning with Cesare Lombroso in the nineteenth century. Together with William Ferrero, his son-in-law, he characterized the female offender as follows:

> . . . we may assert that if female born criminals are fewer in number than males, they are often much more ferocious. . . . What is the explanation? We have seen that the normal woman is naturally less sensitive to pain than a man, and compassion is the offspring of sensitiveness. If the one be wanting, so will the other be. . . . women have many traits in common with children; . . . their moral sense is deficient;[10] . . . they are revengeful, jealous, inclined to vengeances of a refined cruelty. . . . when a morbid activity of the physical centres intensifies the bad qualities of women, and induces them to seek relief in evil deeds; when piety and maternal sentiments are wanting, and in their place are strong passions and intensely erotic tendencies, much muscular strength and a superior intelligence for the conception

and execution of evil, it is clear that the innocuous semi-criminal present in the normal woman must be transformed into a born criminal more terrible than any man.

   . . . women are big children; their evil tendencies are more numerous and more varied than men's, but generally remain latent. When they are awakened and excited they produce results proportionately greater. . . . the born female criminal is, so to speak, doubly exceptional, as a woman and as a criminal. . . . As a double exception, the criminal woman is consequently a monster.[11]

Variations on Lombroso's theories are found in the work of most scholars who wrote on the female offender prior to the 1960s, e.g. Freud, Kingsley Davis, the Gluecks, Otto Pollak et al.[12] (For a critique of some of the major theorists, see Gavigan in this volume.) And whereas Lombroso's theme of biological determinism is modified by the sociological orientation of most subsequent scholarship on the female offender, misogynist speculations on women's hidden capacity for evil and cunning prevailed in the literature. Most notably, the 1975 work of Freda Adler[13] was based on her prediction that the women's liberation movement would have the effect of masculinizing female crime. This was a daring theory, contradicting all the evidence and prior speculation. Wolfgang and Ferracutti, for example, had noted in 1967 that the overall homicide rate had declined steadily between the 1920s and the 1960s, during which time the status differential between the sexes had also declined. Observing "an increasing feminization of the culture," they comment: "Instead of females becoming more like males, males have increasingly taken on some of the roles and attributes formerly assigned to females."[14]

From a feminist perspective one would conclude that liberation could not be equated with the imitation of "masculine" crime[15] and that some women engage in crime precisely because they lack the social and private conditions for liberation. Adler, however, argues that the new "liberated" criminal woman (a contradiction in terms) would imitate criminal men and would therefore exhibit the same aggressive and violent behaviours as her male counterpart. Her anti-feminist theory, and the sensationalized headlines it evoked, revived fears that if women were liberated the world would be overrun by Amazon terrorists inflicting violent mayhem on innocent people. The concern that women will become "masculine" has been an argument against the emancipation of women in every historical period, so we should perhaps not be surprised at its reappearance in the 1970s: the perplexity, in this case, is that the prediction is offered by a contemporary "career woman."[16]

One positive result of Adler's work was the challenge it offered to feminist scholars to disprove the basic tenets of her analysis. In the past decade a plethora of books and articles have appeared in the United Kingdom and in North America which bring a feminist analysis to bear on the study of the female offender.[17] As stated by Steffensmeier, ". . . the new female criminal is more a social invention than an empirical reality and . . . the proposed relationship between the women's movement and crime is, indeed, tenuous and even vacuous.'[18] Indeed, since Adler's alarmist predictions, the low rate of violent crime committed by females has remained relatively stable in both Canada and the U.S.[19] Moreover, women who are sent to prison for violent crime include a significant percentage who have killed an abusive spouse as an expression of delayed revenge or self-defence, or as a way to be safe from his violence at any cost.[20] Such women are not generally characterized as violent, and prison authorities have observed them to be among their most cooperative prisoners.[21]

The essential point is that women's prisons differ markedly from men's institutions. The majority of the population does not have a history of inflicting violence and rarely does a woman become violent as a consequence of imprisonment, as will be further discussed. Also, contrary to Adler's predictions, women entering prison seldom bring with them a history of involvement with the women's movement.[22]

THE LESBIAN AS VILLAIN

Reality to the contrary, women's prison movies are blatant imitations of movies about men's prisons, insofar as violence is the pervasive theme. Consistent with this paradigm, the typical rape victim in movies about men's prisons is a young, vulnerable man who has "feminine" qualities, and the rapists are burly, savage brutes.[23] Substitute for these roles the young, pretty, feminine woman and the "masculine" and unattractive butch-lesbian and you have a mirror image of the male prison in which genders are simply switched with a scriptwriter's sleight of hand.

To the uninformed viewer, there is reason to believe that women in prison would be just as terrifying as the men depicted in prison films. From the images presented one could easily draw the following conclusions:

• Criminal women are masculine;

• Criminal women are violent;

• Criminal women are lesbians;

• Lesbians are masculine and violent.

In reality, criminal women represent a full range of conventional female types. Some are extremely "feminine" and delicate, others are strong and athletic. Many of the women are mothers whose worst punishment is the suffering of their children while they are incarcerated. Some women are creative, others seem to lack imagination. Some women are healthy and others are chronically ill. Some exhibit a lively sense of humour, others are depressed, withdrawn or bitter. And so on. Very few call themselves lesbians and those who do are as likely to be nurturing and supportive as any other woman. For the most part, women in prison are an ordinary range of women who have been exceptionally desperate, foolish or unlucky. Their lawbreaking is a futile response to the continuum of private and/or social abuse to which females are commonly subjected.[24]

The misrepresentations that accrue from formula plots based on myths of female masculinization denigrate males as well as females when masculinity is equated with violence and aggression.[25] And whereas it is well-documented that far more men engage in violence than women,[26] many men do not engage in or even value violence. Thus, as a conventional social construct, "masculinity" could more properly refer to strength, capability, self-control and assertiveness, qualities which may also be attributed to women. [27] Gender characteristics and values are culturally-defined and socially variable concepts,[28] and when the media portray women as cliché, dependent "feminine" types, they play into the narrowest kind of sex-role stereotyping. When the media switch those roles, presenting female criminals as parodies of the worst possible stereotyped male criminals, the message is that females are decent only insofar as they are feminine, and a feminine woman, in this view, would not be a criminal any more than she would be a lesbian.

Since there are no physical characteristics by which one can distinguish a lesbian from other women, and since many lesbians are "closeted," there is no fully accurate means of gauging the numbers of lesbians who commit crime or who are incarcerated, and Canadian agencies do not attempt estimates. Officials at the California Institution for Women estimated that nineteen per cent of their prisoners were lesbian, based on self-report and speculation by the intake officer.[29] Of the women in my sample, approximately ten per cent were self-defined as lesbians, which was somewhat closer to the Kinsey estimate for the national female population.[30] Most of the women, approximately eighty per cent, had experienced some consensual physical intimacy with a "best friend" at some time during incarceration, but the majority did not regard themselves as lesbians and expected to return to heterosexual relationships upon release.[31] Conversely, a number of lesbians who participated in the study avoided any physical involvement with other women for the duration of their imprisonment. The penalties for women discovered in a "P.C." (Physical Contact) were stringent, including solitary confinement. Women who entered the prison with an "H on their jacket," identified as homosexual in their prison file, were subject to particular scrutiny in this regard.[32] In any case, there was not a single instance in the prison of a lesbian (or any woman) metamorphosing into the kind of demented, sex-crazed people shown on our movie and television screens.[33]

There is no correlation between lesbianism and violence [34] and lesbians in the California prison felt grossly maligned by any suggestion that they would want to behave that way. The following quotes from incarcerated women make the point:[35]

> *Kathryn*: I'm one of those with an H on my jacket, so I'm really considered a detriment to the prison society, even though I live very quietly in here.... They told me if I was ever caught in my room with a woman I'd go to rack (solitary). It would go with me to the board and hold up my (release). I'm not in here for being a lesbian, but you'd think I was because of the way they carried on about it when I went to the board for my time. They didn't talk to me at all about my crime (fraud). They talked to me about my homosexuality.
> I really don't think they understand about love . . . two people just

loving each other. It has to be something nasty, and it has to be physical. All love isn't physical.

Norma: The institutional policy on homosexuality is "Don't Get Caught." Otherwise you get a write-up and disciplinary action. They can't officially condone it even though it's no longer against the law on the outside.

There's no such thing as rape in here, the way they play it up in books and movies. "Homosexuality in Prison." They make it sound like prison invented it. If a woman cuts her hair, they figure she's turned gay. Sex is always the headliner.

Susan: I never felt threatened by it, nor did anyone ever express to me that they did. There were none of the horror stories you hear of or see in the movies. Stories of being raped, having brooms stuck up them, held down, forced to do it. I never, never saw any intimidation to be involved sexually. I never saw or experienced it ever happening except between two consenting adult women who both wanted to become sexually close with another woman.

. . . Everybody knows what a relationship is, and sex is not the primary part of any relationship, and it isn't in prison either. Sex is a very important part of a relationship—when all the barriers are gone, and you're really exposed to another person. But what is more primary is the friendship, how you share dealing with the world. . . . Women are able to comfort each other emotionally and physically. To hold each other, to touch and be gentle and listen and care. To love each other. In a prison situation—that is a very beautiful thing.

GOOD WOMEN/BAD WOMEN

Females do have an aptitude for violence; we know this. The question is why filmmakers grossly exaggerate the level of violence that women commit and, in the process, reinforce myths of increasing violence by women—women who are categorically portrayed as the antithesis of the feminine woman. Why would filmmakers be so cavalier in bypassing the ordinary prisoner, the woman who is altogether female in her appearance, attitudes and concerns?

The answer, in a word, is profit. Sensationalistic drama is perceived as more interesting and, therefore, more lucrative than ordinary human experience—and stereotypes are more easily sensationalized than ordinary people. But along with the apparent dollar value, the insidious message of the prison-monster films is that women who are segregated from men go completely out of control and start attacking one another.

That sex-role propaganda in movies such as *Turning to Stone* should be delivered so blatantly in the 1980s is reason to believe that the idea of women's liberation is still, perhaps more than ever, seen as a threat to the male-dominant status quo. This is also indicated by the rash of violent pornography that has surfaced since the second-wave of the women's movement.[36] Indeed, *Turning to Stone* could be appropriately termed pornography, in that violent images of women in connection with sexuality and vulnerability are central to the story.[37] The pornographic "eroticization" of violence against women is compounded rather than diminished by the ploy of casting females as both perpetrators and victims. By virtue of their absence, men are shown as bearing no responsibility at all. The film suggests that if there are no men around to do it to them, women will do it to one another.

Turning to Stone is disturbing because, while females do have the capability for violence, the reality is that women are far more often victims. The reasons attributed to women's low violence rates relate to the low rank of females on the power scale, fear of the generally greater physical strength of men, a desire for social approval, and habits from years of strict gender training. In other words, female passivity is learned primarily through socialization, rather than biologically inherited.[38] Women may be idealized as having innate gentleness due to the child-bearing function, but mothers have certainly, in most cultures, felt free to physically punish their children — ostensibly for the children's own good. Women, no less than men, in socially approved circumstances, have justified violence as necessary to achieve some desired end.[39] There is, nevertheless, a close association between maleness and legal or illegal violence. It is generally men who are expected to go to war;[40] it is men who rape.[41] Indeed, in Canada alone, according to frequency calculations by the Canadian Advisory Council on the Status of Women, a woman is forcibly raped (by a man) every seventeen minutes.[42]

Women in most Anglo, western cultures have been expected to suffer from passivity, irrationality, lack of objectivity and heavy emotionalism. In women's prison films, socially acceptable "feminine" tears are replaced with "masculine" expressions of anger and, whereas anger is an appropriate response to an unjust circumstance, the anger expressed by the film characters is unfocussed, displaced or depicted as an obsessive rage. Some of these loathsome and terrifying characters are so extraordinarily aggressive that everyone succumbs to their wishes from sheer fear: their prison-mates serve them as if they were their slaves; their outside connections smuggle drugs to them or assist with other criminal activities; even guards are intimidated into colluding with their schemes. The idea that prison social organization is governed not by the warden and staff but by powerful prisoners is also taken from a media cliché about male prisons. In male prison films these leaders are cool and detached; in women's prison films, on the other hand, the Queen Bee is a seething cauldron of female hysteria, forever on the verge of exploding with a reign of terror.

Although the reality is very different, the duplicity of the media and misogynist scholars has entrenched these stock characterizations of women in prison in the public mind. It is assumed these fearsome fictional women reflect actual criminal women, and it is further assumed that whatever ill treatment they receive in prison is justified and deserved.

One significant contrast between the film *Caged*, which was produced in 1950 and the 1986 film *Turning to Stone* is that sexuality is now a much more explicit theme. Sexuality is depicted in connection with pain, humiliation and power, with rape and the threat of death the ultimate terror. By attributing criminal women with evils more realistically associated with the worst of male behaviours, filmmakers confirm society's satisfied conviction that normal women and criminal women are very different from one another; only very bad, i.e.sexually deviant, women would behave that way. In this view, which is as anti-male as it is misogynist, women in prison are isolated for good reasons, including public safety: good, normal women don't break the law unless they've been duped by some bad man; evil, abnormal women have an insatiable lust for "masculine" violence and sexual aggression.

Popular culture exploits the dichotomous good vs. evil view of the world. To simplify the distinction, the contemporary "good" woman is stereotypically white, well-mannered and middle-class. Bad women, by contrast, are drawn from stereo-types of the poor and minority and other groups which fail to conform to the dominant culture. Certainly there is a correlation in real life between class position and vulnerability to imprison-ment. No such correlation has been determined, however, between law-breaking and class; that is, crime is committed by all classes but it is primarily the working or unemployed poor who are incarcerated. [43]

And just as the criminal justice system and sentencing judge-ments may be biased in favour of the middle-class offender, so do the media reflect that bias in fictional characterizations of offenders. Allison, as the woman who goes to prison by mistake as a consequence of involvement with a criminal man, is perceived as "innocent" because good girls from good middle-class families wouldn't instigate crime. The class bias of filmmakers shows through in such films, projecting assumptions drawn from a middle-class world view and capitalizing on structural class antagonisms.

The good woman in prison, according to the movies, endeav-ours to isolate herself from the other prisoners, with a sense of being very different from them, and much better. Those who offer to "protect" her from others paradoxically contribute to her "difference" by cultivating her dependency on themselves.

It is consistent with the stereotypes in *Turning to Stone* that the most "masculine" characters would offer protection to the most "feminine" character, based on a traditional heterosexual model in which "helpless" women seek out strong men to protect them (from other men). The incongruity of prison movies is that these "men" are not men, but rather masculinated women. And also, just as in real life, there is danger in relying on a protector because protection can be withdrawn or the protector may turn out to be the greatest threat of all. Allison's misfortunes all stemmed from her inability to depend on those upon whom she was nevertheless dependent. Finally her attempt at isolation resulted only in a complete lack of autonomy, the ultimate price one might pay for femininity.

ACTUAL VIOLENCE
IN WOMEN'S PRISONS

A man in prison once said to me that the worst humiliation he suffered through imprisonment was being "treated like a woman," meaning that he was expected to be submissive to any institutional demand. Women in prison, similarly, complain that they are treated "like children," because they are expected to respond with unquestioning obedience to those who have power over them. Predictably, discipline problems in women's prisons are much less serious than those in men's institutions since women's rebellions are rarely as threatening as those of their male counterparts. The frustrations inherent to prison life may be no less serious for female than for male prisoners, but the means of expressing those frustrations are reflective of gender socialization; men are expected to direct rage into physical expressions, and women are expected to either not experience rage at all (it is "natural," after all, for women to passively acquiesce) or to direct their anger toward themselves.

A number of women in prison have remarked to me variations on the statement that "prison is the one place where I don't have to worry about getting raped or beaten up." The atmosphere in women's institutions may be deadly boring and depressing, and institutional violations of what society perceives to be human rights are commonplace,[44] but physical danger is not a common concern among imprisoned women, as scriptwriters would have us believe.

As noted in one study, "Women don't riot; thus media attention is minimal."[45] The authors of another study of the effects of incarceration observe: "Factors such as racial conflict and violence, normative violence, and predatory sexual aggression, typically associated with male institutions . . . are rarely manifested within the female prisoner community."[46] There has not yet been any study focussed on comparative violence levels between male and female institutions, but male prison literature confirms that violence is a significant problem among men whereas the subject doesn't even arise in most women's prison studies.[47] (In this regard, one California female prisoner remarked, "At least in the movies, as compared to academic studies, we seem interesting!") Indeed, the ill effects of programs such as *Turning to Stone* on public perception of women's prisons are exacerbated by the fact that so little authentic attention is given by the media to women's institutions. It would seem that, apart from real or more "interesting" fabricated violence, the media are not interested in prisons at all.

Certainly there are mean-spirited women (and men) whose aggressive attitudes and threatening behaviours are intimidating. When women do commit assault (inside or outside) their victim is most often another woman,[48] although these assaults rarely result in serious injury; conversely, in cases of homicide women's victims are ninety-eight per cent adult male.[49] Most often, however, and consistent with "importation" theories of prison social organization, women in prison do not bring with them a cultural habit of violent behaviour. The absence of routine violence in women's prisons is consistent with the absence of violence between women generally. When violence does occur in women's prisons, there is no evidence that the perpetrators are the same women who have been incarcerated on a violent charge. If this were to be the case, it could be speculated that prison violence among women would occur in Canada more frequently than in the U.S. since a proportionately greater number of (federal) Canadian female prisoners have been convicted of a violent offence; that is, U.S. courts show a significantly greater propensity for incarcerating women for lesser offences. In any case, it is reasonable to assume that women in Canadian and U.S. prisons do not behave differently from one another, regardless of offence distribution patterns.

Focussing on a three year period (1972-1975) for which I kept a journal account of unusual occurrences at the California prison, there were approximately a dozen incidents of prisoner-initiated violence, the most serious of which (resulting in solitary confinement) were as follows:

• A prisoner punched a staff member who refused to mail a letter for her, knocking her to the floor.

• A normally calm woman, who was denied her expected parole, shoved her fist through a window in the administrative building.

• Two women (unsuccessfully) attempted suicide.[50]

Other women complained of pushing and shoving, and women who became "unmanageable" sometimes got involved in physical scuffles with staff en route to the hospital or solitary confinement. These situations were distressing to everyone, prisoners and staff alike, and their infrequent occurrence was in stark contrast to the commonplace violence at the Soledad men's prison where I had worked previously. (On one particularly dramatic occasion at Soledad, an administrator was stabbed to death in his office adjacent to the room where I was teaching.)

The rationale offered to me by both staff and prisoners when I remarked on the relatively small number of violent disturbances at CIW was that those women who had a history of violence upon entering the institution, or those who showed signs of tension which caused others uneasiness,were invariably assigned to a strict medication regime—generally thorazine or one of the other strong tranquillizers. Tranquillizers and sedatives were also dispensed to most women who requested them, including those who had a history of drug abuse, and medication would surely be a factor in the low occurrence of violence.

Women in the much smaller Prison for Women in Kingston also have access to behaviour-modifying drugs, although my impression from conversations with staff and ex-prisoners is that there is less drugging in Canada than in the California institution and that drugs are dispensed upon request with much less frequency. A woman experiencing serious adjustment problems can request a transfer to the treatment centre inside the walls of the Kingston men's penitentiary located a very short distance from P4W, where five beds are reserved for women. It is observed that in some cases, this change of milieu assists in improving a woman's outlook and better enables her to complete her sentence. In selected cases, when a woman experiences certifiable mental health problems, she may be transferred to the mental hospital in St. Thomas, on the recommendation of the psychiatrist for assessment and medication-centred treatment. Other women who show violent tendencies may be placed in administrative segregation, although this cautionary measure is applied as readily to those perceived as a potential target of violence as to those perceived as potential inflicters of violence against others or themselves. The women themselves sometimes request placement in the segregation unit.

In 1977 the Sub-Committee on the Penitentiary System in Canada reported that seventy-five per cent of the crimes of women at P4W did not involve violence, and they comment as follows: "Most of the women are in reality medium or minimum security inmates in that their character and behaviour conform to the criteria set out for these lesser degrees of custody. Certainly a very small number require maximum security custody [but most]. . . do not require equality in punishment because most of them are not true 'crims' who commit offences against others."[51]

A number of women who have served time at provincial jails in Canada have reported to me that there are more "incidents" in these institutions than at the Prison for Women. When asked for an explanation of this variance, it was explained by one woman as follows:

> Rowdies come in for overnights or weekends and they bring all that heavy street energy with them—they yell and carry on. Maybe they don't actually attack anybody but they create an atmosphere. Women who have to put in a lot of time there—like up to two years less a day—or the exchange women—they like to get into a quiet routine. It's the transients who cause these problems.

In a recently published book by a woman serving a life sentence at P4W for murder, the author acknowledges that there are women at the institution who have "bad attitudes." She carefully avoids, however, the common exaggerations about violence. As she describes it:

> Life here is pleasant enough really—for a prison, I mean. Short-termers are usually the ones who get into fights and find themselves locked up in the segregation unit.[52]
>
> There are a few 'toughs' but they generally turn out to be big softies. . . When I first came here I thought, "Oh my God, I'm going to be among murderers!" I suppose I expected to be with huge, butch broads, with scars, tattoos, wicked grins and knives in their jeans. Television fosters such misconceptions!. . . The media has misrepresented us so much that even outside professionals have misconceptions about us [but] very few..are actually violent [and the] warden will tell you that the lifers are the most agreeable, stable and well-behaved group in the prison.[53]

Other women who have served time at P4W[54] believe that there is more minor violence at the institution than is ever reported and that it is the "young broads," as one woman put it, who try to push other people around. There are rumours of women getting punched and both staff and ex-prisoners report that occasionally there is an attempted stabbing of one woman by another, purportedly with cutlery stolen from the cafeteria. None of those reporting such incidents to me has been witness to one but that such incidents do occur to some extent I have no reason to doubt. It seems, however, that violence of this kind is neither common nor random nor even remotely of the serious consequence portrayed in the film *Turning to Stone*. The most compelling basis for my belief that the rumours of physical violence are exaggerated is that none of the prisoners or ex-prisoners with whom I have spoken on this subject had ever experienced themselves as being in danger of physical harm by any other prisoner.

A P4W administrator reports, in an informal conversation, that there are few actual assaults but that in 1986-87, over a period of a year and a half, there was one knifing attack (which did not result in serious injury) and there was one serious incident in which a prisoner scalded another with boiling water. There have also been minor physical altercations, not involving weapons, over various personal disputes between two women. He cautioned against being non-specific in talking about violence, and stressed that verbal coercion, abuse or intimidation is inflicted by some women against others as a form of "psychological violence."[55]

According to staff, prisoners and outside observers alike, the most serious form of violence at P4W is self-mutilation, specifically "slashing" of the skin with any available sharp object. (This behaviour also occurs in male institutions.)[56] The incidents of slashing are apparently frequent but a member of the health services staff observed that it is the same few women who do this to themselves on a repeated basis. This same staff member explained that after repeated slashings, the nerves are so badly damaged that subsequent pain is minimal, although considerable blood may flow and the woman is usually sent to hospital. And although self-mutilation would be appropriately diagnosed as masochism, one woman said she slashed herself often because she preferred being in hospital to being in prison. Certainly this behaviour is empowering in the negative sense that it allows the perpetrator to "own" her own body. Also, whether or not it is her intent, it causes other people to pay more attention to her. What is sometimes perceived as simple desire for attention, however, must be indicative of some deep torment. In the most dramatic instance of which I'm aware, a Native woman slashed her breast upon receiving the news that her infant child, in outside care, had died. According to the staff, in this instance the woman was not seeking attention but rather honouring a tribal custom for the expression of grief.

There is, finally, no basis for believing that the violence that does occur in P4W is of the kind depicted by John Kastner in *Turning to Stone*. No one is raped by predators or stalked by gangs of vicious madwomen. There is no social or even structural latitude within the institution for the kind of sickening attacks that Kastner portrayed so graphically, as if they were real. He claimed in the screen credits that the story was "fiction based on fact" but to the prisoners he was representing, it was a betrayal of their actual experience. By capitalizing on the hostile, media-mythologized themes of good vs. evil, masculine vs. feminine and low-class vs. middle-class, all embraced by violent fantasy, he obscures and distorts the very real problems endured by women in prison as well as those guarding over them.

No one enjoys any genuine autonomy or choice while in prison, and by and large women acquiesce to this reality simply because they want to get out. Some women protest or appeal through proper channels when there are grievances, but most go according to schedule to their jobs, school, the cafeteria, the pill line, the recreation room—and within these parameters attempt to neither cause nor get involved with any kind of trouble. Together they're stranded in a time-warped tension between loss of personal freedom and the necessity to act out daily institutional require-ments. Alone they're locked in their cells several times a day to be counted, and there they watch TV (if their families are able to provide them with a set), read, write letters, worry about their kids, listen to music on the radio and, when the day is done and the lights are out, toss and turn and sometimes cry. Just like a woman.

THE GOOD NEWS:
FILM AS TRUTH-SAYING

In general, in the past decade, North American movies and television have introduced more honest and positive images of women in both traditional and contemporary roles—due in part to some excellent female writers and directors. It is now possible to turn on the television set and find female characters with whom women in the audience can realistically identify, and this is most obviously true of documentaries. In Canada three films on women in prison have been produced in the 1980s, two of which have been shown on national TV.

The first of these, titled *P4W*, was produced by Holly Dale and Janis Cole in 1981. The film focusses on a number of individual women serving time in Kingston, each of whom has a remarkable story to tell. Indeed, if the film has a weakness it is that the prisoners to whom the audience is introduced are so exceptional; it features, for example, the woman who was the first Canadian to receive a twenty-five year sentence without possibility of parole even though she did not have a hand in the shoot-out in which she was implicated. The film also features a woman who in her life had killed not just one abusive husband, but two of them, and a young woman who speaks poignantly of why she slashes herself. For comic relief there is the woman for whom all the world is a stage, and who channels her energy into hilarious entertainments for her prison-mates. Another talented prisoner entertains the viewer with bizarre stories from her "kinky" life on the street; she also dances in the prison corridor and performs music she's written while in prison. All together these women convey a sense of the rich variety of personality that converges in a prison, and because most of them are so likeable and attractive they certainly dispense with stereotypes. An added value of *P4W* is the footage of the physical structure— full shots of the ranges and the interminable hallways and the suffocating sense of concrete containment in this archaic fortress, even if their cells do look like dorm rooms.

In my view, the most realistic film produced on incarcerated women to date (and, therefore, the film with the least commercial appeal) is *C'est pas parce que c'est un chateau qu'on est des princesses"(Castle/No Princess)*, directed by Lise Bonenfant and Louise Giguere at Maison Gomin in Quebec in 1986 and produced and distributed by Video Femmes. Like *P4W*, this film focusses on interviews with women locked up, but these women and their crimes are altogether conventional and the problems they describe are problems with which most working-class and poor women could identify. They present an altogether realistic account of a prison experience—the intense boredom, lethargy and frustration, the arbitrariness of rule enforcements, the paucity of resources, the loneliness and the value of having close friends upon whom to depend for comfort and companionship.

The third documentary which depicts Canadian women in prison with accuracy as well as sensitivity was produced, ironically, by John Kastner. This was the third film of his prison documentary trilogy, the first of which was *The Parole Dance*, an uncanny bird's eye view of the problems of men seeking to gain and sustain parole status; the second, *The Lifer and the Lady*, followed life events of a male prisoner whose girlfriend waited patiently for his release and unsuccessfully attempted to help him adjust to life on the outside after many years in lock-up.

The third of the series, *Prison Mother, Prison Daughter*, (aired on CBC Jan. 11, 1987) focusses on two women at P4W. Darlene Baldwin is a very pretty, blonde twenty-four year old middle-class woman convicted of drug-smuggling; her parents are horrified by what they perceive to be the injustices and double-binds of the system, and they expend great time and devotion to ultimately obtaining her early release. Kastner claims to have based Allison, the character in *Turning to Stone*, on Darlene.[57] However, there is nothing in *Prison Mother, Prison Daughter* to suggest that Darlene was ever subjected to harassment by other women, much less the horrific tortures inflicted on the fictional character for which she was the alleged model. As a young, sheltered middle-class person she may well have entered the prison with naive fear and trepidation but, if so, it appears in the film as if she overcame it.

The second woman featured in this film by Kastner is Marilyn St. Pierre, who epitomizes the social victim whose self-destructive choices—with men, booze, dishonesty and petty crime—lock her into a system from which she can't escape and to which she ultimately loses the one person in the world for whom she experiences unconditional love, her infant son. Her story is a heartbreaker, and so are the social realities from which her tragedy is constructed. In this film Kastner surely succeeds in telling it like it is, which may or may not be enough to redeem him for the travesty of *Turning to Stone*. Throughout the segments with St. Pierre in various settings, the viewer hears the off-camera voice of Kastner as he talks with her about each new difficult development in her unsuccessful attempt to reclaim her life. It is fair to note that his presence in St. Pierre's story reveals a compassionate human being who has clearly gained the trust of his subject.

CONCLUSIONS

Film is a powerful medium with significant potential for educating the public about the social causes and consequences of imprisonment and about the women whose lives are directly affected by this anachronistic response to crime.[58] Conversely, the stigma which women carry with them from the time of their first arrest is grossly exacerbated by fictionalized film images of criminal women which defy all reasonable understanding of women's lives. Films which exploit negative female stereotypes based on class, race and/or lesbianism, and which presume with Lombroso that "the criminal woman is a monster," only serve to confirm in the public view the idea that prisons are an essential institution for separating the bad people from the good. Moreover, when women are erroneously portrayed as having a great attraction for evil as expressed through violent behaviour, all women in effect are misrepresented and the gap between knowledge and ignorance is widened.

Women's liberation depends not at all on women learning to be "more terrible than any man," as Lombroso put it. Rather, women's liberation depends on the balancing of all social relations through the elimination of arbitrary gender imperatives, class and racial hierarchies and categories of subordination. In such an ideal world, women would no longer serve as fodder for filmmakers' frightening fantasies.

NOTES

1 My appreciation to the following: Della McCreary and Barbara Kuhne of Press Gang Publishers, Shelley Gavigan, who suggested the title, Starla Anderson and Penny Goldsmith. I also wish to thank the many imprisoned women who have facilitated my understanding and a number of prison staff and administrators, including George Caron, Warden of P4W.

2 Having previously worked with male prisoners (see K. Faith (ed.), *Soledad Prison: University of the Poor* (Palo Alto, CA: Science & Behavior Books, 1975)), my work with women in prison began in 1972. At this time I was teaching courses on women and criminal justice at the University of California at Santa Cruz and also teaching women's studies courses in the state prison, the California Institution for Women (CIW). During the subsequent decade, I co-ordinated a university-credit program at CIW and cultural events at other women's prisons, helped organize statewide support systems for women on parole, and produced video and radio programs for public education on women in prison. I also did research, including questionnaire surveys of the general prison population and life history interviews with one hundred women. While conducting this research, I lived at the prison for most of four months as a participant-observer. The gathered material is being developed in manuscripts-in-progress: "Curtain Over the Bars," "13 Women: Parables from Prison," and "Prisoners in the Classroom."

3 There are important similarities between Canadian and American women in conflict with the law and the criminal justice apparatus that governs them. The only significant disparity is in the numbers. The state of California and Canada as a nation have almost the same total populations (approximately twenty-five million) and the female crime patterns are parallel. [See Johnson in this volume, and for comparative data, A. Hatch and K. Faith, "The Female Offender in Canada," paper presented at the Annual General Meeting of the American Society of Criminology, San Diego, CA, November 13-17, 1985.] However, at any given time, over 6,000 women are incarcerated in California state and federal prisons and in local jails, while in Canada the total number of women in federal and provincial institutions is generally less than 1,000. In both Canada and the U.S., at least half of all female prisoners are mothers of dependent children. [MacLeod estimates that during 1983-84, ". . . the mothers of at least 5,400 children were admitted to a (Canadian) correctional facility. . ." (L. MacLeod, *Sentenced to Separation: An Exploration of the Needs and Problems of Mothers Who Are Offenders and Their Children* (Ottawa: Ministry of the Solicitor General of Canada, Research Division No. 1986-25, 1986), p. 12.) Baunach indicates that in the U.S., a range from 56 to 68 per cent of incarcerated women have dependent children (P. Baunach, *Mothers in Prison* (New Brunswick, NJ: Transaction, Inc., 1985), p. 11, n. 1.)] In both contexts,

racial minorities are severely over represented in prison: black women, who constitute ten per cent of the California female population, represent over forty per cent of the female prisoners; Native women constitute just 2.5 per cent of the total female population in Canada, but, depending on the province and the institution, Native women comprise between thirteen and one hundred per cent of female admissions to prison. [Estimate obtained from California Dept. of Corrections for 1982. Re: Native women in Canada, see C. LaPrairie, "Selected Criminal Justice and Socio-Demographic Data on Native Women," *Canadian Journal of Criminology/Revue Canadienne de Criminologie* 26 (April/Avril 1984): 162-163.]

4 L. Steele, "A Capital Idea: Gendering in the Mass Media," in *Women Against Censorship*, ed. V. Burstyn (Vancouver and Toronto: Douglas & McIntyre, 1985), p. 74.

5 This is not to deny that historically women in prison have been the victims of considerable violence committed by guards and authorities as institutional punishment. There is also abundant evidence of the "widespread rape of imprisoned women" historically, by male guards as well as male inmates in mixed institutions. (J. Klaits, *Servants of Satan: The Age of the Witch Hunts* (Bloomington: Indiana University Press, 1985), p. 149.) See also N. Rafter,*Partial Justice: Women in State Prisons, 1800-1935* (Boston: Northeastern University Press, 1985), pp. 8, 20, 57, 73, 80, 97 and E. Freedman, *Their Sisters' Keepers: Women's Prison Reform in America, 1830-1930* (Ann Arbor: The University of Michigan Press, 1981), pp. 15, 60, 99. One of the most frequently articulated reasons for nineteenth century reformers of women's prisons advocating separate institutions for females was to save them from sexual exploitation. (Freedman, op. cit., this note, pp. 40-45.) Whereas anecdotal hearsay suggests that male sexual abuse of female prisoners still occurs as isolated incidents (see, for example, the story of Joan Little in J. Reston, *The Innocence of Joan Little: A Southern Mystery* (New York: Bantam Books, 1977)), it can no longer be perceived as commonplace. The preponderance of female guards in female institutions is one factor in this regard.

6 The fictionalized setting for *Caged* was modelled on the actual state prison for women in California, then located in Tehachapi. In 1952 the prison was destroyed in an earthquake.The present California Institution for Women was constructed at Frontera.

7 Examples include *Girls in Prison* (1956), in which the good chaplain takes the pretty young protagonist under his protective wing and *Reform School Girl* (1957), in which the hero, a kindly male teacher, feels he can justify his futile efforts in the prison classroom "if I can just save this one girl." The genre was dormant during the 1960s, but was revived in the 1970s with strong messages against "women's lib." The most graphic representation of this message was *Jackson County Jail* (1977) starring Yvette Mimieux as a liberated woman who is wrongly jailed, and then violently raped by the deputy sheriff whom she kills in self-defence.

Also released in 1977 was *Chain Gang Women*, an exceptionally misogynous film fraught with sex and violence. Tipping the scales for sheer pornographic content is the 1983 film *Chained Heat*, starring Linda Blair, in which women are raped and beaten, cut with hooks (in the neck) and razor blades and inflicted with a whole potpourri of atrocities, mayhem and death.

8 In an article in *TV Guide* ("The dangerous world of women behind bars," 22 February 1986, pp. 20-23) Kastner is attributed with a remarkable statement: "We have a playwright (Judith Thompson) who's never been to prison writing dialogue that, in some cases, is more poetic than what real inmates would say. There are things that are a little more dramatic in the way the characters speak, but not in what they'd do, because what they'd do is actually *worse* than what's in the script." (emphasis in original) Presumably Kastner supplied the violent imagery on which Thompson based her script.

9 This impression was gained through personal conversation with a P4W authority following the airing of the program, and through conversation with women subsequently released from P4W.

10 The theme of moral deficiency in the female has been perpetrated by contemporary scholars, including Lawrence Kohlberg, whose theories were effectively challenged by his student Carol Gilligan in her landmark study *In a Different Voice* (Cambridge, Mass: Harvard University Press, 1982).

11 C. Lombroso and W. Ferrero, *The Female Offender* (New York: Appleton and Company, 1899), pp. 150-152.

12 S. Freud, *New Introductory Lectures on Psychoanalysis*, trans. and ed. J. Strachey (New York: W.W. Norton & Company Inc., 1965); S. Glueck and E. Glueck, *Five Hundred Delinquent Women* (New York: Alfred A. Knopf, 1934); O. Pollak, *The Criminality of Women* (Philadelphia: University of Pennsylvania Press, 1950); K. Davis, "The Sociology of Prostitution," *American Sociological Review* II (1937): 744-755.

13 F. Adler, *Sisters in Crime: The Rise of the New Female Criminal* (New York: McGraw-Hill, 1975).

14 M. Wolfgang and F. Ferracutti, *The Subculture of Violence: Towards an Integrated Theory in Criminology* (London: Tavistock Publications, 1967), p. 259.

15 "Masculine" crime refers to offences such as burglary, robbery and auto theft. Prostitution, shoplifting and infanticide are the only crimes which are perceived as "feminine." However, prostitution involves the participation of a man and, although shoplifting comprises a significant share of the offences for which females are indicted, more males than females engage in this activity. See D. Steffensmeier, "Crime and the Contemporary Woman: An Analysis of Changing Levels of Female

Property Crimes, 1960-1975," in *Women and Crime in America*, ed. L. Bowker (New York: Macmillan, 1981), pp. 39-59 and Hatch and Faith, op. cit., note 3.

16 An example of how Adler's theory entered the realm of conventional wisdom came to me during a 1986 radio talk show in which I was responding to listeners' questions and comments about women in prison. One apparently middle-aged woman called to say that "women's lib" was the problem and that women in prison "should have had more spankings" when they were children. She went on to say that "If these kinds of women can't behave themselves, we should just hang them."

17 See, for example, C. Smart, *Women, Crime and Criminology: A Feminist Critique* (Boston: Routledge & Kegan Paul Ltd., 1976); S. Norland and N. Shover, "Gender Roles and Female Criminality: Some Critical Comments," *Criminology* 15 (1977): 87-104; F. Cullen, K. Golden and J. Cullen, "Sex and Delinquency: A Partial Test of the Masculinity Hypothesis," *Criminology* 17 (1979): 301-310; P. Giordano and S. Cernkovich, "On Complicating the Relationship Between Liberation and Delinquency," *Social Problems* 26 (1979): 467-481; Steffensmeier, op. cit., note 15; E. Miller, "International Trends in the Study of Female Criminality: An Essay Review," *Contemporary Crises* 7 (1983): 59-70; S. Box and C. Hale, "Liberation and Female Criminality in England and Wales Revisited," *British Journal of Criminology* 22 (1983): 35-49; N. Wolfe, F. Cullen and J. Cullen, "Describing the Female Offender: A Note on the Demographics of Arrests," *Journal of Criminal Justice* 12 (1984): 483-492; J. Messerschmidt, *Capitalism, Patriarchy and Crime: Toward a Socialist Feminist Criminology* (Totowa, New Jersey: Rowan & Littlefield, 1986).

18 Steffensmeier, op. cit., note 15, p. 54.

19 See Johnson, this volume and Hatch and Faith, op. cit., note 3.

20 See A. Browne and R. Flewelling, "Women as Victims or Perpetrators of Homicide," paper presented at the Annual General Meeting of the American Society of Criminology, Atlanta, GA, October 29-November 1, 1986 and A. Browne, *When Battered Women Kill* (New York: The Free Press, 1987). From my own research in 1972, sixteen women of six hundred in the California Institution for Women were imprisoned for first-degree murder; half of these women had killed a violent spouse after years of being battered.

21 Comments to this effect have been offered to me in conversations with staff at four institutions: California Institution for Women; Pleasanton Correctional Facility (federal prison, California); Purdy Treatment Center for Women (Washington state) and Prison for Women in Kingston, Ontario.

22 In my work as an organizer of prisoner support groups (1972-1982), volunteers frequently expressed disappointment that the women they

met within the institutions were so traditional in their outlook and values. However, contacts between feminists and women inside often resulted in some attitude change. The most striking example of this, in my experience, came through teaching women's studies in the prison in the early 1970s. The textbooks for the course included the early anthology of feminist writing by Robin Morgan, *Sisterhood is Powerful: An Anthology of Writings From the Women's Liberation Movement* (New York: Vintage Books, 1970). This was their favourite book and the fifty women taking the course would carry it around the prison "campus" with them; the book evoked curiosity among the other women and eventually we brought in a new supply to respond to the demand.

This was an anomalous situation. More commonly, women in prison randomly express the view that feminism is a movement for middle-class women who want to compete with men for straight jobs. This opinion was expressed strongly by a discussion group at the Washington state prison (October 1984); they were disgruntled because feminist volunteers who had come to the prison to help establish support services had gone away without following up on their promises because, as one woman put it, "they were too busy with their careers."

23 For a succinct and eloquent analysis of how the rule of force is manifest in male institutions, see J. Lowman, "Images of Discipline in Prison," in *The Social Dimensions of Law*, ed. N. Boyd (Scarborough, Ontario: Prentice-Hall Canada Inc., 1986), pp. 237-259. For a discussion of masculine dominance and feminine submission as a component of heterosexual eroticism, see E. Morgan, "The Eroticization of Male Dominance/Female Submission," *Papers in Women's Studies*, Vol. 11, No. 1 (Ann Arbor: The University of Michigan, Women's Studies Program, September, 1975), pp. 112-145.

24 Analysis of female victimization proliferated during the 1970s (and to the present). Notable examples which helped chart the course for subsequent work would include: P. Chesler, *Women and Madness* (New York: Avon Books, 1972); S. Brownmiller, *Against Our Will: Men, Women and Rape* (New York: Simon and Schuster, 1975); D. Russell, *The Politics of Rape* (New York: Stein & Day, 1975); D. Martin, *Battered Wives* (San Francisco: Glide Publications, 1976); R. Dobash and R. Dobash, "Wives: The 'Appropriate' Victims of Marital Violence," *Victimology: An International Journal* 2 (1977): 426-442; S. Griffin, "Rape: The All-American Crime," in *Feminism and Philosophy*, eds. M. Vetterling-Braggin, F. Elliston and J. English (Totowa, New Jersey: Littlefield, Adams & Co., 1977), pp. 313-332; L. Clark and D. Lewis, *Rape: The Price of Coercive Sexuality* (Toronto: The Women's Press, 1977); E. Pizzey, *Scream Quietly or the Neighbors Will Hear* (England: Ridley Enslow, 1977); K. Barry, *Female Sexual Slavery* (New York: Avon Books, 1979); and C. MacKinnon, *Sexual Harassment of Working Women* (New Haven and London: Yale University Press, 1979). Also see L. Clark, "Boys Will Be Boys: Beyond the Badgley Report, A Critical Review," in *Regulating Sex: An Anthology of Commentaries on the*

Findings and Recommendations of the Badgley and Fraser Reports, eds. J. Lowman, M. Jackson, T. Palys and S. Gavigan (Burnaby, B.C.: School of Criminology, Simon Fraser University, 1986, pp. 93-106 and N. Davis and K. Faith, "Women and the State: Changing Models of Social Control," in *Transcarceration and the Modern State of Penalty*, eds. J. Lowman, R. Menzies and T. Palys, (Aldershot, England: Gower Publishers, 1987). Staff in female custodial institutions and social workers frequently speculate that girls and women in conflict with the law have a high rate of prior victimization and sexual abuse, including incest. For a review of studies concerned with this issue, see M. Chesney-Lind, "Girls' Crime and Woman's Place: Toward a Feminist Model of Female Delinquency," (University of Hawaii: Youth Development and Research Center, Report No. 334, May 1987).

25 For a criminological perspective on "masculinity" and violence as a product of culture, rather than as a behaviour determined by biological sex, see, for example, Wolfgang and Ferracutti, op. cit., note 14, pp. 147-163; 305-308.

26 S. Steinmetz, "The Battered Husband Syndrome," *Victimology* 2 (1977/78): 499-509 and M. Straus, R. Gelles and S. Steinmetz, *Behind Closed Doors* (Garden City, New York: Anchor Books, 1980) provoked controversy with the thesis that in spousal assault, women are the most frequent attackers, even though they generally lack the physical capacity to cause serious harm. For a discussion of this controversy, and a review of the literature, see M. Schwartz, "Gender and Injury in Spousal Assault," *Sociological Focus* 20, (January 1987): 61-75.

27 See *The Bem Sex Role Inventory* in S. Bem, "The Measurement of Psychological Androgyny," *Journal of Consulting and Clinical Psychology*, 1974.

28 D. Russell hypothesizes that male violence against women can be construed as over-conformity to the gender-constructed male sex role by men who feel inadequate in their masculinity (Russell, op. cit., note 24, p. 260). Also, see S. Hills, "Rape and the Masculine Mystique," in *Gender Roles: Doing What Comes Naturally?*, eds. E. Salamon and B. Robinson (Toronto: Methuen Publications (Carswell Company, Ltd.), 1987), pp. 296-307. Additional work on the causes and processes of gender construction includes: R. Stoller, *Sex and Gender: On the Development of Masculinity and Femininity* (London: Hogarth, 1968); J. Money and A. Erhardt, *Man and Woman, Boy and Girl* (Baltimore, Maryland: John Hopkins University Press, 1972); J. Money and P. Tucker, *Sexual Signatures: On Being a Man or a Woman* (Boston: Little, Brown and Company, 1975); E. Morgan, op. cit., note 23; M. Teitelbaum, *Sex Differences: Social and Biological Perspectives* (Garden City: Doubleday, 1976); N. Henley, *Body Politics: Power, Sex and Nonverbal Communication* (Englewood Cliffs: Prentice-Hall, 1977); J. Laws and P. Schwartz, *Sexual Scripts: The Social Construction of Female Sexuality* (Hinsdale, Illinois: The Dryden Press, 1977); C. Smart and B.

Smart, *Women, Sexuality and Social Control* (London: Routledge & Kegan Paul Ltd., 1978) and R. Bleier, *Science and Gender: A Critique of Biology and Its Theories on Women* (New York: Pergamon Press, Inc., 1984). Salamon and Robinson argue that the interminable (and ideologically loaded) debate between biological and socialization explanations for gender behaviour is ultimately a false issue and that ". . . one must consider both influences to understand the development of gender identity and gender behaviour" (op. cit., this note, p. 8). In an analysis of feminist politics, I. Young, "Humanism, Gynocentrism and Feminist Politics," *Women's Studies International Forum* 8 (1985): 173-183, cites Gilligan (op. cit., note 10), N. Chodorow, *The Reproduction of Mothering* (Berkeley, California: University of California Press, 1978) and S. Griffin, *Women and Nature: The Roaring Inside Her* (New York: Harper and Row, 1978) as examples of feminist theorists who stress the positive moral valuation of feminine gender socialization, in contradistinction to the equation of femininity with victimization and inferiority, a model for which de Beauvoir's pioneering work, *The Second Sex* (New York: Vintage Books, 1952) may be seen as a prototype.

29 The intake officer told me that estimates are based on a woman's appearance, whether or not she shows a "normal interest in the opposite sex," and reports of involvement with another woman during a prior incarceration.

30 In 1953, at a time when lesbianism was virtually a hidden reality, the Kinsey report shocked many people with the revelation that twenty-eight per cent of their sample had experienced a "homosexual response" with another woman and that thirteen per cent had been actively involved. (A. Kinsey, W. Pomeroy, C. Martin and P. Gebhard, *Sexual Behavior in the Human Female* (Philadelphia: W.B. Saunders Company, 1953), pp. 474-475.) *The Hite Report: A Nationwide Study of Female Sexuality* (New York: Dell Publishing Co. Inc., 1976), pp. 389-418, indicates eight per cent as active lesbians, and an additional nine per cent who had sexual experience with both men and women. Kinsey et al, Hite and Masters and Johnson (*Human Sexual Inadequacy* (Boston: Little, Brown and Co., 1970)) all indicate that sexuality is a continuum of response and that the world cannot be clearly divided into homosexual or heterosexual populations.

31 Two studies conducted in the 1960s, D. Ward and G. Kassebaum, *Women's Prison: Sex and Social Structure* (Chicago: Aldine Publishing Company, 1965) and R. Giallombardo, *Society of Women: A Study of a Women's Prison* (New York: John Wiley & Sons, Inc., 1966) agree that "homosexuality" in women's prisons is based not on sexuality per se, but rather on the need for affectional relationships.

32 The attitudes of authorities toward "homosexuality" varied according to professional specialization; accordingly, the medical staff regarded it as a disease (which could be cured), the chaplain considered it a sin (which could be forgiven through repentance), and the counsellors

viewed it as a deviance (from which one could be rehabilitated). The overriding priority, within the context of the custody-oriented institution, was to curtail the incidence through control and surveillance. Self-identified lesbians reported feeling persecuted in this regard but they did not suffer the indignities experienced by lesbians who are processed by the mental health system. For a remarkable account of the phenomenon, see P. Blackbridge and S. Gilhooly, *Still Sane* (Vancouver: Press Gang Publishers, 1985).

33 F. Pearce, "How to be Immoral and Ill, Pathetic and Dangerous, All at the Same Time: Mass Media and the Homosexual," in *The Manufacture of News: Social Problems, Deviance and the Mass Media*, eds. S. Cohen and J. Young (London: Constable and Company, Ltd., 1973), pp. 284-301, analyzes the impact of the media on public attitudes concerning (male) homosexuality, noting that the characterization of homosexuals as dangerous deviants who threaten the moral order provides a rationale for the persecution of homosexuals and, in that process, supports a limited view of sexuality in which heterosexuality is perceived as the only "normal" or "natural" sexual expression.

34 Indeed, lesbians and gay men are remarkably "normal," despite social, political and family pressures and hostilities. A. Barfield, "Biological Influences on Sex Differences in Behavior," in *Sex Differences: Social and Biological Perspectives*, ed. M. Teitelbaum (Garden City, New York: Anchor Books, 1976), pp. 62-121, reports on research indicating that "Almost all homosexuals have normal chromosomal constitutions...[and] There is also no known correlation between homosexuality and adult levels of sex hormones." (pp. 94-95).

E. Genders and E. Player, "Women's Imprisonment: The Effects of Youth Custody," *British Journal of Criminology* 26 (October 1986): 357-371, in their study of a youth institution in Britain, state: "Lesbian relationships, as with other forms of friendship in prison, tended to occur between consenting partners of a similar age." (p. 363). The consensual element of intimate relationships within women's prisons is also emphasized by Ward and Kassebaum (op. cit., note 31), R. Giallombardo, (op. cit., note 31) and A. Propper, *Prison Homosexuality: Myth and Reality* (Lexington, Mass: D.C. Heath and Company (Lexington Books), 1981). Propper cites isolated self-reported incidents in youth facilities in which physical aggressions had sexual implications and she also reports on hearsay evidence that women in adult institutions in New York and California expressed fears of "lesbian" attacks (pp. 182-183). There is no indication that these alleged incidents/perceived threats were attributable to lesbian inmates.

For a thorough review of the literature concerning lesbianism, see V. Brooks, *Minority Stress and Lesbian Women* (Toronto: D.C. Heath and Company, 1981). She emphasizes the fallacies of the stereotypes of lesbians as "masculine," effectively refutes the standard mythologies regarding lesbian behaviour, and cites evidence that in general lesbians have greater self-esteem and educational/occupational achievement. See also A. Bell, M. Weinberg and S. Hammersmith, *Sexual Preference: Its Development in Men and Women* (Bloomington: Indiana University Press, 1981). For biographies and first-person accounts, see for example, B. Grier and C. Reid, *Lesbian Lives: Biographies of Women from the Ladder* (Oakland, CA: Diana Press, 1976) and R. Curb and N. Manahan, *Lesbian Nuns: Breaking Silence* (New York: Warner Books, Inc., 1985). For accounts of lesbians in academia, see M. Cruikshank, *Lesbian Studies: Present and Future* (Old Westbury, New York: The Feminist Press, 1982).

35 K. Faith, "Love Between Women in Prison," in *Lesbian Studies: Present and Future*, ed. M. Cruikshank (Old Westbury, New York: The Feminist Press, 1982), pp. 187-193.

36 Feminists in the 1960s commonly referred to themselves as "second wave" to distinguish themselves from the turn-of-the-century suffragists who fought for the vote, with the implication that considerable work remained to be done if women were to be truly emancipated.

37 The question of censorship inevitably arises and, given the exceptionally horrific violence depicted in *Turning to Stone*, one might well have expected that it would have been withheld from prime time national broadcast on the grounds that it violated the Criminal Code (s. 159(8)), which deals with definitions of obscenity that deal with sex, crime, horror, cruelty and violence. For further discussion of the Canadian censorship debate, see V. Burstyn (ed.), *Women Against Censorship* (Vancouver and Toronto: Douglas & McIntyre, 1985); D. Copp and S. Wendell, *Pornography and Censorship* (Buffalo, New York: Prometheus Books, 1983); W. Coons and P. McFarland, "Obscenity and Community Tolerance," *Canadian Psychology/Psychologie Canadienne* 26 (1985): 30-38 and N. Boyd, "Pornography, Prostitution, and the Control of Gender Relations," in *The Social Dimensions of Law*, ed. N. Boyd (Scarborough, Ontario: Prentice-Hall Canada Inc., 1986), p. 130.

38 Op. cit., note 28. See especially Bleier, op. cit., note 28, pp. 182-190.

39 Apart from disciplinary abuse against children in the domestic realm, consider, for example, Margaret Thatcher's decision to invade the Falklands in 1982, female participants in what are described as "terrorist" movements, and the support among right-wing women for capital punishment.

40 One of the central arguments in opposition to the attempt in the U.S. to pass the Equal Rights Amendment was that it would result in women playing combat roles in the armed forces. This phenomenon has already occurred in numerous developing nations, and it was perceived by ERA opponents as antithetical to women's ordained functions as sustainers of the nuclear family upon which, in this view, capitalism depends. The entire debate begs the question of the appropriateness of militarism as a means of conflict resolution.

41 As reported in Clark, op. cit., note 24, p. 95, females comprise 2.8 per cent of sex offenders according to the National Population Survey, and 1.1 per cent of all convicted sex offenders in Canada are female. See also Clark and Lewis, op. cit., note 24; C. Shafer and M. Frye, "Rape and Respect," in *Feminism and Philosophy*, eds. M. Vetterling-Braggin, F. Elliston and J. English (Totowa, New Jersey: Littlefield, Adams & Co., 1977); Russell, op. cit., note 24 and D. Russell, *Marital Rape* (New York: Macmillan/Collier, 1982); Brownmiller, op. cit., note 24; Messerschmidt, op. cit., note 17, pp. 130-156; Bleier, op. cit., note 28; and further references cited in note 24.

42 Canadian Advisory Council on the Status of Women, Ottawa. "Sexual Assault" pamphlet, February, 1985.

43 Women comprise only about four per cent of the North American imprisoned population, even though women are more apt than men to be economically disadvantaged. Among female defendants, there is ample evidence that it is the poor, the working-class/unemployed and, by extension, women of colour, who are most vulnerable in most American constituencies in which studies have been conducted. See, for example, I. Bernstein, J. Cardascia and C. Rose, "Defendants' Sex and Criminal Court Decisions," in *Discrimination in Organizations*, eds. R. Alvarez and K. Lutterman (San Francisco: Jossey-Bass, 1979); M. Chesney-Lind, "Chivalry Reexamined: Women and the Criminal Justice System," in *Women, Crime and the Criminal Justice System*, ed. L. Bowker (Lexington, Mass.: D.C. Heath and Company, 1978), pp. 197-223; D. Lewis, "Black Women Offenders and Criminal Justice," in *Comparing Female and Male Offenders*, ed. M. Warren (Beverly Hills, CA: Sage Publications, 1981), pp. 89-105; Rafter, op. cit., note 5, p. 143; D. Bishop and C. Frazier, "The Effects of Gender on Charge Reduction," *The Sociological Quarterly* 25 (Summer, 1984): 385-396; I. Nagel and J. Hagan, "Gender and Crime: Offense Patterns and Criminal Court Sanctions," in *Crime and Justice: An Annual Review of Research*, eds. N. Morris and M. Tonry (Chicago: University of Chicago Press, 1983); C. Spohn, J. Gruhl and S. Welch, "The Impact of Ethnicity and Gender of Defendants on the Decision to Reject or Dismiss Felony Charges," *Criminology* 25 (February 1987): 175-191. J. Gruhl and S. Welch, "Women as Criminal Defendants: A Test for Paternalism," *The Western Political Quarterly*, 37 (September 1984): 456-467, suggest that women are most apt to be treated with chivalry if they can be shown to be responsible mothers. For a study of the "effects of sexism on sentencing" in the Canadian context, see C. Boyle, M-A. Bertrand, C. Lacerte-Lamontagne and R. Shamai, "Effects of Sexism on Sentencing," *A Feminist Review of Criminal Law* (Ottawa: Ministry of Supply and Services Canada, December 1985), pp. 139-147.

44 On March 19, 1976, over a thousand women rallied outside a hearing in the California state capitol to protest abuses of the human rights of women in prison. Within the chambers, legal advisers documented abuses as follows: solitary confinement without a hearing; arbitrary removal of

women from the general prison population to the prison hospital for non-medical reasons; failure to provide translators for non-English-speaking prisoners, and the withholding of mail written in other languages; separation of mothers from infants; inadequate visitation programs; harassment of lesbian prisoners; the failure of foster families to facilitate communication between imprisoned mothers and their children; internal disciplinary hearings in which women are denied advocacy; reclassification procedures in which women are assigned to more restrictive custody status without due cause; inaccessibility of the prison law library to women in closed custody; improper medical procedures and inadequate health care; the arbitrary assignment of "troublesome" women to a behaviour modification unit. (See K. Faith, *Inside/Outside* (Culver City, CA: Peace Press, 1976), pp. 27-29). This and subsequent public hearings did result in some effort to improve policies and conditions in the state institution, but women inside are still vulnerable to the traditionally legal position that convicted felons lose all civil rights. See M. Haft, "Women in Prison: Discriminatory Practices and Some Legal Solutions," *Clearinghouse Review*, May 1974; D.C. Commission on the Status of Women, "Female Offenders in the District of Columbia," Washington, D.C.: District Building, April 1972; K. Krause, "Denial of Work Release Programs to Women: A Violation of Equal Protection," *Southern California Law Review* 47 (1974): 14-18; N. Shaw, "Female Patients and the Medical Profession in Jails and Prisons: A Case of Quintuple Jeopardy," in *Judge Lawyer Victim Thief: Women, Gender Roles and Criminal Justice*, eds. N. Rafter and E. Stanko (Boston: Northeastern University Press, 1982), pp. 261-273.

45. J. Larson and J. Nelson, "Women, Friendship and Adaptation to Prison," *Journal of Criminal Justice* 12 (1984): 601-615. That men do riot is of great interest to the media, as evidenced by the voluminous attention in the past decade in Canada to major riots, incidents, and disturbances at the B.C. penitentiary, the Matsqui psychiatric centre, the Saanich, Prince Albert and Thunder Bay institutions where hostages were taken, Archambault, where in 1978 the warden was killed (resulting in the assigning of body guards to wardens in federal institutions), not to mention the highly publicized outbreaks of violence at Laval, Kingston (male), Orsainville, Dorchester, Joyceville and Millhaven. The response to these events is to provide more maximum security cells, more weapons training for guards, more searches and lock-ups and other repressive measures which, in turn, exacerbate tensions. For selected samples of scholarly analysis of violence in male institutions, see J. Fox, *Organizational and Racial Conflict in Maximum Security Prisons* (Lexington, Mass.: D.C. Heath and Company, 1982); J. Gibbs, "Violence in Prison: Its Extent, Nature and Consequences," in *Critical Issues in Corrections: Problems, Trends and Prospects*, eds. R. Roberg and V. Webb (St. Paul, Minnesota: West, 1981), pp. 110-149; J. Irwin, *Prisons in Turmoil* (Boston: Little, Brown and Company, 1980); D. Lockwood, *Prison Sexual Violence* (New York: Elsevier, 1980). Also see the following autobiographical accounts: R. Caron, *Go-Boy!* (Don Mills, Ont.: Thomas

Nelson & Sons, 1979); A. Schroeder, *Shaking it Rough: A Prison Memoir* (Toronto and New York: Doubleday, 1976); J. Abbott, *In the Belly of the Beast: Letters from Prison* (New York: Vintage Books, 1982).

46 Fox, op. cit., note 45, p. 205.

47 The exception is Propper, who offers one and a half pages of discussion of primarily hearsay incidents. See op. cit, note 34.

48 Hatch and Faith, op. cit., note 3, p. 2.

49 Browne and Flewelling, op. cit., note 20, p. 8. The common explanation for this phenomenon is that since women are usually unable to physically defend themselves against men by conventional means, when they do commit violence (usually against a mate) they do not want to risk retaliation and murder is committed as an absolute final resort. For such women, the murder is often their one criminal offence. We can reasonably speculate that the female homicide rate would decline significantly if women received more support, in the form of community shelters, to leave abusive relationships before they culminate in irrevocable damage.

50 In the year 1980 there were two deaths of women in all state and federal institutions in the United States (total approximately 14,000 female prisoners): one suicide in Florida and one "death by injury caused by another" in Pennsylvania; it is not specified as to whether the perpetrator of the injury was another prisoner or a staff member. U.S. Department of Justice, *Sourcebook of Criminal Justice Statistics*, 1982, p. 567.

51 Ministry of Supply and Services Canada, *Report to Parliament: The Sub-Committee on the Penitentiary System in Canada*, 1977, p. 135.

52 B. Walford, *Lifers: The Stories of Eleven Women Serving Life Sentences for Murder* (Montreal: Eden Press, 1987), p. 15.

53 Ibid., pp. 96-98.

54 I have held conversations with approximately a dozen women who have served time at P4W and at least twice that number who have served time in provincial facilities, all since 1982. These were not formal interviews but this account seems accurate in that individuals report virtually the same experiences.

55 Private conversation, July 9, 1987. Anonymity respected.

56 See, for example, M. Jackson, *Prisoners of Isolation: Solitary Confinement in Canada* (Toronto: University of Toronto Press, 1983), p. 51.

57 *TV Guide*, 22 February, 1986, p. 23.

58 It is my strong personal view that prisons are appropriate only for individuals who have demonstrated through violent actions that they are a genuine danger to society, and that the commonplace problems that result in imprisonment for some people must be resolved at the community level.

Women Inside:
P4W
Kingston, Ontario

Bibliography

Abbott, J. *In the Belly of the Beast: Letters From Prison.* New York: Vintage Books, 1982.

Ackerman, Nathan W. "Sexual Delinquency and Middle Class Girls," in *Family Dynamics and Female Sexual Delinquency*, edited by Otto Pollak and Alfred Friedman. Palo Alto, CA: Science and Behavior Books, Inc., 1969.

Adelberg, Ellen. *A Forgotten Minority: Women in Conflict with the Law.* Ottawa: Canadian Association of Elizabeth Fry Societies, 1985.

Adler, Freda. *Sisters in Crime: The Rise of the New Female Criminal.* New York: McGraw-Hill, 1975.

Barfield, A. "Biological Influences on Sex Differences in Behavior," in *Sex Differences: Social and Biological Perspectives*, by M. Teitelbaum. Garden City, New York: Anchor Books, 1976.

Barrett, Michele. *Women's Oppression Today: Problems in Marxist Feminist Analysis.* London: Verso & NLB, 1978.

Barry, K. *Female Sexual Slavery.* New York: Avon Books, 1979.

Baunach, P. *Mothers in Prison.* New Brunswick, NJ: Transaction, Inc., 1985.

Beattie, John M. "The Criminality of Women in Eighteenth-Century England." *Journal of Social History* 8, (Summer 1974-75):80-116.

Beauvoir, Simone de. *The Second Sex.* Translated by H.M. Parshley. New York: Vintage Books, (1952) 1974.

Bell, A.; Weinberg, M.; and Hammersmith, S. *Sexual Preference: Its Development in Men and Women.* Bloomington: Indiana University Press, 1981.

Bem, S. "The Measurement of Psychological Androgyny." *Journal of Consulting and Clinical Psychology*, (1974).

Berkely, Heather et al. *Children's Rights: Legal and Educational Issues.* Toronto: Ontario Institute for Studies in Education Press, 1978.

Bernstein, I.; Cardascia, J.; and Rose, C. "Defendants' Sex and Criminal Court Decisions," in *Discrimination in Organizations*, edited by R. Alvarez and K. Lutterman. San Francisco: Jossey-Bass, 1979.

Berzins, Lorraine and Cooper, Sheelagh. "The Political Economy of Correctional Planning for Women: The Case of the Bankrupt Bureaucracy." *The Canadian Journal of Criminology* 24 (October 1982).

Bienvenue, Rita M. and Latif, A.H. "Arrests, Disposition and Recidivism: A Comparison of Indians and Whites." *Canadian Journal of Criminology and Corrections* 16 (1984):105-116.

Birkenmeyer, A.C. and Jolly, Stan. *The Native Inmate in Ontario.* Toronto: Ontario Ministry of Correctional Services and the Ontario Native Council on Justice, 1981.

Bishop, D. and Frazier, C. "The Effects of Gender on Charge Reduction." *The Sociological Quarterly* 25 (Summer, 1984):385-396.

Blackbridge, Persimmon and Gilhooly, Sheila. *Still Sane.* Vancouver: Press Gang Publishers, 1985.

Bleier, R. *Science and Gender: A Critique of Biology and Its Theories on Women.* New York: Pergamon Press Inc., 1984.

Box, S. and Hale, C. "Liberation and Female Criminality in England and Wales Revisited." *British Journal of Criminology* 22 (1983):35-49.

Boyd, N. "Pornography, Prostitution, and the Control of Gender Relations," in *The Social Dimensions of Law*, edited by N. Boyd. Scarborough, Ont.: Prentice-Hall Canada Inc., 1986.

Boyle, C.; Bertrand, M-A.; Lacerte-Lamontagne, C.; and Shamai, R. "Effects of Sexism on Sentencing," in *A Feminist Review of Criminal Law*, edited by J. Russell. Ottawa: Minister of Supply and Services Canada, December 1985.

Brooks, V. *Minority Stress and Lesbian Women.* Toronto: D.C. Heath and Co., 1981.

Browne, A. and Flewelling, R. "Women as Victims or Perpetrators of Homicide." Paper presented at the Annual General Meeting of the American Society of Criminology, Atlanta, GA, October 29 -November 1, 1986.

Browne, A. *When Battered Women Kill.* New York: The Free Press, 1987.

Brownmiller, Susan. *Against Our Will: Men, Women and Rape.* New York: Bantam Books, 1975.

Burstyn, Varda, ed. *Women Against Censorship.* Vancouver and Toronto: Douglas & McIntyre, 1985.

Canada, *Annual Reports of the Directors of Penitentiaries in the Dominion of Canada.* 1868-1874.

Canada, *Annual Reports of the Inspectors of Penitentiaries.* 1914-1918.

Canada, *Annual Reports of the Minister of Justice as to Penitentiaries in Canada.* 1875-1913.

Canada, *Annual Reports of the Superintendent of Penitentiaries.* 1864-1867.

Canada, *Annual Reports of the Superintendent of Penitentiaries.* 1919-1938.

Canada, *Childhood Experiences as Causes of Criminal Behaviour.* Ottawa: Proceedings of the Senate of Canada, Issue No. 7, 1978.

Canada, Correctional Service of Canada. *Basic Facts About Corrections in Canada.* Ottawa: Correctional Service of Canada, 1986.

Canada, Correctional Service of Canada. "History of Crime and Punishment in Canada." *Crime and Punishment Journal* 10 (August 15, 1985):6-7.

Canada, Correctional Service of Canada. "Non-Native Population Profile Report and Native Population Profile Report." Ottawa: Solicitor General of Canada, Information Services Branch, March 1982.

Canada, Correctional Service of Canada. *Progress Report on the Federal Female Offender Program.* Ottawa: Solicitor General of Canada, 1978.

Canada, Department of Indian Affairs and Northern Development. *Indian Conditions: A Survey.* Ottawa: Supply and Services, 1980.

Canada, Government of Canada, House of Commons, *Minutes of Proceedings and Evidence of the Standing Committee on Justice and Legal Affairs.* Ottawa: House of Commons, Dec. 6, 1979, 13:9-13:10.

Canada, *Journals of the Legislative Assembly.* 1840-1849.

Canada, (Province of), *Journals of the Legislative Assembly.* 1849, Appendix BBBBB.

Canada, *Report of the Canadian Committee on Corrections* (Ouimet Report). Ottawa: Queen's Printer, 1969.

Canada, *Report of the Commission on Equality in Employment.* Ottawa: Supply and Services, 1985.

Canada, *Report of the Committee Appointed to Inquire into the Principles and Procedures Followed in the Remission Service of the Department of Justice of Canada* (Fauteux Report). Ottawa: Supply and Services, 1956.

Canada, *Report of the Committee on Sexual Offences Against Children and Youths* (Badgely Report). Ottawa: Supply and Services, 1984.

Canada, *Report of the National Advisory Committee on the Female Offender.* Ottawa: Solicitor General of Canada, 1977.

Canada, *Report of the Royal Commission on Penitentiaries.* Sessional Paper No. 252, 1914.

Canada, *Report of the Royal Commission on the Status of Women in Canada.* Ottawa: Supply and Services, 1970.

Canada, *Report of the Royal Commission to Inquire and then Report upon the Conduct, Economy, Discipline and Management of the Provincial Penitentiary* (Brown Report). 1849.

Canada, *Report of the Royal Commission to Investigate the Penal System of Canada* (Archambault Report). Ottawa: King's Printer, 1938.

Canada, *Report of the Special Committee on Pornography and Prostitution*. Ottawa: Supply and Services, 1985.

Canada, *Report on the State and Management of the Female Prison*. 1921.

Canada, *Report to Parliament by the Sub-Committee on the Penitentiary System in Canada* (MacGuigan Report). Ottawa: Supply and Services, 1977.

Canada, Statistics Canada. *Adult Correctional Services in Canada* (Annual, Cat. no. 85-211). Ottawa: Supply and Services, 1985.

Canada, Statistics Canada. *Canada's Native People*. Ottawa: Supply and Services, 1984.

Canada, Statistics Canada. *Canadian Crime Statistics* (Annual, Cat. no. 85-205). Ottawa: Supply and Services, 1985.

Canada, Statistics Canada. *Juvenile Delinquents*. Ottawa: Supply and Services, 1983.

Canada, Statistics Canada. *Women in Canada: A Statistical Report* (Cat. no. 89-503E). Ottawa: Supply and Services, 1985.

Canada, *The Female Offender—Selected Statistics: Report of the National Advisory Committee on the Female Offender*. Ottawa: Solicitor General of Canada, 1977.

Canada (Upper), *Journals of the House of Assembly*. 1833-1839.

Canadian Advisory Council on the Status of Women. *The Shocking Pink Paper*. Ottawa: Canadian Advisory Council on the Status of Women, 1984.

Canadian Advisory Council on the Status of Women. *Ten Years Later*. Ottawa: Canadian Advisory Council on the Status of Women, 1979.

Canadian Association of Elizabeth Fry Societies. "Brief to the Solicitor General of Canada." Ottawa: Canadian Association of Elizabeth Fry Societies, 1979.

Canadian Council on Social Development. "Native Crime Victims Research." Ottawa: Canadian Council on Social Development, 1984 (unpublished working paper).

Carlen, Pat, ed. *Criminal Women*. Cambridge: Polity Press, 1985.

Carlen, Pat. *Women's Imprisonment: A Study in Social Control.* London: Routledge & Kegan Paul, 1983.

Caron, R. *Go-Boy!* Don Mills, Ont.: Thomas Nelson & Sons, 1979.

Chesler, Phyllis. *Women and Madness.* New York: Doubleday & Co., 1972.

Chesney-Lind, Meda. "Chivalry Re-examined: Women and the Criminal Justice System," in *Women, Crime and the Criminal Justice System,* edited by Lee H. Bowker. Lexington: D.C. Heath, 1978.

Chesney-Lind, Meda. "Girls' Crime and Woman's Place: Towards a Feminist Model of Female Delinquency." University of Hawaii: Youth Development and Research Center, Report no. 334, May 1987.

Chesney-Lind, Meda. "Is Sexism a Dead Issue?" Paper presented at the Annual General Meeting of the American Society of Criminology, San Diego, CA, November 13-16, 1985.

Chesney-Lind, Meda. "Judicial Enforcement of the Female Sex Role, the Family Court and the Female Delinquent." *Issues in Criminology* 8 (Fall 1973).

Chesney-Lind, Meda. "Re-discovering Lilith: Misogyny and the New Female Criminal," in *The Female Offender: Selected Papers from an International Symposium,* edited by Curt Taylor Griffiths and Margit Nance. Vancouver: Criminology Research Centre, Simon Fraser University, 1980.

Chesney-Lind, Meda. "Sexist Juvenile Justice: A Continuing International Problem."*Resources for Feminist Research* 13 (December/January 1985-6).

Chesney-Lind, Meda. "Women and Crime: The Female Offender." *Signs* 12 (Autumn 1986):78-96.

Chodorow, N. *The Reproduction of Mothering.* Berkeley, CA: University of California Press, 1978.

Clark, G.S. and Associates. *Native Victims in Canada: Issues in Providing Effective Assistance* (User Report). Ottawa: Solicitor General of Canada, 1986.

Clark, Lorenne. "Boys Will Be Boys: Beyond the Badgley Report, A Critical Review," in *Regulating Sex: An Anthology of Commentaries on the Findings and Recommendations of the Badgley and Fraser Reports,* edited by J. Lowman, et al. Burnaby, B.C.: School of Criminology, Simon Fraser University. 1986.

Clark, Lorenne and Lewis, Debra. *Rape: The Price of Coercive Sexuality.* Toronto: The Women's Press, 1977.

Cole, Susan. "Child Battery," in *No Safe Place,* edited by Connie Guberman and Margie Wolfe. Toronto: The Women's Press, 1985.

Conference Internationale sur la situation des filles (1985). *Le Temps d'y voir*. Montreal: Guerin, 1986.

Coons, W. and McFarland, P. "Obscenity and Community Tolerance." *Canadian Psychology/Psychologie Canadienne* 26:1 (1985):30-38.

Copp, D. and Wendell, S. *Pornography and Censorship*. Buffalo, New York: Prometheus Books, 1983.

Cousins, Mark. "Mens Rea: Sexual Difference and the Criminal Law," in *Radical Issues in Criminology*, edited by Pat Carlen and Mike Collison. Oxford: Martin Robertson, 1980.

Covenant House. *The Street is No Place for a Kid: A Symposium on Street Youth*. Symposium Proceedings. Toronto: Convenant House, 1986.

Cruikshank, M. *Lesbian Studies: Present and Future*. Old Westbury, NY: The Feminist Press, 1982.

Culhane, Claire. *Barred From Prison*. Vancouver: Pulp Press, 1979.

Cullen, F.; Golden, K.; and Cullen, J. "Sex and Delinquency: A Partial Test of the Masculinity Hypothesis." *Criminology* 17 (1979):301-310.

Curb, R. and Manahan, N. *Lesbian Nuns: Breaking Silence*. New York: Warner Books, Inc., 1985.

Dalton, Katharina. *Once a Month*. Glasgow: Fontana, 1978.

Davis, K. "The Sociology of Prostitution." *American Sociological Review* II, No. 1-6 (1937):744-755.

Davis, N. and Faith, K. "Women and the State: Changing Models of Social Control," in *Transcarceration and the Modern State of Penalty*, edited by J. Lowman, R. Menzies and T. Palys. Aldershot, England: Gower Publishers, 1987.

D.C. Commission on the Status of Women. "Female Offenders in the District of Columbia," Washington, D.C.: District Building, April 1972.

Dobash, R. and Dobash, R. "Wives: The 'Appropriate' Victims of Marital Violence." *Victimology: An International Journal* 2, No. 3-4 (1977):426-442.

Dubec, Bernice. "Native Women and the Criminal Justice System: An Increasing Minority." Mimeographed. Thunder Bay: Ontario Native Women's Association, 1982.

Eaton, Mary. "Documenting the Defendant: Placing Women in Social Inquiry Reports," in *Women in Law: Explorations in Law, Family and Sexuality*, edited by Julia Brophy and Carol Smart. London: Routledge & Kegan Paul, 1985.

Eaton, Mary. "Mitigating Circumstances: Familiar Rhetoric." *International Journal of the Sociology of Law* 11 (November 1983): 385-400.

Edwards, Susan. *Female Sexuality and the Law*. Oxford: Martin Robertson, 1981.

Ekstedt, John W. and Griffiths, Curt T. *Corrections in Canada: Policy and Practice*. Toronto: Butterworths, 1984.

Faith, Karlene. *Inside/Outside*. Culver City, CA: Peace Press, 1976.

Faith, Karlene. "Love Between Women in Prison," in *Lesbian Studies: Present and Future*, edited by M. Cruikshank. Old Westbury, New York: The Feminist Press, 1982.

Faith, Karlene, ed. *Soledad Prison: University of the Poor*. Palo Alto, CA: Science & Behavior Books, 1975.

Feinman, Clarice. *Women in the Criminal Justice System*. New York: Praeger, 1980.

Figueira-Mcdonough, Josephina. "Are Girls Different? Discrepancies Between Delinquent Behaviour and Control." *Child Welfare* LXIV (May/June 1985).

Firestone, Shulamith. *The Dialectic of Sex*. New York: Bantam Books, 1970.

Fox, J. *Organizational and Racial Conflict in Maximum Security Prisons*. Lexington, Mass.: D.C. Heath and Co., 1982.

Freedman, Estelle. *Their Sister's Keepers: Women's Prison Reform in America, 1830-1930*. Ann Arbor: University of Michigan Press, 1981.

Freedman, Lisa. "Wife Assault," in *No Safe Place*, edited by Connie Guberman and Margie Wolfe. Toronto: The Women's Press, 1985.

Freud, Sigmund. *New Introductory Lectures on Psychoanalysis*. Translated and edited by J. Strachey. New York: W.W. Norton & Co. Inc., 1933.

Geller, Gloria. "Streaming of Males and Females in the Juvenile Justice System." Ph.D. dissertation, University of Toronto, 1981.

Genders, E. and Player, E. "Women's Imprisonment: The Effects of Youth Custody." *British Journal of Criminology* 26 (October 1986):357-371.

Giallombardo, R. *Society of Women: A Study of a Women's Prison*. New York: John Wiley & Sons, Inc., 1966.

Gibbs, J. "Violence in Prison: Its Extent, Nature and Consequences," in *Critical Issues in Corrections: Problems, Trends and Prospects*, edited by R. Roberg and V. Webb. St. Paul, Minnesota: West, 1981.

Gilligan, C. *In a Different Voice.* Cambridge, Mass.: Harvard University Press, 1982.

Giordano, P. and Cernkovich, S. "On Complicating the Relationship Between Liberation and Delinquency." *Social Problems* 26 (1979): 467-481.

Glueck, S. and Glueck, E. *Five Hundred Delinquent Women.* New York: Alfred A. Knopf, 1934.

Gomme, Ian M. et al. "Rates, Types and Patterns of Male and Female Delinquency in an Ontario County." *Canadian Journal of Criminology* 26 (July 1984).

Greenwood, Victoria. "The Myths of Female Crime," in *Women and Crime* (Cropwood Conference Series No. 13), edited by A. Morris and L. Gelsthorpe. Cambridge: Institute of Criminology, 1981.

Gregory, Jean. "Sex, Class and Crime: Towards a Non-Sexist Criminology," in *The Political Economy of Crime: Readings for a Critical Criminology,* edited by Brian D. Maclean. Scarborough, Ont.: Prentice Hall, 1986.

Grier, Barbara and Reid, C. *Lesbian Lives: Biographies of Women From The Ladder.* Oakland, CA: Diana Press, 1976.

Griffin, Susan. "Rape: The All American Crime," in *Feminism and Philosophy,* edited by M. Vetterling-Braggin, F. Elliston and J. English. Totowa, New Jersey: Littlefield, Adams & Co., 1977.

Griffin, Susan. *Women and Nature: The Roaring Inside Her.* New York: Harper & Row, 1978.

Gruhl, J. and Welch, S. "Women as Criminal Defendants: A Test for Paternalism." *The Western Political Quarterly* 37 (September 1984): 456-467.

Haft, M. "Women in Prison: Discriminatory Practices and Some Legal Solutions." *Clearinghouse Review* (May 1974).

Halleck, Seymour L. *Psychiatry and the Dilemma of Crime.* New York: Harper & Row, Hollier Medical Books, 1967.

Hann, R. and Harman, W. "Full Parole Release: An Historical Descriptive Analysis." Ottawa: Ministry of the Solicitor General, 1986.

Harding, Jim. "Unemployment, Racial Discrimination and Public Drunkenness in Regina." Unpublished paper. Regina: Faculty of Social Work, University of Regina, 1984.

Hatch, Alison and Faith, Karlene. "The Female Offender in Canada." Paper presented at the Annual Meeting of the American Society of Criminology, San Diego, California, November 13-17, 1985.

Hawthorn, Felicity, et al. *Report to the Fraser Committee from the*

Elizabeth Fry Society of Kingston. Kingston: Elizabeth Fry Society, 1984.

Henley, N. *Body Politics: Power, Sex and Nonverbal Communication.* Englewood Cliffs: Prentice-Hall, 1977.

Henriques, Z.W. *Imprisoned Mothers and Their Children.* New York: University Press of America, 1982.

Herskovitz, Herbert H. "A Psychodynamic View of Sexual Promiscuity," in *Family Dynamics and Female Delinquency,* edited by Otto Pollak and Alfred Friedman. Palo Alto, CA: Science and Behavior Books, Inc., 1969.

Hill, Christina M. "Women in the Canadian Economy," in *The Political Economy of Dependency,* edited by Robert Laxer. Toronto: McClelland and Stewart, 1973.

Hills, S. "Rape and the Masculine Mystique," in *Gender Roles: Doing What Comes Naturally?,* edited by E. Salamon and B. Robinson. Toronto: Methuen Publications (Carswell Co. Ltd.), 1987.

Hite, S. *The Hite Report: A Nationwide Study of Female Sexuality.* New York: Dell Publishing Co. Inc., 1976.

Irwin, J. *Prisons in Turmoil.* Boston: Little, Brown and Co., 1980.

Jackson, M. *Prisoners of Isolation: Solitary Confinement in Canada.* Toronto: University of Toronto Press, 1983.

Jefferson, Christie. "The Female Offender: A Status of Women Issue." *Canadian Association of Elizabeth Fry Societies Newsletter* 10 (March 1984).

Johnson, Brian. "Women Behind Bars." *Equinox* (March/April 1984).

Johnson, Holly. *Women and Crime in Canada.* Ottawa: Solicitor General of Canada, 1986.

Jones, Ann. *Women Who Kill.* New York: Holt, Rinehart & Winston, 1980.

Kellough, Gail. "From Colonialism to Imperialism: The Experience of Canadian Indians," in *Structured Inequality in Canada,* edited by John Harp and John R. Hofley. Scarborough, Ont.: Prentice-Hall, 1980.

Kinsey, A.; Pomeroy, C.; Martin, C.; and Gebhard, P. *Sexual Behavior in the Human Female.* Philadelphia: W.B. Saunders Co., 1953.

Klaits, J. *Servants of Satan: The Age of the Witch Hunts.* Bloomington: Indiana University Press, 1985.

Klein, Dorie. "The Etiology of Women's Crime: A Review of the Literature." *Issues in Criminology* 8 (Fall 1973):3-30.

Klein, Dorie and Kress, June. "Any Woman's Blues: A Critical Over-view of Women, Crime and the Criminal Justice System." *Crime and Social Justice* 5 (Spring-Summer 1976):34-49.

Krause, K. "Denial of Work Release Programs to Women: A Violation of Equal Protection." *Southern California Law Review* 47 (1974): 14-18.

Landau B. "The Adolescent Female Offender: Our Dilemma." *Canadian Journal of Criminology and Corrections* 17 (1975):146-153.

LaPrairie, Carol Pitcher. "Native Women and Crime." *Perception* 7 (1984):25-27.

LaPrairie, Carol Pitcher. "Selected Criminal Justice and Socio-Demo-graphic Data on Native Women." *Canadian Journal of Criminology* 26 (April 1984):161-169.

Larason Schneider, Anne, et al. "Divestiture of Court Jurisdictions over Status Offences," in *An Assessment of Juvenile Justice System Reform in Washington State*, by Institute of Policy Analysis and Urban Policy Research. Eugene, Oregon: Institute of Policy Analysis; and Seattle, WA: Urban Policy Research, March 1983.

Larson, J. and Nelson, J. "Women, Friendship, and Adaptation to Prison." *Journal of Criminal Justice* 12 (1984):601-615.

Lavell, Alfred. "The History of Prisons of Upper Canada." Mimeo-graphed. Kingston: Queen's University, 1948.

Laws, J. and Schwartz, P. *Sexual Scripts: The Social Construction of Female Sexuality*. Hinsdale, Illinois: The Dryden Press, 1977.

Leonard, Eileen. *Women, Crime and Society: A Critique of Theoretical Criminology*. New York: Longman Inc., 1982.

Levine, Helen. "Feminist Counselling: Approach or Technique?" in *Perspectives on Women in the 1980s*, edited by J. Turner and L. Emery. Winnipeg: University of Manitoba Press, 1983.

Lewis, D. "Black Women Offenders and Criminal Justice," in *Compar-ing Female and Male Offenders*, edited by M. Warren. Beverly Hills, CA: Sage Publications, 1981.

Lockwood, D. *Prison Sexual Violence*. New York: Elsevier, 1980.

Lombroso, Cesare and Ferrero, Enrico. *The Female Offender*. New York: D. Appleton, 1900.

Lowman, J. "Images of Discipline in Prison," in *The Social Dimensions of Law*, edited by N. Boyd. Scarborough, Ont.: Prentice-Hall Canada Inc., 1986.

Lowman, J.; Jackson, M.; Palys, T.; and Gavigan, S., eds. *Regulating Sex: An Anthology of Commentaries on the Findings and Recom-*

mendations of the Badgley and Fraser Reports. Burnaby, B.C.: School of Criminology, Simon Fraser University, 1986.

MacKinnon, Catherine. *Sexual Harassment of Working Women.* New Haven and London: Yale University Press, 1979.

MacLeod, Linda. *Battered But Not Beaten: Preventing Wife Battering in Canada.* Ottawa: Canadian Advisory Council on the Status of Women, 1987.

MacLeod, Linda. *Sentenced to Separation: An Exploration of the Needs and Problems of Mothers Who are Offenders and their Children* (User Report No. 1986-25). Ottawa: Solicitor General of Canada, 1986.

MacLeod, Linda. *Wife Battering in Canada: The Vicious Circle.* Ottawa: Canadian Advisory Council on the Status of Women, 1980.

McIntosh, Mary. "Review Symposium: Women, Crime and Criminology." *British Journal of Criminology* 17 (October 1977).

McNeil, Gerard and Vance, Sharon. *Cruel and Unusual.* Toronto: Deneau & Greenberg, 1978.

Martin, Del. *Battered Wives.* San Francisco: Glide Publications, 1976.

Masters, W. and Johnson, V. *Human Sexual Inadequacy.* Boston: Little, Brown and Co., 1970.

Mendelsohn, Robert S. *Mal(e)practice: How Doctors Manipulate Women.* Chicago: Contemporary Books, 1981.

Messerschmidt, J. *Capitalism, Patriarchy and Crime: Toward a Socialist Feminist Criminology.* Totowa, NJ: Rowman & Littlefield, 1986.

Miller, E. "International Trends in the Study of Female Criminality: An Essay Review." *Contemporary Crises* 7 (1983):59-70.

Miller, Jean Baker. *Toward a New Psychology of Women.* Boston: Beacon Press, 1976.

Misch, Cindy et al. *National Survey Concerning Female Inmates in Provincial and Territorial Institutions.* Ottawa: Canadian Association of Elizabeth Fry Societies, 1982.

Money, J. and Erhardt, A. *Man and Woman, Boy and Girl.* Baltimore, Maryland: Johns Hopkins University Press, 1972.

Money, J. and Tucker, P. *Sexual Signatures: On Being a Man or a Woman.* Boston: Little, Brown and Co., 1975.

Morgan, E. "The Eroticization of Male Dominance/Female Submission." *Papers in Women's Studies* 11 (September 1975):112-145. Ann Arbor: The University of Michigan, Women's Studies Program.

Morgan, Robin. *Sisterhood is Powerful: An Anthology of Writings*

From the Women's Liberation Movement. New York: Vintage Books, 1970.

Morris, Alison and Gelsthorpe, Lorraine. "False Clues and Female Crime," in *Women and Crime* (Cropwood Conference Series No. 13), edited by Alison Morris and Lorraine Gelsthorpe. Cambridge: Institute of Criminology, 1981.

Nagel, I. and Hagan, J. "Gender and Crime: Offense Patterns and Criminal Court Sanctions," in *Crime and Justice: An Annual Review of Research,* edited by N. Morris and M. Tonry. Chicago: University of Chicago Press, 1983.

Native Counselling Services of Alberta. "Submission to the Federal-Provincial Task Force on Victims of Crime." Edmonton: Native Counselling Services of Alberta, 1982.

Nease, Barbara. "Measuring Juvenile Delinquents in Hamilton," in *Deviant Behaviour and Societal Reaction,* edited by Craig L. Boydall et al. Toronto: Holt, Rinehart and Winston of Canada, Ltd., 1972.

Norland, S. and Shover, N. "Gender Roles and Female Criminality: Some Critical Comments." *Criminology* 15 (1977):87-104.

Northwest Territories, Department of Health and Social Services. *Female Offender Study Committee Report to the Minister.* Government of the Northwest Territories, 1985.

Ontario, Ministry of Community and Social Services and Ministry of Correctional Services. *Young Offenders.* Toronto, 1984.

Ontario, Ministry of Correctional Services. *Annual Report 1984-5.* Toronto: Ministry of Correctional Services, 1986.

Pearce, F. "How to be Immoral and Ill, Pathetic and Dangerous, All at the Same Time: Mass Media and the Homosexual," in *The Manufacture of News: Social Problems, Deviance and the Mass Media,* edited by S. Cohen and J. Young. London: Constable and Co., Ltd., 1973.

Penfold, P. Susan and Walker, Gillian. *Women and the Psychiatric Paradox.* Montreal: Eden Press, 1983.

Pizzey, Erin. *Scream Quietly or the Neighbors Will Hear.* Harmondsworth, Middlesex: Penguin Books, 1974.

Pollak, Otto. *The Criminality of Women.* Philadelphia: University of Pennsylvania Press, 1950.

Prins, Herschel. *Offenders: Deviants or Patients?* London: Tavistock Publications, 1980.

Propper, A. *Prison Homosexuality: Myth and Reality.* Lexington, Mass.: D.C. Heath and Co. (Lexington Books), 1981.

Rafter, Nicole H. *Partial Justice: Women in State Prisons, 1800-1935.* Boston: Northeastern University Press, 1985.

Rafter, Nicole H. and Natalizia, Elena. "Marxist Feminism: Implications for Criminal Justice." *Crime and Delinquency* 27 (January 1981).

Rawlings, Edna and Carter, Diane, eds. *Psychotherapy for Women: Treatment Towards Equality.* Springfield, IL: Charles C. Thomas, 1977.

Reston, J. *The Innocence of Joan Little: A Southern Mystery.* New York: Bantam Books, 1977.

Robertson, Heather. *Reservations are for Indians.* Toronto: James Lewis and Samuel, 1970.

Rosenblatt, E. and Greenland, C. "Female Crimes of Violence." *Canadian Journal of Criminology and Corrections* 16 (1974):173-180.

Rosenbluth, V. "Women in Prison," in *Women in Canada,* edited by Marylee Stephenson. Don Mills, Ont.: General Publishing, 1977.

Ross, Robert R. and Fabiano, E.A. *Correctional Afterthoughts: Programs for Female Offenders* (User Report). Ottawa: Solicitor General of Canada, 1985.

Russell, D. *Marital Rape.* New York: Macmillan/Collier, 1982.

Russell, D. *The Politics of Rape.* New York: Stein & Day, 1975.

Ryan, William. *Blaming the Victim.* New York: Vintage Books, 1976.

Salamon, E. and Robinson, B., eds. *Gender Roles: Doing What Comes Naturally?* Toronto: Methuen Publications (Carswell Co. Ltd.), 1987.

Schroeder, Andreas. *Shaking it Rough: A Prison Memoir.* Toronto and New York: Doubleday, 1976.

Schur, Edwin. *Labeling Women Deviant.* Philadelphia: Temple University Press, 1984.

Schwartz, M. "Gender and Injury in Spousal Assault." *Sociological Focus* 20 (January 1987):61-75.

Scutt, Jocelynne A. "Debunking the Theory of the Female 'Masked Criminal.'" *Australia and New Zealand Journal of Criminology* 11 (March 1978):23-42.

Scutt, Jocelynne A. "Sexism in Criminal Law," in *Women and Crime,* edited by S.K. Mukerjee and Jocelynne A. Scutt. Sydney: Australia Institute of Criminology/George Allen and Unwin, 1981.

Shafer, C. and Frye, M. "Rape and Respect," in *Feminism and Philosophy,* edited by M. Vetterling-Braggin, F. Elliston and J. English. Totawa, NJ: Littlefield, Adams & Co., 1977.

Shaw, Nancy. "The Female Offender," in *Judge, Lawyer, Victim, Thief: Women, Gender Roles and Criminal Justice,* edited by Nicole H. Rafter and Elizabeth A. Stanko. Boston: Northeastern University Press, 1982.

Shaw, Nancy. "Female Patients and the Medical Profession in Jails and Prisons: A Case of Quintuple Jeopardy," in *Judge, Lawyer, Victim, Thief: Women, Gender Roles and Criminal Justice*, edited by Nicole H. Rafter and Elizabeth A. Stanko. Boston: Northeastern University Press, 1982.

Simon, Rita. *Women and Crime*. Toronto: Lexington Books, 1975.

Smart, Carol. "Legal Subjects and Sexual Objects: Ideology, Law and Female Sexuality," in *Women in Law: Explorations in Law, Family and Sexuality*, edited by Julia Brophy and Carol Smart. London: Routledge & Kegan Paul, 1985.

Smart, Carol. "The New Female Criminal: Reality or Myth?" *British Journal of Criminology* 19 (January 1979):40-59.

Smart, Carol. *Women, Crime and Criminology: A Feminist Critique*. Boston: Routledge & Kegan Paul, 1976.

Smart Carol and Smart, Barry. *Women, Sexuality and Social Control*. London: Routledge & Kegan Paul, 1978.

Smith, Dorothy and David, Sara, eds. *Women Look at Psychiatry*. Vancouver: Press Gang Publishers, 1975.

Spohn, C.; Gruhl, J.; and Welch, S. "The Impact of the Ethnicity and Gender of Defendants on the Decision to Reject or Dismiss Felony Charges." *Criminology* 25 (February 1987):175-191.

Steele, Lisa. "A Capital Idea: Gendering in the Mass Media," in *Women Against Censorship*, edited by Varda Burstyn. Vancouver and Toronto: Douglas & McIntyre, 1985.

Steffensmeier, D. "Crime and the Contemporary Woman: An Analysis of Changing Levels of Female Property Crimes, 1960-1975," in *Women and Crime in America*, edited by L. Bowker. New York: Macmillan, 1981.

Steinmetz, S. "The Battered Husband Syndrome." *Victimology* 2 (1977/78):499-509.

Stoller, R. *Sex and Gender: On the Development of Masculinity and Femininity*. London: Hogarth Press, 1968.

Straus, M.; Gelles, R.; and Steinmetz, S. *Behind Closed Doors*. Garden City, NY: Anchor Books, 1980.

Taylor, Ian. *Law and Order: Arguments for Socialism*. London: Macmillan, 1981.

Teitelbaum, M. *Sex Differences: Social and Biological Perspectives*. Garden City, NY: Doubleday, 1976.

Toronto Rape Crisis Centre. "Rape," in *No Safe Place*, edited by Connie Guberman and Margie Wolfe. Toronto: The Women's Press, 1985.

Usher, Peter J. "A Northern Perspective on the Informal Economy." *Perspectives* (1980).

Valentine, Victor. "Native People and Canadian Society: A Profile of Issues and Trends," in *Cultural Boundaries and the Cohesion of Canada*, edited by R. Breton, J. Reitz and V. Valentine. Montreal: Institute of Research on Public Policy, 1980.

Van Bibber, Marilyn. "Term Paper." Unpublished. Ottawa: Department of Sociology and Anthropology, Carleton University, 1985.

Walford, Bonnie. *Lifers: The Stories of Eleven Women Serving Life Sentences for Murder*. Montreal: Eden Press, 1987.

Walker, Nigel. *Crime and Insanity in England, Vol. 1: The Historical Perspective*. Edinburgh: Edinburgh University Press, 1968.

Ward, D. and Kassebaum, G. *Women's Prison: Sex and Social Structure*. Chicago: Aldine Publishing Co., 1965.

Wardell, Walter I. "The Reduction of Strain in a Marginal Social Role," in *Problems in Social Psychology*, edited by Carl W. Backman and Paul S. Secord. New York: McGraw-Hill, 1966.

Weiler, Karen. "Unmanageable Children and Section 8." *Interchange* 8 (1977-78).

Weis, Joseph G. "Liberation and Crime: The Invention of the New Female Criminal." *Crime and Social Justice* 6 (Fall-Winter 1976):17-27.

West, Gordon. *Young Offenders and the State: A Canadian Perspective on Delinquency*. Toronto: Butterworths, 1984.

Widom, Cathy Spatz. "Perspectives of Female Criminality: A Critical Examination of Assumptions," in *Women and Crime* (Cropwood Conference Series No. 13), edited by Alison Morris and Lorraine Gelsthorpe. Cambridge: Institute of Criminology, 1981.

Wolfe, N.; Cullen, F.; and Cullen, J. "Describing the Female Offender: A Note on the Demographics of Arrests." *Journal of Criminal Justice* 12 (1984):483-492.

Wolfgang, M. and Ferracutti, F. *The Subculture of Violence: Towards an Integrated Theory in Criminology*. London: Tavistock Publications, 1967.

Women for Justice. "Brief to the Canadian Human Rights Commission." Ottawa: Women for Justice, 1980.

"Women in Prison: The Human Rights Connection." *Liaison* 8 (1982).

Young, I. "Humanism, Gynocentrism and Feminist Politics." *Women's Studies International Forum* 8 (1985):173-183.

Young, Joanne. "Confessions of a Jail Bird." *Arthur* 23 (March 1983).

Lobby and Advocacy Groups

*Association for Women in the
Justice System*
P.O. Box 69579, Station K
Vancouver, B.C.   V5K 4W7
(604) 872-5651

*B.C. Federation of Women
Prison Committee*
c/o Vancouver Women's
Bookstore
315 Cambie Street
Vancouver, B.C.   V6B 2N4
(604) 684-0523

Correctional Law Project
295 Brock Street
Kingston, Ontario   K7L 1S5
(613) 546-1171

Friends of Jezebel
P.O. Box 1075
Edmonton, Alberta   T5J 2M1
(403) 429-4291, pager 2883

*Groupe de défense des droits
des Détenus*
570, rue de Roi
Quebec, P.Q.   G1K 2X2
(418) 522-4343

Inmate Committee
Prison for Women
P.O. Box 515
Kingston, Ont.   K7L 4W7

*Legal Education and Action Fund
(LEAF)*
344 Bloor St. W., Ste. 403
Toronto, Ont.   M5S 1W9
(416) 963-9654

*National Association of Women
and the Law*
323 Chapel Street
Ottawa, Ont.   K1N 7Z2
(613) 238-1544

*L'Office des droits des détenus/
Prisoners Rights Bureau*
1825 rue de Champlain
Montreal, Quebec
(514) 527-8551

*Student Legal Services
of Edmonton*
Room 114, Law Centre
University of Alberta
111th Street and 88th Avenue
Edmonton, Alberta   T6G 2H5
(403) 432-2226

Women for Justice
P.O. Box 3187, Station D
Ottawa, Ont.   K1P 6H6

ELIZABETH FRY SOCIETIES

*The Canadian Association
of Elizabeth Fry Societies*
302-151 Slater Street
Ottawa, Ont.   K1P 5H3
(613) 238-2422

Unison Society of Cape Breton
106 Townsend Street
Sydney, N.S.   B1P 5E1
(902) 539-6165

Elizabeth Fry Society of Halifax
P.O. Box 3351, Halifax South
Postal Stn.
Halifax, N.S.   B3J 3J1
(902) 469-6590

*Elizabeth Fry Society
of New Brunswick, Inc.*
18 Botsford Street
Moncton, N.B.   E1C 4W7
(506) 855-7781

Elizabeth Fry Society
of Greater Montreal
3836 rue St-Hubert
Montreal, Quebec   H2L 4A5
(514) 284-2125

Elizabeth Fry Society of Ottawa
195A Bank Street
Ottawa, Ont.   K2P 1W7
(613) 238-1171

Elizabeth Fry Society of Sudbury
240 Elm Street West
Sudbury, Ont.   P3C 1V3
(705) 673-1364

Elizabeth Fry Society of Kingston
503A Princess Street
Kingston, Ont.   K7L 1C3
(613) 544-1744

Toronto Elizabeth Fry Society
215 Wellesley Street East
Toronto, Ont.   M4X 1G1
(416) 924-3708

Elizabeth Fry Society
—Peel-Halton Branch
203-14 George Street North
Brampton, Ont.   L6X 1R2
(416) 459-1315

Elizabeth Fry Society
of Hamilton
103 John Street South
Hamilton, Ont.   L8N 2C2
(416) 527-3097

Elizabeth Fry Society
of Manitoba
51 Osborne Street South
Winnipeg, Manitoba   R3L 1Y2
(204) 474-2469

Elizabeth Fry Society
of Saskatchewan
301, 219-22nd Street East
Saskatoon, Sask.   S7K 0G3
(306) 934-4606

Elizabeth Fry Society of Calgary
1009-7 Avenue S.W.
Calgary, Alberta   T2P 1A8
(403) 294-0737

Elizabeth Fry Society of Edmonton
702 McLeod Bldg.
10136-100 Street
Edmonton, Alta.   T5J 0P1
(403) 421-1175

Central Okanagan Elizabeth Fry
Society
202-1610 Bertram Street
Kelowna, B.C.   V1Y 2G4
(604) 763-4613

Kamloops and District
Elizabeth Fry Society
200-142 Victoria Street
Kamloops, B.C.   V2C 1Z7
(604) 374-2119

Elizabeth Fry Society
of British Columbia
(Vancouver)
2412 Columbia Street
Vancouver, B.C.   V5Y 3E6
(604) 873-5501

Elizabeth Fry Society
of British Columbia
Prince George Branch
315-1717 Third Avenue
Prince George, B.C.   V2L 3G7
(604) 563-1113

South Cariboo
Elizabeth Fry Society
Box 603
Ashcroft, B.C.   V0K 1A0
(604) 453-9656

Index

Biographical Notes

photo: Jim Davidson

Ellen Adelberg is a freelance print and radio journalist. She has a Masters in Social Work, has done research and written articles on women offenders, and worked for two years as a halfway house director for the Elizabeth Fry Society of Ottawa.

Claudia Currie has a Masters in Applied Criminology and ten years experience working in corrections and criminology, in the area of the female offender. She has managed community programs for offenders, conducted research and currently teaches at Algonquin College in Ottawa.

251

Lorraine Berzins has worked with offenders in federal penitentiaries and on their behalf for the government and national voluntary organizations for sixteen years. She now works with the Church Council on Justice and Corrections in Ottawa as an educator and advocate.

Sheelagh (Dunn) Cooper has a Masters in Criminology. She worked for the Canadian Penitentiary Service and served as co-co-ordinator of the Female Offender Program at the Ministry of the Solicitor General in the 1970s. She now lives in Bermuda, teaches sociology and is active in the Nuclear Awareness Association.

Liz Elliot has worked with women and men in conflict with the law for four years as a social worker and advocate. She lives in Vancouver, where she is enrolled in the doctoral program in criminology at Simon Fraser University.

Karlene Faith has been doing research and working with women in prison since the early 1960s in the United States and Canada. She has a PhD in Humanities and Social Sciences from the University of California at Santa Cruz and is an associate professor at Simon Fraser University. She also organizes courses in women's prisons in British Columbia and at P4W in Kingston, Ontario.

Shelley Gavigan is an assistant professor of law at Osgoode Hall Law School, York University, where she directs the student program at Parkdale Community Legal Services Clinic. Her research centres on women, law and the state, and she has written journal articles in this area.

Gloria Geller is an assistant professor at the School of Social Work, University of Regina. After working as a school teacher and at a settlement house in the mid-'60s, she completed a doctorate at the Ontario Institute for Studies in Education on the streaming of males and females in the juvenile justice system.

Brigid Hayes was the spokeswoman for Women for Justice, a lobby group, for four years in the early 1980s. She lives in

Ottawa, where she has been active with the Elizabeth Fry Society, and works for the federal government.

Holly Johnson is a research criminologist with the federal Ministry of the Solicitor General. Her work centres on women offenders and victims of crime. She is the author of the ministry publication *Women and Crime in Canada*.

Carol Pitcher LaPrairie is a senior researcher for the Solicitor General of Canada. She has a PhD in Sociology from the University of British Columbia, a Masters degree in Criminology from the University of Toronto, and has worked on aboriginal rights and criminal justice for the past nine years.

Ruth Morris has spent the past fifteen years as a prison abolitionist and has founded three community agencies for offenders. She has a PhD, has taught university courses and has written extensively on prison issues and homelessness. Two of her books will be released by Mosaic Press this year.

Press Gang Publishers
is a feminist collective.
We publish non-fiction and fiction
that challenges traditional assumptions
about women in society.

For a free catalogue
of our books and posters write to:
Press Gang Publishers,
603 Powell Street,
Vancouver, B.C.
V6A 1H2 Canada